STRUCK

AMANDA CARLSON

STRUCK

A PHOEBE MEADOWS NOVEL: BOOK ONE

Copyright © 2016 Amanda Carlson

ISBN-13: 978-1-530849-13-0
ISBN-10: 1-530849-13-6

For Mom. My biggest fan.

1

I blinked open my eyes to find two concerned faces hovering above me. I shifted my body, and a cascade of shoeboxes tumbled around me. "What happened?" I swallowed a few times. My throat felt funny.

"You tell us," Sam said, hands on her hips, her blonde curls bouncing in agitation. "I was minding my own business helping a seventy-five-year-old lady cram her corns into a pair of high heels when all of a sudden what sounds like a sonic boom goes off. I run back to find you out cold, crumpled like a rag doll on top of a pile of Steve Maddens." She extended her arm to help me up. Samantha Reed, my co-worker and recent best friend, was not amused. I grabbed on to her hand, scattering boxes and shoes as I went. "When I saw you lying here, I thought you were dead, Phoebe. Don't scare me like that again. Ever."

"Yeah," Tom echoed in his standard monotone. "Don't scare us like that." Tom Levine, Macy's resident eighteen-year-old stock boy, took a few steps back so I had enough room to fully clear myself of the mess. Apparently, I'd passed out, but I had no recollection of the event at all. "But, dude, at the same time it was freakin' awesome. I thought the whole building was going to cave in or something. There was this huge *kaboom*." Both his hands went out in front of him, mimicking an explosion. The story ended with a whooshing noise out of the side of his mouth. It was the most animated I'd ever seen the guy. "Then the lights flickered and…you were lying here."

"Honestly," I said, trying to smooth down my now static-frizzed hair, "I don't remember much. I heard a noise and glanced up, right as a bolt of something shot out of the lights. It must've hit me, which is weird, because I didn't feel anything and I'm not hurt. Next thing I knew, you guys were looking down on me."

We all tilted our heads up to the ceiling.

Several long, narrow fluorescent bulbs hung from their fixtures at odd angles, rocking slowly back and forth. It was the only indication that my convoluted story held a kernel of truth.

"No way." Tom moved under one of the bulbs and tried to reach it, jumping twice, but it was too high. He glanced over his shoulder, flipping his brown hair off his forehead in a single flick. "I wish this kind of stuff happened to me. It's boring as hell back here."

"I had no idea fluorescent lights could shock someone like that." I rubbed my arms. My extremities were a little tingly, but other than that I felt fine. My throat was better after a couple of swallows. "A big store like Macy's should insulate their lights better or check the circuits or hire better maintenance people." I gestured to the broken fixtures. "That's a lawsuit waiting to happen."

"Please, fluorescent lights can't shock you like that." Sam's voice was full of authority as she marched forward to investigate. "It's completely impossible. Electricity doesn't arc that far at one hundred and ten volts, and even if it did, fluorescent lights are made up of electrons and gas, not wire filament. So essentially there's no way on earth those light bulbs or that fixture"—she directed an angry finger toward the hanging bulbs that still had the audacity to rock back and forth—"shocked you from way up there."

Sam was an aspiring actress, but she should've been an engineer. Her brain was vast and held more factoids than I thought possible for one person. She was one of the smartest people I'd ever met.

A sharp acidic smell hit the air.

I glanced down. The hemline of my skirt was smoking.

"Oh." I licked my fingers and pressed them against the frayed edge, and a soft *psst* sounded as the tiny coal of heat was extinguished.

Sam met my eyes, her expression shocked. "Holy crap, Phoebe!" she cried, moving in front of me. "We need to get you to the doctor right away. Your skirt is *smoking*. How is that even possible?" She twisted her head up toward the ceiling and then back to look at me, her face incredulous.

"Dude, that's freakin' crazy." Tom was giddy as he shuffled toward us. "I've never seen anyone on fire before."

"I'm not on fire," I answered testily as I checked the rest of my body for any other indication that I may, in fact, be on fire. This was beyond insane. "I'm totally fine. I promise. I have a great idea. Let's call maintenance, and they can come in and check it out and we can all go back to work. The customers are probably crawling up the walls by now, and Nancy is going to be mad we've both been back here so long. I can't afford to lose my job."

"I don't care if Nancy's pissed or not. She can wait." Sam placed her hands firmly on her hips. "This is much more important. Phoebe, if your clothes are smoking, that's a pretty big indication that something calamitous just happened. People don't just *catch on fire*. Something could be really wrong with you. I think we need to get you to a hospital, pronto."

She might be right, except I felt better with each passing second.

In the short amount of time we'd been standing here, my body had become somehow more...energized. Like I'd downed an entire bag of Skittles, and the sugar high was kicking in. My fingers twitched, and my feet almost bounced on their own.

"Sam, I'm fine," I reassured her. "I feel more awake, but that's it. I actually feel like I could go for a run right now. Whatever happened, it didn't hurt me. It worked the opposite."

Sam wasn't buying what I was selling. "It's the middle of winter in New York City, and you hate running. You refer to runners as self-torturers who love inflicting pain on themselves. That alone means we should take you in. You're not yourself, and this proves it."

"Well, *hm*, you might be right about the running part," I said. "But according to how I feel right now, I might have to alter my definition of self-torture. I could be missing out by not giving it a try." She crossed her arms. "Seriously, Sam. I'm not lying. I feel amazing. I have no explanation for what happened, but I have no scorch marks on my body, no gaping holes in my chest, and nothing else is smoking. Let's not make this a big deal, okay? Even though you said the noise was loud, you two seem to be the only ones who heard it. No one else is here." I glanced at Tom. The kid had four looks: bored, ultra-bored, slightly happy, and confused. He was giving us confused now—the same expression he wore whenever we tried to explain how invoicing worked. I turned back to Sam. "Let's get back to work. This entire thing is

4

embarrassing, and we've been gone so long the customers are going to riot. Please, Sam. I can't afford to have Nancy fire me. I can barely cover rent as it is."

Sam rolled her eyes, dropping her arms. "Fine, but I'm keeping an eye on you for the rest of the day. If you so much as sneeze in the wrong direction, I'm calling an ambulance. I mean it, Phoebe. I'm not taking any chances."

"Deal."

"Dude, you know"—Tom shoved his hands in his front jean pockets, tugging them down impossibly lower—"when you were lying there, you looked totally dead. I've only seen one other dead guy before, but you looked just like him. Kinda freaked me out."

"Thanks, Tom. That's really helpful." Judging by the artful green leaves proudly displayed all over his attire, he was a real poster boy for Sherlock Holmes. Anything could look dead if it wasn't moving. "I was clearly breathing the entire time, since I'm standing here alive. Fainting can look an awful lot like dead. The subtle difference would be in the chest movement." I nodded to Sam. "I'll just clean up these boxes and meet you out on the floor." Macy's didn't mess around with their shoe department in New York. It spanned two floors, and it was always busy.

"Okay," she relented. "If you're not out in ten minutes, I'm coming back to find you."

"Got it." I was relieved when she finally walked out of the stock room. I wanted to forget this craziness had ever occurred.

Tom bent over to help me as I gathered up the errant shoes. "Dude," he said, "can I touch your arm? I've never touched anyone who's died before."

I hurried down the block toward Penn Station, buttoning up my wool coat against the wind as I went. The temperature had dropped since I'd started my shift at nine this morning, and my cheeks were already windburned.

Nothing else had happened during the rest of my shift, so I was chalking the entire ordeal up as a freak event, which I could add to the long laundry list of other strange New York City occurrences I'd witnessed since I'd arrived eight months ago.

In the short time I'd been here, I'd seen more unique things than I had in my entire life: guys dressed like monsters, people who seemed to shimmer, strange animals running around without leashes.

You name it, I'd seen it.

Once I was inside Penn Station, my train was just rolling up, which was a gift. At the fourth stop, I exited, hurrying up the stairs, eager to finally get home.

As I neared the top, a shoulder slammed into me.

I managed to grab on to the handrail in time to save myself from tumbling backward down the flight of steps. "Goodness…I'm sorry," I sputtered. "I didn't mean to bump into you. I wasn't watching—"

A large face loomed above me.

The man wore a dark blue knit cap pulled down low, almost covering his eyes. But the hat wasn't enough to conceal the huge jagged scar that ran across his entire face, spanning from one eyelid, marring his nose, and finishing at the opposite jawline. It was grisly up close, dark pink and puckered, like something had dug in deep before it ripped free.

He stood unmoving, glaring down at me.

The mystery man was a good two feet taller than I was. Three at the moment, because he was elevated on the step above me. His clothes were tattered, and he stank like stale food and body odor.

"Again…I wasn't looking…" I stammered, trying my best to maneuver around him. People were coming and going around us, but no one seemed to notice this man had trapped me. "I promise to be more careful next time." I managed to squeeze by him, joining someone else who was coming up on my right, barely refraining from grabbing on to the new stranger.

As I slipped by, the scarred man's meaty fist latched on to my forearm.

His grip was painful, even through my woolen coat.

Abruptly, he turned and headed up the stairs, practically lifting me off my feet as he tugged me behind him.

Once we emerged on the street, I gasped, trying to yank my arm back. "What are you doing?" His iron grip held firmly. "Let me go!" I turned my head frantically, trying to search for help.

People passed us on both sides, but nobody noticed my plight. Typical New York. If I'd been in my hometown, there would've been an uproar, with folks swarming to help me.

Before I could shout my distress again, the man snapped me tightly to his chest. His breath carried the scent of coffee and something rancid. "New York is no longer safe," he growled, his face not even an inch from mine. "You must get…*away*. They will be coming soon."

No crap I needed to get away! Like right now.

"Let go of me!" I braced both hands against his chest and heaved backward. "If you need money, I have a few dollars in my pocket. I'm happy to give it to you. Just…let…me…*go*!" One more push, and he finally released me.

I pivoted away, twisting into the pulse of people on the crowded sidewalk. I wove in and out manically, ducking and bobbing. Only a full block later, with many bodies separating us, did I stop and venture a glance over my shoulder. The mystery man stood where I'd left him. Even at this distance I could see his eyes were focused on mine. I had no trouble picking him out of the crowd because he was a head taller than anyone else on the entire street.

One arm rose in some sort of salute, and his jacket cuff fell away.

He was missing his right hand.

"*Ohmygods!*" I ducked around the next corner, my breath coming in short, staccato bursts. I didn't linger. Instead, I hurried down the street, heading for home, dodging groups of pedestrians, and checking furtively behind me at regular intervals to make sure he wasn't following.

When I finally arrived at my corner, I turned back and scanned the street one last time.

It was clear.

There was no way I was leading that guy to my doorstep.

With relief, I rushed the last few paces to my building. I rented a small studio on the top floor of a five-story complex. I keyed the door open and raced up the threadbare steps to my apartment, unlocking my door as fast as I could.

I slammed it behind me, tossing my purse and keys onto the small table next to the door, my back braced against the wood as I tried to catch my breath and calm down. My heart raced a million miles an hour.

I began to unbutton my coat with shaky fingers.

CA-CAW CA-CAW.

2

My head snapped toward my tiny kitchen. The room was partitioned off from my main living space by a flimsy wall that rose only ten feet up.

CA-CAW. CA-CAW.

Holy crap!

A cool breeze wafted by my cheeks. There's no way I'd left my window open. It was the middle of winter. I fisted my hands at my sides. Not knowing what else to do, I crept slowly toward the kitchen. There wasn't a door—it was just an opening that led from one space to another.

CA-CAW. CA-CAAAW.

I stopped just shy of the doorway, gathering all my strength. Then I leaned over and peered slowly into the tiny galley space that held a small fridge, a stove, and two cupboards. There, perched on my ugly gray Formica counter top, was the biggest raven I'd ever seen in my life.

And I knew birds.

You couldn't be raised on a farm in small-town America and not know the difference between a crow and a raven—

and this was no crow. This raven was so big it looked like it could swallow a fat raccoon and still be hungry.

It met my gaze, staring at me for a few beats before it cocked its head at a crazy angle and let out a big, loud *CA-CAW*.

"What've you got in there?" a voice said behind me.

"*Argh!*" I leaped back, shrieking, covering my face with both hands.

"Sorry, Phoebe," my neighbor Ingrid said in soothing tones. "I didn't mean to scare you. Hey, calm down there." Her hands patted my shoulders. I began to relax. "The door was unlocked, so I let myself in. I heard noises."

After a few more inhales and exhales, I managed to slide my hands away from my face. I placed one of my palms over my thumping heart and tried not to pass out for the second time today.

I was glad Ingrid had arrived. She could help me get rid of the giant avian sitting in my kitchen. I started to tell her that very thing, but all thought left my brain once I took in her outfit. "Ingrid…what are you wearing?"

I'd met Ingrid, who lived across the hall, the very first day I moved to New York City. She had bounded into my apartment, introduced herself, and then, without being asked, lugged box after box up five flights of stairs, assuring me that helping people she'd just met move was what she loved to do in her free time.

But this wasn't the Ingrid I'd come to know and love.

This Ingrid was dressed like a gladiator in some time-gone-by era where people smote one another for a living. Or at the very least, they impaled their opponents with wicked-looking spears, like the one she held tightly in her left fist.

Ingrid glanced down the front of herself like she was noticing her bronze breastplate, white tunic, leather arm guards, and full-length lace-up moccasins for the first time. "Well, I can't very well protect you if I'm not armed and ready for battle, can I?"

"Protect me? Why would I need protection?" Right then, the raven soared over the partition with a huge flap of its wings, screeching loudly.

CA-CAW. CA-CAW.

I shrieked and hit the floor.

Okay, maybe I needed a little protecting.

"Use your spear, Ingrid!" I gestured wildly at the ornate weapon. "That bird is not going back out that window without a fight. Hurry, before it pecks us to death!"

Instead of impaling the flying beast with her spear, Ingrid chuckled warmly. "Huggie, it's nice to see you again." Her tone was affable as she nodded to the bird, which had managed to find a new perch on one of the wooden bedposts of my bed, which sat in the middle of the small studio room. "It's been a while, old friend, hasn't it?"

The bird gave a giant squawk in response.

I blinked a few times.

I was crouched on the floor, arms comically wrapped around my head. I was certain the bird was going to peck out my brain, so I was doing what any logical person would do in my place. I was shielding it. I sat there, pretending I hadn't just heard what Ingrid had said to the killer bird.

The urge to run screaming out of my apartment pressed down on me.

That, combined with the jitters and near constant heart-hammering, made it hard for me to keep still. My legs quaked, and my heart felt close to bursting. Instead of fleeing my apartment, screaming like a madwoman, I managed, "Did you just call that bird *Huggie*?"

"Yep, this here is Hugin," she answered matter-of-factly.

"Your dad sent him to help you. Kind of like your own personal animal totem. Huggie can relay thoughts. You should be able to feel something from him once you get to know him a little better."

"Huh?" I needed to find a different position, or I was going to fall over. Instead of collapsing in a heap on the floor, which I pondered for a long, sweet moment, I edged onto my knees and shuffled over to my one and only piece of furniture that wasn't a bed—a shabby-chic chair I'd found at a thrift store—and pulled myself onto the thing, sitting down with a thump. I bent over and rubbed my temples. "Um, Ingrid," I mumbled, "I hate to burst your bubble, but my dad runs an Ace Hardware store in rural Wisconsin. He couldn't possibly have sent me a gigantic raven as an *animal totem*. And even if the sky did fall, and the world spun wildly on its axis, why would he sneak all the way to New York, break into my apartment, and drop a man-eating raptor in my kitchen without even sticking around to say hello?"

Why I was trying to make sense of this was the bigger mystery.

Ingrid was obviously delusional.

"Huggie came here of his own accord. Your dad only *asked* him to come. Well, he likely made it an official order, but the bird makes his own decisions. You can't be this old without gaining your own power, and Huggie here is as old as they come. Isn't that right?"

The bird gave a loud squawk in answer.

I lifted my head, staring at her with an open mouth. With mock enthusiasm, I said, "Well, that's a huge relief. I wouldn't want the bird terrorizing us to be robbed of its own free will."

"Free will. That's a good one, Phoebe." Ingrid chuckled as she strode over to my closet door and pulled it open. "Okay, enough dillydallying around. We have to make haste.

They're already tracking you, and time is of the essence."

Make haste? Time is of the essence?

Ingrid wore lumberjack shirts exclusively. Her hair was military short, and she rarely left her apartment. She had a hard edge and most certainly did not use words like *dillydally*.

"*Who*…exactly is tracking me?" I glanced warily at the raven. It had its beady eyes pinned on me.

Ingrid poked her head out of the closet, duffel bag in hand. "When you got struck today, the Norns found out about you for the first time—and let me tell you, they are biting mad. Pulling the wool over their eyes for the last twenty-four years was no small feat. Manipulating them is nearly impossible for us regular people to do—and only *barely* possible for a god." Ingrid began yanking clothes off hangers and tossing them into the duffel bag she'd set on my bed. "If they get to you before I can get you to the Valkyrie stronghold, you'll either be killed or tossed into one of the Nine Worlds quicker than you can say, 'Odin's my dad.'"

"Okay, Ingrid, I have to stop you right there." Wearily, I stood, one hand out in front of me, partly to ward off the giant raven from coming any closer and partly because I had no idea what else to do. "I'm not quite sure how you know I got a weird shock today. I was sort of saving that to tell you over popcorn during our movie tonight, but this entire conversation is making me crazy. More crazy than usual. I don't understand why you're dressed up in a toga like a Roman Coliseum fighter, or why there's a raptor perched on my bedpost, or why you're telling me these odd things, but just to be clear, my parents go by the names Frank and Janette Meadows, and they live in Prospect, Wisconsin. They do not breed ravens, I have no idea what a Norn is, and I'm not going to any Valkyrie stronghold—whatever that is. And, better yet, if you don't mind, I'd love to continue this entire conversation later. Maybe, say, in a week or two when we're both feeling back to our normal selves?" I wanted so badly for my life to be normal again. "I know we were supposed to hang out tonight, but I'm okay with rescheduling so you can go back to...your play practice...or whatever it is you're working on. How does that sound?" I nodded hopefully.

It sounded like a perfect plan to me. Maybe the best one I'd ever had.

"Not your real parents, Phoebe. I hate to break it to you like this, but as I said before, time is of the essence." She tapped her bare wrist right below her leather arm cuff. "Your real dad fell in love with one of his shieldmaidens twenty-five years ago—which is highly forbidden, by the way. You do *not* mess with the help. They had no choice but to give you to the Meadows family when you were born. Frank and Janette did a bang-up job, if you're interested in hearing my opinion. But there's no more time to explain. We need to move."

Ingrid had never given off an insane vibe before, but this was seriously over the top. "Ingrid," I started very slowly, "how is it that you know so much about me? Or, let me rephrase—the *me* you seem to think I am." Did that even make sense? "We've never met before I moved here. I would've remembered you. There's no way you can know anything about me or where I come from. This is madness, and I don't know why we're having this conversation. I think it's time for you to go." I paused, remembering my unusual situation. "You know, after you help me get the bird out." I gestured casually to the raven, which seemed content to sit and watch us, its head bouncing between us as we talked.

Ingrid was completely unfazed by my order for her to leave the premises. She kept talking like I hadn't said anything of importance. "I know about you because Leela was my sister—*is* my sister. I was sworn to protect you the day you were born, and I take that oath very seriously." She threw more stuff into the duffel bag.

"I take it Leela is the shieldmaiden who gave birth to me?"

Ingrid nodded.

My fake real mother. "Just to humor me—if she's still alive, why didn't she raise me herself? You'd think a loving mother would reject the idea of her offspring being given away by her forbidden lover." I crossed my arms. I was tired and wanted badly to lie down.

On a bed that didn't have a raven perched on it.

"Odin had no choice but to seal her away. It was either that or instant death. And a baby wouldn't have survived the transition process, and even if you had, most of the Nine Worlds are harsh and unforgiving. No place to raise a child. Your survival rate would've been nil to none. He made the best choice he could for both of you at the time. They both love you, Phoebe, and that's why we need to leave right now."

"Sealed her where *exactly*?" Morbid curiosity was apparently now in charge.

Ingrid moved to my dresser and opened my underwear drawer and began shoveling things into the bag. "Well, we've pretty much narrowed it down to Svartalfheim, which is the only world we haven't been able to fully search yet. Those bastards guard their entrances like rabid dogs. If she's there, let me tell you, it's going to be hard work to spring her. Dark elves are nasty, and tricky with their magic. We've been trying to find a way in for the past eight years with no luck, but we're getting closer each day. Invaldi recently made a very big mistake, and he owes one of my sisters a favor. We're bargaining for entrance right now."

My head spun like someone had clocked me right in the face.

Why had I asked?

I thumped down on the edge of the chair to steady myself. "*Svartalfheim*? Come on, Ingrid!" I tossed out my arms. I had to find a way to get her to put my undies back in my drawer and leave. "I can't believe you're actually trying to convince me this story is real, and you can stop packing now. I'm not going anywhere, except to sleep. For like a week."

"Yes, Svartalfheim. It's one of the Nine Worlds. Covered in dark elves. Highly dangerous." She zipped the now full duffel like I hadn't said anything and slung it over her shoulder like it weighed nothing. "Enough talking. We're wasting time. We need to get out of here. It's not safe for you in the city any longer."

There were so many things wrong with those sentences.

I stood, shaking my head. "I'm really, really sorry, Ingrid, but I'm not going to join you tonight. What I need is a hot cup of soup and some honest-to-goodness sleep. If you could just help me get the bird out, I promise I'll be a good audience the next time you need another run-through with your lines. But, I'm going to stay here and crash."

Before Ingrid could answer, the raven swooped off the bedpost, barely flapping its wings, and landed on the table next to me.

I stifled a scream as the lamp clattered to the ground.

That thing was *huge*.

CAW-CA. CAAA-CAW.

The sound was deafening this close.

"Sorry, big guy," I squeaked, slowly standing and backing against the wall behind the chair, edging as far away as I possibly could. "I'm not really picking up on any mind action, so I think your communication lines might be broken. If I open the window a little more, do you think you could make it back out by yourself?"

Leave...now.

The words fluttered through my brain like actual feathers tickling my gray matter.

I gasped, stumbling to the side, trying to catch myself before I fell. My head snapped to Ingrid, who now wore a devilish grin, and then back to the raven perched on my tiny table.

"Huggie start talking to you? Good job, bird. Whatever it takes. Now we really have to go. You don't want to come face-to-face with the Norns, Phoebe. There's nothing worse. Those hags will tear you apart with their bare hands and cackle while they do it."

Instead of moving, I responded in a monotone, my eyes locked on the bird. "What exactly is a Norn, Ingrid?"

"The Norns are sister goddesses—or witches—depending on who you talk to. They control, manipulate, and foresee what goes on with us, and tend to Yggdrasil, the tree of life. They don't really care what goes on in Midgard." She motioned out the window, I guessed to indicate the rest of the world. "But if you go behind their backs like we did for all those years, you're going to pay in spades. Not even Odin is strong enough to take them on all at once. Nasty bunch of ladies. Come on. I'll fill you in more on the road." Ingrid whipped open my front door and disappeared through the opening.

I glanced wearily at the huge raven.

It snapped its beak a few times, and I flinched, my fingernails scrabbling on the wall.

Today, after I'd been struck, I'd felt energized. Now, with everything that had happened, from the mystery one-handed man accosting me on the subway stairs, to right this minute, I felt totally drained.

I just wanted to lie down. I *needed* to rest.

"This can't be happening," I muttered to myself. My twenty-fourth birthday was in less than a week. Maybe this was some sort of elaborate practical joke Ingrid was playing on me, starting with exploding fluorescent lights and ending with a telepathic raven and a mad escape from the Norns. I glanced directly at the raven, meeting its beady stare, human to bird. "Ingrid is just taking me to a costume surprise party. I'm going to look back on all of this in a few days and laugh. Isn't that right, big, scary bird?"

There was no way this raven was going to answer me.

I brought a hand up and pressed it against my neck, checking my pulse to make sure I was actually alive and breathing, and made my decision. I was going to shut the door behind Ingrid, lock it, and crawl into bed. Then I was going to pile an army of pillows over my head so the raven didn't peck me to death. I was pretty sure once it got hungry enough, it would leave through the window from whence it came.

If not, I'd deal with it in the morning.

Leave…now.

The words fluttered through my brain, same as before, with a small tickle and a poof of air.

My eyebrows shot above my hairline right as Ingrid stuck her head through my still open door. "Phoebe, let's go! Right now! If you want to live, follow me. If you want to die, then, by all means, stay here. But I wouldn't wish that kind of death on anyone."

I glanced from Ingrid to the raven.

"Fine. I'll go," I squeaked. "But you have to promise me that when we get to where we're going, I get a drink, possibly with a pineapple slice or two and definitely with an umbrella. I need an umbrella."

3

I trailed Ingrid down the stairs. She moved fast, but I managed to keep up. The lighting in my hallway sucked, but the leather crisscrosses holding her breastplate in place stood out starkly over her white tunic.

"Ingrid," I said to her quickly retreating back. "Don't you think it would be a good idea to change into regular clothes? You know, before we actually encounter the general public on the street? Plus, I don't think spears are allowed on the subway. I'm pretty sure they're considered deadly weapons."

"This is New York, Phoebe. Nobody gives a crap what I'm wearing," she tossed over her shoulder. "If anybody asks, I'll tell them I'm an extra in a movie, and they won't blink twice. Don't worry about the spear." She shook the weapon once, and it flexed, snapping smoothly down on its own to the size of a baton.

When she was done, she holstered it at her waist.

It must be a trick spear. "That was neat." I was out of breath by the time we came to a stop in front of the door leading outside. "Can anyone buy one of those? It looked so real before."

Ingrid ignored my foolish question, peering sideways through the glass, her back up against the wall. "Huggie's in place already. The plan is to follow him. He chooses which tunnel we go down, understood? You have to stay close to me. Are you sure you can keep up?" She gave me a critical once-over.

I glanced down at my own attire, still laboring hard, like I'd sprinted a lap.

Underneath my wool coat I had on a gray work skirt, black tights, a blue blouse, and fairly sturdy black boots. On my head I wore a black knit hat. A black and white checked scarf finished the ensemble.

It was winter after all.

I reached up and rearranged my scarf so it covered half of my face and pulled my black knit cap down over my ears. "I think I can keep up. I mean, I don't see why not. I'm not exactly in your kind of shape." Ingrid obviously worked out a lot. She was a good foot taller than I was and all brawn. If it weren't for a set of thick, curly eyelashes framing a pair of clear hazel eyes, she could almost pass for a man. My dull chestnut hair and gray eyes seemed boring in comparison. "But I can most likely get to a subway station without collapsing." I tried to stop breathing hard to further prove my point, but my lungs weren't cooperating. I was a swimmer in high school, and I walked the city streets regularly. I wasn't totally incapable.

She nodded once and made her move.

I followed her out onto the street. It was full dark already. Early December brought on the short days.

I spotted Huggie perched on a flagpole across the street.

The bird turned toward us, its feathers catching the

orange glow of the streetlights, making it shimmer in the low light. It was more than a bit surreal.

In fact, this whole day had been surreal.

I guess it seemed apropos that I was going to end my very strange day trailing a huge, gleaming raven named Huggie through the streets of New York City.

The bird took off, soaring down the street with unusual grace. Its powerful wings flapped fluidly and soundlessly in the dark. Ingrid followed and I jogged behind.

"Ingrid," I panted after a while, the cold air stinging my lungs. "We've passed three stations so far, and it's a friggin' meat locker out here. Are we heading down anytime soon?"

Up ahead, the raven chose that moment to plunge into a stairwell at the corner of 72nd Street.

I stopped mid-jog.

People should be screaming their heads off right now.

If a bird that big buzzed by me as I was emerging from a subway station, I would've hit the ground, shouting for animal control and Valium.

Nobody noticed the bird at all.

"Come on, Phoebe. Hurry up. Time to head down," Ingrid called over her shoulder.

I picked up the pace. "Why aren't people freaking out about Huggie?" I asked. "He's a big, black, terrifying bird. It should be pandemonium down there."

Ingrid scoffed. "They don't see him, of course. What? You think people in Midgard can see stuff from Asgard? Ha! Only if they have Aesir or Vanir blood flowing through their veins. Or if Huggie chooses to let them. But why would he? That would be courting chaos."

I grabbed on to the handrail, yelling after her, "I have no idea what you're talking about! As usual," I muttered under my breath. This was so crazy. "Midgard, Asgard,

Vanir…*whatever*." I shuffled down the steps. "I need an umbrella."

The subway car Ingrid entered was fairly empty. Other than a few curiously raised eyebrows about her choice of attire, no one said a word, which wasn't a surprise.

Huggie had either disappeared or flown off, and I was relieved.

"Where are we headed to now?" I asked as I took a bench seat opposite Ingrid. My duffel was sprawled out next to her. The subway doors closed, and the train took off.

"We're heading to the airport."

"*The airport*? Are you serious?"

"How else are we supposed to get out of town? Well, other than a portal. But those are too risky at the moment. The shieldmaidens have a private jet parked in New Jersey at Teterboro. The modern human world has forced us to adjust over the past hundred years. Even though it's not our preferred mode of transportation, it works fine. Usually." Her voice ominous.

"But…" I trailed off. "Ingrid, I can't leave town. I'm sorry, but I can't do it. I've played along with you thus far, but honestly, I have to go home. I have a job and a life, and I like it in New York. I can't just jet off on some mad tangent with you! This is so insane."

Ingrid leaned forward, resting her forearms on her thighs, her face serious. "Phoebe, listen to me. I understand this has been a lot to take in and you're freaked out. But what's happening here is real. I'm not known for my soothing nature or my subtleness. I'm known for kicking someone's ass four ways from Friday. That's why I'm here. I'm the best protection you've got. When, and if, this blows over, you can think about returning to New York, but until then—"

The lights in the car flickered, and the car was thrown into complete darkness.

"What's going on?" I whispered as my blood began to gallop in my veins. When she didn't answer, I urged, "Ingrid, this isn't funny!" I grabbed on to the handrail beside me, wrapping a hand around the metal bar. I tried to wait patiently for her to get back to me, but when no emergency lights blinked on, panic bubbled in my chest like carbonation out of a shaken can of soda.

The only illumination came from the occasional dim light outside the tunnel, giving the inside of the car a sporadic strobe of artificial light. There were some quiet murmurings from the other passengers, but it was going to take a lot more than a blackout to freak out a seasoned New Yorker.

I, however, was not seasoned. "Ingrid!" My voice was shrill because she still hadn't answered me. "I can't take any more! What's going on?"

"Stay right where you are." Ingrid's order came from a space over by the doors closest to us. As we passed another light, I saw her crouched down.

I was restless, so I glanced out the window.

A face stared back at me.

I screamed.

The head was leathery, and it had gleaming yellow eyes. It opened its maw and snarled at me, revealing rows of sharp, pointy teeth.

Several things happened at once.

My head snapped to Ingrid, who was shouting something I couldn't understand. In the next flicker of light, I saw an object hurtling toward me. Instinctively, I stretched out my hand, and a rock the size of a walnut landed in my palm. As

I closed my fist around it, Huggie soared down the aisle, his eyes brilliant, like two clear, glowing orbs of gleaming mercury in the dark.

The raven landed on the rail next to me, squawking loudly, and I bravely shot another gaze out the window.

Mercifully, it was clear.

Ingrid was still yelling at me, and I jerked my head in her direction, but I was having trouble focusing on anything.

"Phoebe! Put the stone in your mouth!"

"Wha—?"

"Just do it!"

I numbly glanced down. It was too dark to see exactly what I was holding, but I brought it up to my lips, hesitating for only a brief moment before I popped it in.

At this point, I was out of options.

Coherent thoughts weren't forming in my mind. Following Ingrid's lead was my only real choice, and at least I had the wherewithal to realize it.

If I couldn't trust her, all was lost.

A warm tingling sensation began to buzz through my body as the "stone" disintegrated on my tongue. The initial flavor was a sweet, buttery rum, but as it spread over my mouth, the aftertaste puckered like citrus.

I pressed my lips together until the gross taste subsided.

After a few moments, I felt calm enough to take inventory of the car. I craned my head around, wondering if any of the other passengers had seen the same face I had. It was unlikely, since I hadn't heard any other screaming.

Surprisingly, everyone was out cold, slumped over in their seats.

I whipped back around. "Ingrid!" I whisper-yelled, stretching into the aisle, hoping not to disturb Huggie. The bird remained quiet. "What's going on? Why is everyone asleep? Don't they know we're in trouble?" That creature's ugly face fluttered through my mind, and the hair on my arms jumped to attention. "And what did I just eat? I feel kind of lightheaded."

Ingrid hadn't moved from her position by the doors. She was still crouched, the trick spear at full length. "Sit down, Phoebe," Ingrid hissed, motioning me back with her free arm. "I gave you a cloak stone. It's made by the white elves, and it's powerful stuff. It's targeted to my blood, so I'm the only one who can see you. The ettins are here, but even if they come aboard, you should stay hidden from them for now. Plus, with Huggie here, they'll think twice about storming the train. As long as the train keeps moving, we should be fine."

Huggie gave a loud caw and flapped his wings.

I sat back on my seat. "But why is everyone asleep?"

"It's a safety precaution, Phoebe. They can't see Huggie or the ettins, but the humans will remember you and me and what went on tonight. We had to put them out. Just sit tight."

"What *exactly* is an ettin?" I assumed she had been referring to the beastie outside my window, but I couldn't be sure. "It looked like something I'd imagine living under a bridge and eating small children for breakfast."

"They are the Norns' primary agents, a mix between lake troll and dark elf, so that's actually not far from the truth. They're hard to kill, the little bastards. They have extremely thick hides, and they're quick. Most likely a bunch of them are out there waiting for an opportunity to snatch you."

"Snatch me? Why would they want to do that?" Before I could ask her to elaborate on their kidnapping plans, the subway car hitched and began to slow.

It rocked back and forth as the speed diminished, tossing me around in my seat.

Crap! Ingrid said we had to keep moving.

Huggie rose off his perch and flew toward the far end of the car. That wasn't a good sign.

"Come on, Phoebe! The ettins are stopping the train. We have to get out of here." Ingrid jumped from her position by the doorway, reaching me in two strides. She hoisted me out of my seat, positioning me in front of her. "Follow Huggie. *Now!*"

We raced toward the far end of the car.

Huggie had already disappeared, so I pulled open the doors, and we took off through to the next one. As we ran, the train slowed until it was only inching along.

In every car we ran through, the passengers were asleep.

I slid to a stop when Huggie appeared out of thin air in front of me and gave a giant squawk. Ingrid twisted me with both hands toward the outside doors.

It was dark and hard to see much of anything.

"We're getting out here." Ingrid stepped in front of me, shoving her spear into the crack between the doors. They burst open with enough force to make them clang back and forth. She jumped onto a very narrow walkway next to the train and scanned the dim darkness like a predator, sniffing and cocking her head from side to side. When she was satisfied, she motioned me out.

As I stepped onto the old broken concrete she drew something out of her tunic. How many things did she have stored in there? "Phoebe, you're going to need to protect yourself from now on."

I glanced shakily around me, trying to locate any more of those little yellow-eyed monsters before focusing on the object Ingrid held out to me.

"This is Gram." She placed the knife carefully on my open palm. "This dagger can cut through just about anything, including the hide of an ettin. The cloak stone should hold, but ettins are tricky. They know you're with me and will look for you in all the obvious places. If you get cornered, go for their eyes."

In a daze, I gazed down at the dagger I held in my hand and then back up at Ingrid stupidly.

Without waiting for a response, Ingrid grabbed on to my arm above the elbow and propelled me down the tunnel after Huggie, who had gone far ahead. "Oh, and don't let them bite you," she told me. "Their saliva is full of hateful poison."

I gripped the hilt of the weapon like a lifeline and allowed myself to be led down the tunnel like a zombie, trying to put one foot in front of the other as quickly as I could without stumbling. When I finally found my voice, it wasn't much more than a squeak. "Ing…" I cleared it and tried again. "Ingrid…I don't understand. All of this is so unreal…I don't think I *can do this*…" My steps faltered, and I almost fell.

Ingrid turned, gripping me by the shoulders. "You have to wake up, Phoebe." She shook me. "You're going into shock, but we don't have time for you to do that right now. I'm just shy of slapping you completely silly. If you don't fight for your life right now, you won't get another chance. Do you understand me? This is it. You have to woman up and fight through this. I know you can. It runs in your blood. You're stronger than you think."

"But, Ingrid…I don't know how to fight," I responded lamely. This couldn't be right. What we were experiencing couldn't be real. "I'm not equipped to handle anything like this. I grew up in a small town. I don't even know how to fire a gun."

"Well, you're just going to have to learn on the job, aren't you? That's why we're heading to the Valkyrie stronghold. I don't have time to explain everything now. We can't wait here like sitting ducks for the ettins to make their move. You're going to have to trust me. We have to keep going, and when they come, we fight." She turned, keeping a firm hand on my arm, guiding me forward. "Phoebe, I know you can do this. You're just going to have to dig deep and find it."

After a few paces, Huggie shrieked in front of us and Ingrid swore, breaking her hold on me and reaching for her spear. She spun and yelled, "Phoebe! Watch out—"

A cold, bony hand latched around my ankle.

One yank, and I was gone.

4

Hands were all over me, grabbing me, pulling me, manhandling me.

It was pitch dark, and we were moving fast. No more tunnel lights. I hadn't noticed when they'd gone out, but it was black as night. I twisted my body, trying to scream, to make some kind of noise, but the leathery fingers covering me held me like iron, including the hand clamped over my mouth.

Huggie was in the distance, his loud, angry squawk echoing through the tunnel. He was moving away from me, not toward me.

"Two can play the same game, little *biiiirdie*," a gravelly voice below me growled. "We, too, can be *cloaaaaked*."

The words had been delivered methodicaly slow and were incredibly awful.

I moaned, still trying to squirm my way free. With some hope, I realized I was still gripping Gram in one fist. Why these little monsters hadn't stripped me of the dagger was a mystery, but I wasn't going to question my good luck now. I tightened my hold around it. It was my only lifeline.

"Phoebe!" Ingrid shouted from what felt like too far away. "I promise I'm going to find you. You're still cloaked! Remember that!"

Still cloaked?

How could I still be hidden when these little beasts had obviously found me?

The bodies under me picked up their pace after Ingrid's words. There must have been at least a dozen of them. We were heading away from Ingrid at a fast clip.

"*Huuuurry*, the shieldmaiden draws near," one of the voices ordered the group. "She must not reach us before we get to the *porrrrtal*."

I thrashed again and got lucky. One of my legs broke free, and it struck something hard. By the echo of the noise, it sounded like the side of a subway car.

I was within reach of help! The subway was right there.

With renewed vigor, I wrested my body back and forth, making it as hard as I could for my captors to keep their filthy grips on me.

Then, without warning, the group took a sharp left.

The beasties' footsteps echoed less now, so we must've entered a smaller area, likely an offshoot tunnel.

"Here it *issss*," a dark and gravelly voice announced to the group.

I could still hear Huggie's angry call out in the main tunnel. If these horrid creatures succeeded in getting me out of New York, I knew my chances for survival were next to nothing.

I screamed.

Straight into the hand covering my mouth.

No sound escaped. Not even a whimper.

The group came to an abrupt halt. More hands wrapped around me, and I was completely immobilized.

STRUCK

One of the creatures broke away from the group, jabbering words I couldn't come close to understanding. To my left, a faint glow erupted on the tunnel wall. Now that I could see, I frantically searched around, trying to get my bearings. It was no use. We were in a small tunnel with nothing else around.

The horrid little beast that faced the wall began to chant.

I wrenched my head toward the glow, and my eyes widened. Light began to flicker and move on its own, slowly swirling. The eddy of light spiraled in a lazy circle—not on the surface of the wall, but *inside* the concrete. I watched in morbid curiosity as the creature took its wickedly sharp fingernail and scratched some geometric patterns into the light.

The sound made my skin crawl.

In a shallow hiss, the creature recited something in English. "By the tree of *Yggdrasillllll*, open your *doorsssss*, we come on a mission, sent from the *Nornsssss*, our entry we pay willingly to thee, bear my blood to the *rootsssss* of your *treeeee*."

Then, it lifted its long, sharp fingernail off the wall and slashed it deeply into its own forearm. The sound was ridiculous, a slurping and rending of skin that would be etched in my mind forever.

A thick stream of liquid erupted out of the wound, but it wasn't red. It was a ghastly, putrid amber. The thing had motor oil for blood. I gagged and closed my eyes, willing myself away—*anywhere* but here.

More sounds from the creature, and my eyes fluttered open. I was riveted, unable to look anywhere else, to the scene unfolding in front of me.

Light swirled even more frenetically on the wall, faster and faster.

Then, to my abject horror, the hideous beast dipped its

nail into the gash it'd torn in its skin and took the thick, dripping mess and smeared it on the wall in the center of the light in circular motions chanting, "*Yggdrasil, yggdrasil, yggdrasil, yggdrasil…*"

From out in the main tunnel, I heard a clattering of footsteps. They were racing quickly in our direction, and they were getting louder by the second.

Ingrid was coming!

"*Hurrrry*, she nears!" one of the voices below me growled with urgency. My body shifted from side to side as the creatures steered me closer to the wall.

Now was my last chance! I flexed all my muscles, forcing my neck upward with all the remaining strength I had left in my body.

A few of the gross leathery fingers covering my mouth slid to the side, and I thrashed my head back and forth with renewed hope. If I could get free, I could yell. If it was loud enough, Ingrid could save me from whatever was about to happen.

A little more, and I broke free, gasping for air. "Ingrid! I'm here! I'm here! They're taking me away—"

"It's too late for *youuuu*," one of the creatures growled. As a group, they lowered me down, tugging harshly on my arms and legs. They swung me twice, cackling, "*Goodbyeeee*."

On the third swing, they tossed me straight into the swirling light.

I screamed as I plunged through it like I'd been thrown into the deep end of a pool. I free-fell into the void, my arms pinwheeling frantically. There was nothing to grasp on to. My stomach dropped to my knees, like a bag of concrete tossed directly on top of my lungs.

I couldn't breathe.

Gaping like a fish, my body was tossed in circles. The

pressure was too much. It was yanking me apart, and it felt like my brain was going to explode.

Just when I thought I couldn't handle any more, things went blessedly black.

⟡

"Where is *she*? I told you not to fail me on this, Bragnon! That little human is doomed. She will not get by us. If the shieldmaiden Ingrid thinks she can outsmart me, she has much to learn. She will not be able to save the girl. None of them will. Not even Odin himself."

"We have not failed you, *missssus.*" The familiar leathery voice jerked me out of my delirium. My head felt like it'd been split open and my gray matter was leaking out. I twitched my hand and felt dirt. "The girl *issss* here, but she is *clooooaked.* Have no fear, she will be found."

I opened one eye.

A pair of old, scuffed shoes passed within an inch of my face. "She better be here. If she came through the other portal, we would've heard her by now. You go to the barracks. Tell them to be on high alert. I'm going to check the receiving room."

The voices trailed out of the room.

I eased my aching head up, making as little noise as possible. I couldn't see anything from my vantage point on the floor. It seemed I was wedged under some kind of bookcase. I craned my neck and peeked out. The first thing I saw was a low fire burning in a stone fireplace. It held a smoking black cauldron, which hung from an iron rod. The fire was crackling, and there was actual steam bubbling out of the pot.

If I hadn't gone through such an ordeal, I would've thought I was on a movie set.

I examined the rest of the room as best I could. It was more like a cave than an actual room. The walls were earthen and dirty and contained a busy network of roots running in every direction, even the ceiling.

It was like we were encased in a tree.

I brought my arm up and touched the rough wood directly above my face. It was old and worn. I was lucky these shelves were big enough to cover most of me, even though that thing had told the woman I was cloaked.

"Insufferable white elves! Their magic should not surpass our own!" The angry voice stalked back into the room. "She could be anywhere by now. We must search the caverns. Put everyone on it. We must find her. My sisters will arrive soon. She will not get by Urd so easily."

"Yes, *missssus*," the creature hissed. How could a horrid thing like that take orders from anyone? The beast should only have to bare its teeth, and the old woman should be screaming in fear.

"Don't fail me again, Bragnon." Something flew through the air and struck the hard-packed wall, exploding into pieces. "I will not tolerate anything less than success. Do you understand me? The cloak stone will wear off in a few hours. I want her brought to me well before then!"

They both left the room again, presumably to scour the caverns. I quietly eased from my spot. My only hope was to find a way out of here. As I stood, my brain threatened to short-circuit for a second as my mind rehashed everything, from getting shocked, to the one-handed man, to finding a raven in my kitchen, to Ingrid dressed as a gladiator, to the horrible face gaping at me in the subway car, to being kidnapped and tossed here.

I reached out to steady myself.

I couldn't allow my brain to rest on any one thing for too

long, or I knew I'd find myself in a fit of ugly tears brought on by total disbelief, soon to be followed by rocking on the floor in a fetal position, unable to function.

That was not going to help me get out of this place.

If I'd made it here, I could find a way out.

I brought my other hand up to my forehead and remembered Gram. Forgetting everything, I dropped to my knees, frantically searching on the ground. It had to be here. Without protection in the form of a hide-cutting dagger, I knew I'd never have a chance to make it out of here alive. "Please, please, be here," I whispered.

Growing up on a farm, before my family moved into town and bought the hardware store, I'd regularly handled tools such as hammers, axes, and crowbars. I'd used them my entire life. But the only knife I'd ever owned was a small, flimsy pocket knife given to me when I started 4H.

I couldn't think about that right now.

With relief, my hand finally closed around the hilt, and I slid the dagger out. "Thank you," I whispered to it, my fingers wrapped over the warm handle. I must not have been out for very long.

I stood.

Okay, now what?

I focused on what Ingrid had told me. I had to woman up. There was no other choice. I had to find a way out.

Think, Phoebe.

Other than the old fireplace with the spooky, bubbling cauldron, and the rickety bookshelves I'd landed under, which I saw upon further inspection held millions of jars with specimens floating in them, the room was sparse.

The only other piece of furniture was a battered old wooden table that sat in the middle. It had a few stools shoved under it.

I turned in a full circle.

Toward the back, a massive expanse of a tree trunk half erupted out of the wall. It took up the entire corner.

In fact, this room looked to have been built purposefully around that exposed trunk. The bark went from the floor to the ceiling, indicating it kept going outside these walls.

The tree was oddly compelling.

I walked toward it with one hand extended before I knew what I was doing.

Once there, my fingertips brushed against the bark. A swirl of light formed instantly at the contact point as a spark of electricity raced up my arm, like a swarm of bees had jumped into my bloodstream.

I snatched my hand away and stumbled back.

The light dimmed before my eyes.

Before I could decide what to do, I heard a loud thumping. It sounded like it was coming from the tree. Something was clanking around inside. I searched for a place to hide and ran, ducking down by the end of the bookcase, right as a massive form tumbled out in a flash of bright, white light.

Right where I'd been standing only two seconds ago.

As it landed, rolling a few times, it shook the room like an earthquake.

I shrank back into the shadows as far as I could go, clutching Gram to my chest.

The thing on the floor was huge. As it rose, it shook its head a few times. The ride must have been rough. At full height, it had to duck down so it didn't scrape its gigantic noggin on the exposed roots dangling from the ceiling.

When I noticed the tusk coming out of its forehead, it was all I could do not to whimper out loud. The thing had to be at least eight feet tall.

"Good, Junnal." The same crisp voice entered the room,

but stopped short of where I could see from my position crouched against the wall. "You came quickly. I am in need of your assistance. We have had a...*misfortune* of sorts. A certain prize of mine has slipped away. I will need the aid of your expert nose. I want you to sniff the creature out and bring her to me. She must smell human after all the time she's spent on Midgard. You're familiar with human scent, aren't you, Junnal?"

"Yes...Verdandi." Its voice was extremely low and filled the room like rumbling thunder, making my head ache.

"Good. Now come with me. We have reason to believe she has made it into the root network. The ettins are busy scouring the caves, but the little urchins have yet to unearth her. She is cloaked, but that shouldn't be a problem for you. You are immune to white-elf magic, are you not?"

The thing nodded its boulder-sized skull.

As they moved to the door, I risked poking my head slightly around the bookcase. I wanted to get a glimpse of the woman, Verdandi. Her voice was harsh and formidable, and I was expecting a librarian or a schoolmarm. At first look, my hand flew up to my mouth to stifle any sound that wanted to erupt without my permission.

The woman was nothing more than a skeleton, gnarled and grizzled.

As she appraised the giant, or the troll, or whatever Junnal was, it took everything I had not to squeal out loud. Her eyes were two sunken orbs in her skull. Her skin was so worn it hung in loose folds, drooping around her face. Her pallor matched the grubby gray dress she wore, and her hair was a tangled mass of charcoal and white hanging limply around her shoulders.

She turned and left, the large beast lumbering after her, each footfall shaking the floor.

I slowly exhaled, but kept a hand cupped over my mouth just in case. I tasted bile in the back of my throat as I sank down to the dirt floor, bringing my knees up, bowing my head on my arms, still clutching Gram in my fist.

What was I supposed to do now?

I wasn't sure why the giant hadn't smelled me already, but I knew my luck would run out once they came back.

That's when I heard the humming.

5

I lifted my head off my knees. The humming wasn't exactly a tangible sound, per se. It was more like a frequency. My blood began to beat at the same rate, like a song.

I stared at the tree.

Ingrid would never forgive me if I didn't try my best to escape. I wouldn't really forgive myself either. I'd be dead, but ultimately unforgiven. I stood up and brushed myself off, cocking my head at the tree as I took a step toward it.

As I drew closer, the thumping in my veins got louder. The humming was coming from *inside* the tree.

Once I was close enough, I brought my hand forward, just like I had before, lightly brushing my fingertips over the rough, aged bark. Shocks and tingles immediately raced up my fingers, electrifying my entire body.

I almost snatched my hand back, until I realized my body *liked* the sensation. It seemed to be absorbing it greedily, like nourishment. The tree was giving me something, and it felt wonderful. I exhaled as I moved closer, resting my forehead against the trunk, splaying my hands across it.

The humming merged effortlessly with my body, and they became one, with the same heartbeat.

This tree is alive.

As soon as the thought entered my mind, I realized this had to be the tree of life Ingrid had mentioned. I was bewildered. What had those creatures called it in the tunnel? Ig-dra...Ig-dras-something?

Nothing rang any bells.

I wasn't up on ancient history or mythology. Ingrid had mentioned Odin. I knew he was a Norse god, but other than that, I had no idea what any of the particular mythology entailed. In rural Wisconsin, we learn about farming and animals. We didn't have much need for detailed accounts of Norse gods—even though a good portion of our population was Scandinavian.

Oh, the irony!

I stepped back, hoping my touch this time had kindled some kind of swirling light. The light had to be a good thing. It's what got me here, if I followed the logic of what the ettins had done. That had been a concrete wall in New York City, not a tree. But maybe the tree had been behind it, since it seemed I'd been spit here just like Junnal? It was hard to know anything for sure.

No light sparked this time.

Shouts came from outside the room.

I eyed the trunk with mounting panic. I leaned into it and whispered, "Okay, I need to get out of here right now." What had the creature said to unlock it? I racked my brain, trying to remember the chant and what it'd been doing with its hands. In an effort to try to make something happen, I placed a hand on the bark, using my fingertips to trace some rectangular shapes while quietly chanting, "Please, please, open for me. I need to get home because...Ingrid's waiting for me."

That was the best I had.

Nothing.

Not even a glimmer of a spark.

The creature had given the portal its blood. That goopy, awful, yellow stuff. I'd been trying hard to forget. I still held on to Gram in one hand. I glanced down at the dagger. Without over-thinking it, I pressed the tip of the knife into a soft spot on my palm.

Bright red blood burst forth.

I blinked a few times at what I'd done. *You didn't have a choice*, I reminded myself. Something had to be done, and this counted as something.

I dipped a single finger into the blood and brought it up to the tree. "I pay my debt willingly in blood," I murmured as I pressed my bloody finger into the bark, which was deeply grooved. "Please open your doors for me and bring me home."

There, before my shocked eyes, a small, bright light started to swirl in the bark. It was small, but it was there.

It was working!

A loud clamor shook the earth under my feet. "The human"—the low, booming voice of the giant moved toward the room—"is in here."

The swirl of light started to lessen. "No! No!" I took more of my blood and frantically rubbed it on the bark in circular motions. "Open! Please, open! I give to you, oh, blessed tree, I give you my blood. I'm paying my toll! Please take me back to where I came from!"

The glowing started to increase once again, but the bark beneath it stayed firm and hard. I rocked my hand into it, trying to force myself inside.

A wicked snarl erupted from behind me. "You think to escape me! There is no escape unless I deem it so. Nobody gets away from here, *human*."

I turned around slowly, pressing my back against the bark, my fist still clutched around Gram.

Verdandi could obviously see me now, so the cloak stone must've worn off. She was livid. Her haunting, skeletal face contorted in some serious angry rage.

To her right and slightly behind her was the ettin who had ripped his arm open to get us through the portal. Bragnon, she'd called him. The giant lurked just outside the room, its head ducked so it could see inside, its pointy tusk curling into the space above the door.

"I'm...I'm not trying to escape," I tried. "See, there's been some kind of mistake. I'm not supposed to be here. You have the wrong girl, and I just want to go home." I glanced down, and I suddenly knew why Verdandi could see me.

I was glowing.

Glowing!

I brought my arm up in front of my face and turned it from side to side. It was shining all the way through. The gash in my palm was still bloody, but instead of red, my blood was pure light, like the inside of a white glow stick.

"You cannot pass through the tree of life without permission!" Verdandi snarled, tearing me out of my shock and awe. "This is *my* domain, bastard child. My sisters and I make the rules here, and you may not pass." She stalked forward, her dirty gray skirts kicking up the earth around her, bringing me back to the crushing reality of my current situation. A situation I had no idea how to get out of, much less *think* I could survive. The pit of hell would've likely been a better place to land.

"I'd really love to get...um...permission to leave," I answered meekly. "If you could grant it, that would be extremely helpful. Honestly, this has all been a mistake. I'm not the girl you're looking for. I grew up in a small town. I don't have anything to offer. I just want to go home."

Verdandi stopped midstride and let out a mirth-filled cackle, flashing a mouthful of broken, horrible teeth. "Oh, human, that is so *endearing*, really. You think to ask me permission to leave and think I'll have *mercy* on you?" She started for me again, still chortling. It sounded like one of those kids toys at a birthday party that unrolled as you blew through it, wheezy and high-pitched. "There is no mercy for you here. We have much better plans…and there is no going *home*."

I let out a small squeak and tried to scoot farther into the tree, willing it to open up and suck me in. Anything to get out of here. Warm energy radiated against my back. That was it, but it was the only thing keeping me from losing my mind. "I don't know why you're so interested in me," I said, trying to stall. "I'm a nobody. I work in the shoe department at Macy's. I've never done anything exceptional in my life, except move to New York City, which I'm actually in the process of regretting. I promise you, the moment I get home I'm going to forget all of this ever happened. I won't tell a soul. Your secret…world…is safe with me."

Verdandi reached me, a snarl on her flaccid face.

She leaned in, her fetid breath reeking as it wafted up my nostrils. I tried to shoo the bile back down my throat as it rose rapidly from my stomach. From this close, I could see her grotesque skin hanging like loose wallpaper. Her irises were a dead, flat black, but worse were the muddy lines radiating out from them, permeating the whites—or, in her case, the yellows—like vines, making it look like black rivulets were leaking back into her brain. "You will never leave here," she whisper-snarled, clearly enjoying her torment. "This is where you *die*."

A noise interrupted Verdandi's reign of terror, and I flicked my eyes away from her terrible face, happy to look just about anywhere else.

Bragnon had scurried up behind her. Up close, he was just as awful as she was. He had leathery skin running in shallow folds around his head like a lizard. His eyes were rheumy, discharging a sickly greenish liquid. He opened his mouth to guffaw at my discomfort, and I glimpsed row after row of pointy shark teeth, immediately remembering what Ingrid had said about them being full of poison.

Oh, Ingrid! What am I doing here? *Where are you?*

"You are *ourssss* now," Bragnon hissed as he came to stand next to his missus. "You will do well to keep *quiiiiet*. No use for talking *nowww*."

"Yes, that's right, dear," Verdandi said in a mockingly sweet tone. "Listen to Bragnon. No more talking." She stepped back slightly, so there was a tiny space between us, and brought her index finger up. Her nail was long and jagged and yellowed with age.

The tip touched my cheek, and I flinched back, arching my head as far as it could go. When my face lost contact with the nastiness, I begged, "Please let me go! I don't know what you want from me, but I'll do anything. Please, don't do this!"

The earth began to shake.

It took me a moment to realize the troll had entered the room.

"Verdandiiiiii," it bellowed. "Human."

"What is it, Junnal?" Verdandi said impatiently, leaving her finger blessedly off my cheek for the moment. "I don't have time for interruptions now. You will be paid as was agreed. Now go away. Use the portal in the barracks to get home."

When the giant didn't go, Verdandi glanced back, irritated.

"Human…hurt," it managed as it thumped closer, my legs vibrating with each step.

"Yes, yes, the human will hurt. We're working on it. If you're patient, I might even give you a turn, Junnal. I will render her useless first, and then you may have her. We will show her together what hiding from the Norns truly means." She turned back to me. "You cannot override your destiny, child…no matter who your father is or where you choose to *hide*."

Out of the corner of my eye, Bragnon smiled in greedy adoration, rubbing his alligatorlike hands together. After the troll had his turn, I'm sure the wonderful ettin would kindly take his. Sinking his poison into me would be the final icing on my death-filled cake.

The earth stopped rocking as Junnal came to a stop next to Verdandi.

Verdandi chose to ignore the giant creature next to her, giving me an evil smirk and staring at me with her chalky, dead eyes. "Now where were we? Ah, yes, punishing the bastard girl who thought to elude us for all these years. We foresee all of what is told, and *you* were not meant to be." She was so close her spittle coated my face, and bile took up residence in the back of my throat, where it had found a permanent new home. "You are a stain on our world, a mixed breed of dirtied blood, an ugliness that must be eradicated. Yggdrasil, our beloved tree, will take your soul as payment for your lies—as payment for being *born*!" She lofted an arm above her head, her nails fanned out like claws, a grimace of pleasure forming on her lips. Her eyes rolled back in their skeletal sockets, her unbridled ecstasy at my impending doom seeping out of every single pore in her body.

My gaze locked on her gnarled hand.

I was pressed back as far as I could go, still trying to will myself through the tree. Verdandi was going to tear me to shreds with her evil, jagged nails, and there wasn't anything I could do. I clenched my muscles, bracing for the impact, my hand tightening around the dagger still in my hand. Sweat had saturated the hilt, dripping onto the floor. I didn't have enough room to strike her.

She was too close.

I had to try. I lifted Gram, but the old woman moved too fast, her hand whipping down like a cat batting at a toy on a string. Her nails landed against my neck, digging deeply as they slashed me, rending open my skin and drawing wet, sticky blood.

I screamed, forcing Gram up between us, the pain searing me as I swung the blade upward. Instead of making its mark, it snagged on the sleeve of my wool jacket.

I didn't have time to be mad at my incompetence, because to my utter relief, Verdandi was suddenly flying backward, away from me. I watched in stunned silence, with my mouth hanging open, as she whizzed through the air, hitting the earthen wall like a bullet, bouncing off, and crashing onto the table.

The wood buckled instantly, collapsing beneath her, covering her with broken pieces.

"Not"—Junnal bellowed as it brought its sledgehammer-sized fist back around in front of its body, looking directly at me—"human."

I nodded dumbly, agreeing with it, as I glanced at the wood-strewn body on the floor, and then back at the giant creature. The thing had just tried to save my life by smashing Verdandi into the wall.

It didn't take Bragnon long to figure this out for himself.

"You *inssssolent* troll!" Bragnon shrieked. "You will pay for *thissss*." Then he dove for the giant's legs. Junnal kicked out, but Bragnon found purchase and pierced his awful shark teeth into the troll's leg, gouging at the hard flesh like a feasting piranha.

The sounds were sickening.

Junnal hardly seemed to notice as he reached down and grabbed Bragnon by the scruff of his rubbery neck. The little beast grinned, holding a mouthful of the giant's bloody flesh between his incisors. Junnal roared, shook Bragnon a few times for good measure, and tossed him away like a reptilian rag doll.

Bragnon crashed against the bookcase. The creepy jars exploded on impact like fireworks, spraying the room with glass and liquid and parts. The smell was immediately toxic.

I covered my mouth, using the inside of my elbow, gasping and coughing as the fumes burned my lungs and tears rolled down my cheeks. The backs of my fingers grazed my neck. I pulled back my hand and saw my blood was still the color of a white glow stick, but it was fading to red as I watched.

Verdandi was still under the table rubble, but I saw a foot twitch. She wouldn't be out for long, and when she awoke, there would be hell to pay for all involved.

I spun around and pounded my fist against the tree. "Please, please, open! I'm begging you!" I screamed. "Open. *Pleeeeeease!*"

A loud, thunderous crash shook the ground, and I peered fearfully over my shoulder.

Junnal now sat on the dirt floor.

His hurt leg was covered in deep magenta blood, thick as paint. It leaked out slowly, like ketchup out of an inverted bottle.

The giant stared straight at me.

I eased around, swiping the blood still trickling out of my neck and rubbing it into my now tattered jacket. It left a long streak of neon pink in its wake. I was forced to lift my arm back over my mouth and nose, because the smell from the broken jars was too intense. My lungs felt like they were on fire.

I quickly glanced over at Bragnon.

He was out cold. The contents of the jars had spread out over his body, and now his clothing, a nondescript brown toga-like thing, was smoking. I hoped it was strong enough to eat through his hide.

"Not. Human." Junnal's voice was quieter now, which meant it was at megaphone level. "Odin."

I froze.

I wasn't sure what to do.

The giant creature shook his head, the boulder rocking back and forth. I shrank back. When he was done, his entire body listed to one side, like he was trying not to pass out after a night of hard drinking.

The giant troll had been poisoned.

Bragnon had bit him.

I took a tentative step forward. This thing had tried to save my life, the least I could do was tell him thank you. I had no idea what to do to help him. "Um, hi, Junnal. I'm Phoebe." I tread a little closer. "Thank you for…helping me. I wasn't expecting that. I see you're in pain. Can I do anything to help you?"

He shook his head as he tried to focus on me, his eyes looking small in proportion to his massive body. He blinked a few times before he opened his cave of a mouth. "Odin. Me."

"You're…Odin?" I had to admit I was a little shocked. "*Really?*"

He pointed to himself and shook his lumbering head. "Send...Junnal. Odin."

Odin sent this giant to help me?

I really hadn't been expecting that. "That was nice of him. So what can I do? If I aid you, can you help me escape?" My voice was filled with hopeful optimism.

Before the giant could answer, an angry shriek filled the room.

It had come from the pile of wood.

6

Verdandi kicked her legs out, and pieces of the table soared around the room like she had superhuman strength. She didn't, because she was probably zero human, but calling her *super* alone seemed wrong.

My eyes locked on her. I was riveted, even though I should be using this precious time to beg the tree to open its portal to take me home.

She rose to a sitting position exactly how I would imagine a dead body would rise out of a coffin: bent perfectly at the waist, the transition effortless.

Her veiny black eyes were wild as they scoured the room, searching for who to punish first.

I regretfully backed away from Junnal, toward the safety of the tree, tugging my scarf over my mouth and nose.

"Troll, what you have done will cost you your life," Verdandi seethed once her eyes lit on Junnal. "I will tear your head from your shoulders and spit into your decaying body as it withers and dies!"

That was a serious threat.

The rest of the wood covering her flung off, like the walls had become magnetized.

Junnal glanced from Verdandi to me, his poor head listing even more. "Grum. Tree." With effort, he lifted his massive hand and gestured to the tree. Then he dug his fists into the dirt and scooted to the side, trying to position himself between me and Verdandi.

I wanted to go give him a bear hug.

Instead, I pondered what *grum tree* meant.

I glanced over my shoulder at the tree. Maybe that was the sacred name of the tree for giant trolls? Possibly a password?

"That's right, Junnal, come closer," Verdandi cackled as she stood. Her dress was tattered and hung in ribbons around her. "I will enjoy making you bleed." She swung her hands out in front of her with an evil grin, her teeth making ugly clacking sounds as she wiggled her fingers, muttering something under her breath.

Her head bobbed once, and poor Junnal arched backward, grabbing on to his massive throat with one hand.

"How does that feel, *troll?*" Verdandi raged as she stalked closer. "You caught me by surprise once, but that will *never* happen again."

My back thumped against the tree, and it startled me. I glanced down at my body. Gram was still thankfully clutched in my hand. The color of my skin was back to normal. I leaned into the tree and immediately felt its energy. As I absorbed whatever it gave me, my hand began to brighten.

"You will die!" Verdandi seethed, continuing her assault on the giant, who so far was not cooperating with her plan.

Junnal, still gripping his neck with one hand, had pulled himself closer to Verdandi. They were almost eye to eye, though Junnal was still taller, even though he sat on the dirty floor.

"How can this be?" Verdandi's voice quaked with anger. "You are not immune to my powers, lesser! You will fall, and then I will kill the human impostor."

Bragnon picked that moment to stagger to his feet, brushing the potions and shattered glass off like they were minor irritants, taking most of his toga along with them. Charred black holes dotted the rest of the fabric, but his skin was unmarred as far as I could see.

That was really too bad.

He came straight for me.

I dropped my scarf and twisted around, bringing both of my hands up to pound on the bark. "Please, grum tree, open up! The nice troll said to ask you. He gave me permission! I don't want to die here. Please open up!"

"You will not leave. You will *dieeee*," Bragnon hissed from right behind me.

There was a loud roar of anger.

I glanced around as Bragnon did the same. Junnal had changed directions and was now making his way toward us.

"Giant, you will not get away from me!" Verdandi shrieked. "Die, die, *die!*"

The big guy just kept coming.

Bragnon turned back to me, his wide mouth curling up in a sinful smile laced with horrible, painful intent. "I will kill you *firsssst*. The giant cannot harm *meeee*."

He sprang.

Before any concrete thought hit my brain, I swung Gram in front of me. But Bragnon's wicked fingers grabbed on to my arm, forcing the knife down.

"Grum. Grum," Junnal wailed impatiently, his voice barely above a whisper, but still echoing like a drum around the room.

Bragnon twisted my arm painfully, and I cried out.

"What is wrong with you? Why won't you die?" Verdandi squealed as she marched up to the injured troll and kicked him. Junnal was almost to Bragnon and me.

It was going to be one big party at the tree.

"Verdandi?" A breathy female voice rang out from the hallway. "What's happening? Urd has rushed us home. She said you were in danger!"

"I know she's in danger, you harpy. I just saw it," another voice added. "The bastard child is here, and Verdi's been felled by a troll." They were almost through the doorway.

My grip began to fail. Bragnon was going to make me drop the dagger, and then he was going to kill me. He knew it and snickered with glee.

I pulled back at the last moment, using the tree as leverage, yanking my arm up. At the same time, Junnal grabbed on to Bragnon and pulled. The beastie's legs went out from under him, but he held on to my wrist in a death clamp that rivaled Hercules.

"Why won't you die, imbecile?" Verdandi screamed. "You are *not* immune to my magic!" It was lucky Junnal was big and sat between me and the hag. I knew without hesitation that Verdandi's attention would transfer to me once she spotted me, and she would rip out my throat with her wicked fingernails.

"Well, this is quite a scene," a breathtakingly beautiful woman said from inside the doorway. "Verdi, how come you didn't invite us?" Her hair looked like spun gold. It was amassed in a halo towering around her head, flowing over her shoulders and tumbling down her chest. Her features were as precise and perfect as Verdandi's were ancient and horrid.

It was hard to believe they were actual sisters.

Right behind her, another figure stepped into view. She

was tall, plain, and remarkably thin, with long, greasy black hair. She wore an actual black pointy hat. "I told you, Skuld, and I'm never wrong. You should know that by now."

"Well, what I'm seeing, Urd, is that this girl will be gone in just a few minutes. Only, I can't quite see where she's going." Skuld, the woman with the Rapunzel hair, cocked her head and studied me. "That's odd."

"This little bastard isn't going *anywhere*!" Verdandi seethed between a very clenched jaw. "Help me kill this troll, and then we'll kill the girl together. And then the stain of her existence will be wiped out for all of time."

Bragnon's tenacity as he held on to my wrist showed no bounds. He was fighting Junnal's tug with gusto, kicking his short legs and arching his body. The giant couldn't get him off. If Junnal tugged any harder, it would take my arm off.

Junnal gave out a loud bellow, his voice ripping through the room.

"The giant is resisting my magic," Verdandi yelled in frustration. "It is impossible for any troll to withstand our power!"

Junnal tightened his grip on Bragnon's leg and snapped him up like a whip. The horrible beastie finally lost his grip on my arm, but managed to latch on to my ankle on the way down, his wicked nails gouging into my leg through my boots.

"This giant is spelled by a god, Verdi," the pointy-hatted Urd said. "It will take all of us to break it. Here, let me put my things down." For the first time, I noticed that each sister carried an armful of bags. I must've interrupted their shopping date.

Junnal glanced up, meeting my eyes. This was it. The cavalry was here. He said, with as much urgency as he could muster, "Grum. *Tree*."

"I don't understand what you're telling me," I pleaded. "Please, this is my only chance. Tell me how to get out of here!"

Junnal struggled to free his hand, but it was the only thing propping him up. Bragnon was in his other hand, still stretched taut between us. I shook my leg, trying to get him off, as Junnal brought a shaky hand up and pointed to my fist.

The one holding Gram.

Then he said, "In...tree."

"*Nooo!*" Verdandi screamed. "You will not leave here! You will not escape me!"

Put the dagger in the tree? Grum was Gram?

I could do that.

I hopped around, kicking out my leg with renewed vigor, but Bragnon held on stubbornly.

Junnal bellowed his frustration. *I'm right there with you, big guy.*

"You will not get *awayyyy*," Bragnon hissed.

"Watch me." I twisted the upper part of my body, slamming Gram home at the same time.

"*Nooo!*" Verdandi screamed.

"Oh, Verdi. You were never supposed to win this round. I told you she'd be gone in a few minutes," Skuld said matter-of-factly. "I'm just puzzled why I can't see what happens next."

Light swirled at the tip of the dagger, and there was a substantial tug from the tree. A moment later, white light blazed out of the hole, and I felt myself being blessedly sucked inside.

At the same time, a shot of pain bloomed up my leg.

The sounds in the room quieted behind me as my body sailed into the vortex. The only things trailing in the darkness were Verdandi's muted screams and Junnal bellowing one last time.

Then I was totally gone.

My body turned in on itself, tumbling, dropping, falling. I went numb, my brain threatened to go black.

Then everything ceased to exist.

Everything except the throbbing in my leg.

Where Bragnon had bitten me.

7

The smell of sulfur stung my nostrils, bringing me back to consciousness with a gasp. Two seconds later, I didn't have room to think about the smell of rotten eggs infecting my nose, because the throbbing in my ankle occupied all of my available brain space.

Bragnon had not only bitten me, but had shredded my boot, which had been lost somewhere in the transfer. The ride through the portal had been rough, like being tossed in a human-sized clothes dryer spinning at warp speed. My faithful scarf was also missing.

I was on my back, dirt coating the ground beneath me. Again.

This was getting old. I moaned as I brought my injured leg up and tried to cradle it against my body. "*Ow!*" I rolled to the side, trying to focus my eyes in the low light, rocking lightly from side to side, urging the pain to go away.

It seemed I was in another cave, but this one had stone walls instead of earthen ones. It was more like a large cavern. It had a high, domed ceiling, and there were outcroppings of boulders piled up against the walls and scattered around the room.

I bent my head around, trying to get a look behind me, expecting to find the tree or some exposed bark, but saw only more rock.

The cave wall was smooth, but I spotted a faded archway set into the wall. That must have been where I'd been jettisoned from.

In a panic, I remembered Gram.

My ticket out of here.

Battling through the pain, I jerked onto my stomach, running my hands along the ground, frantically searching for the dagger. It wasn't anywhere near me. "No, no," I cried. "It can't be gone!"

I scrabbled some more in the dirt, pulling myself along like a crab.

It wasn't here.

I finally gave up and struggled to sit. The pain in my ankle ignited like wildfire. I cried out, reaching to put pressure on my leg, anywhere, just to try to stop the throbbing. My brain reeled from the intensity of it. I'd never experienced anything this painful in my life.

But I couldn't give up. I had to find my lifeline. Gritting my teeth, I started to inch my way forward, running my hands around, upturning rocks and stones, hoping it had just been covered when we landed. "Please, please," I whispered. "Please be here."

"Looking for something?" A low, throaty growl, decidedly male, sparked from the shadows to my left. "I can tell you right now, you're not going to find it."

My head shot up, and I cringed. I wasn't ready to fight another big bad.

Using all my strength, I propelled myself backward as

quickly as I could go, fighting through the blazing pain that had become my leg, until I was pressed against the smooth part of the rock wall, right where I thought the portal opening was.

I exhaled and slumped over.

My energy was spent. I took in another lungful of hateful air and was reminded that all around me was the smell of stinky, potent rotten eggs.

Could I be in actual *hell*?

I'd been joking about it being a better place to land. Now I wasn't so sure. I glanced around. It was just a cave. It likely wasn't hell, but this was definitely what I imagined hell would smell like. Rancid sulfur with a side of vomity gag.

I braced my head against the wall and listened. All was quiet from the direction I'd heard the voice. But it'd definitely been male. I couldn't see into the shadows. The lighting was dim, and there were too many places to hide. The only illumination seemed to come from a distant opening across the cave floor.

There could be an army of ettins out there waiting to rip me apart, or better yet, something new and equally as haunting, and I wouldn't even know it.

I shuddered and closed my eyes.

Think.

I needed that dagger, and whoever had taken it may be able to be reasoned with. The voice had sounded human, so that was a plus. At least, I was hoping it was. It had sounded rusty, like the man hadn't spoken in a while, with maybe a hint of an unfamiliar accent? It was hard to know. He hadn't said much.

The possibility of having only one thing to contend with right now made me feel a little bit more optimistic. Maybe humanlike people lived in this place. Maybe the inhabitants of *this* particular world weren't insane and hell-bent on trying to kill me. That was a nice thought. I was going to hold on to that.

Sweat beaded on my face.

Not only was it stinky, it was steaming hot. But there was a chance I might be running a fever from Bragnon's poison. The pain in my ankle had ratcheted up to, and was quickly passing, unbearable. I had to find something else to focus on. Trying to talk the stranger out of my blade was a good place to start. "Hello," I called in a thin voice. "I'm so sorry I've landed in your…space. But I really need what you've taken from me so I can go home. Without it…I'm trapped here."

"I will not give it up." The sound came from about twenty paces to my left. Closer this time. It was still too dark and shadowy for me to pinpoint exactly where. The voice was still rough and raspy around the edges.

I sighed. I was not in any shape to deal with another monster. "It's mine, and I need it back!" I called. "Where I'm from, people don't take what's not theirs." Usually. Sometimes. Okay, most *nice* people.

"It's been a long time since I've received a gift of this magnitude," the voice replied hoarsely. "I will not part with it."

"It wasn't a gift. It belongs to me," I insisted, bringing my injured leg up, gritting my teeth as I wrapped my hands around my knee, lofting it in the air to take the weight off my ankle. I was running out of time. I was either going to black out or die from the poison. "In order to *receive* a gift, one has to give it willingly. I did not *give* you anything. You took it while I was out cold. That's called stealing."

"I take what the fates give me," he growled. "I do not regret it."

"If you keep that dagger, I will die," I said flatly. "While that may be an enjoyable option to you, I promise my death will rest on your shoulders for all eternity. Depending on what sort of world I've landed in, and what kind of species you are, that might be a very long time."

"I will not aid in killing you," he called. "Your death is your own."

"If you don't help me, it's the same as killing me. Maybe down here you guys don't take honor lightly, but from where I'm from, not helping another person is equal to signing their death certificate. You don't leave someone to rot in the street. You help them if you can. And you *can*. Give me back my dagger!"

"Do not talk to me about honor!" His voice became stronger each time he spoke. "They have stripped me of everything in this wretched place. All I have left is my honor."

"Could've fooled me." I coughed. The pain had climbed to mid-thigh. It was blinding. It was a miracle I was still conscious, but I wasn't going to be for much longer. Once the poison hit my vital organs, I knew I would die, and then Verdandi and Bragnon would win.

I tried to concentrate, focusing on Ingrid and what she would want me to do.

She would want me to fight. It wasn't even up for debate. That was a good, concrete thought. I latched on to it greedily. Fight. I had to fight. "Quit being a coward and give me back my knife!" I shouted. "You're a dirty thief with no honor and nothing more!" That took more effort than I'd thought, and I slumped to the side, gravity tugging me to the dirty floor.

"I am no coward," the voice answered as a shape finally stepped from the shadows. "I have been bound by gods, cast out of my rightful world, tied up like a dog, and have bested the fire demons again and again, and yet I still live. I am *no* coward." Each syllable had been spoken with purpose.

He walked—more like *stalked*—toward me.

My eyes blurred, the pain eating away at my ability to discern much of anything, but he seemed to have only one head, so that was a relief. Even if he'd had ten heads, I wasn't in a position to do anything about it. My body was spent, and the bastard had my trusty blade. If his plans included chopping me up, or flaying me open, there would be no stopping him.

He dropped to a crouch in front of me, peering at me, his eyes narrowing like a predator's. The fact that he was shirtless was the first thing I noticed. It was hard to miss, even with my failing vision. His body was large, full of corded muscle. He wore a ragged pair of shorts, which looked vaguely like they used to be pants. They were caked with dirt. Sweat beaded all over his body, making it shine.

He had the right idea. You really shouldn't wear clothes here. It was too hot. Deliriously, I wished he would take my jacket off since I was pretty much burning up.

He leaned in closer.

I could tell he was a big guy, even crouched down. He had intricate dark patterns etched on his stomach like flames. They were beautiful. "Pretty lines," I slurred, my body beginning to shut down. "Dagger. I need it. Please…my only chance."

He lifted my ankle. I muffled a scream and bit the insides of my cheeks, my hands scrabbling in the dirt. In a rough voice, he asked, "What bit you here?"

I moaned. "A shark…with lots of teeth."

"A shark?" He cocked his head, his long, blond hair dropping over one shoulder, obscuring the black tattoos I noticed ran along his huge biceps. "I don't understand."

"Short and mean…icky green eyes…lots of sharp, pointy

teeth…just like a shark." He turned my ankle, and I cried out, tears springing to my eyes.

"An ettin?" he asked. "The Norns' agents? You were bitten by an ettin?"

"Yes, yes, an ettin!" I chortled. It rhymed. Bitten by an ettin. "His name was…Bragnon." I was proud I could remember the shark's name.

"They are full of poison," he added gravely.

"No…crap," I gasped. "Hurts!"

He rocked my ankle, still inspecting it.

"Stop…touching…*me*!" I was too weak to pull out of his grip, or kick him, which is what I wanted to do.

He finally set it down and then decisively tore open what was left of my tights. I was still dressed in my skirt from this morning, my wool jacket, and one winter boot. I moaned and tried to focus my eyes, but they kept rolling back in my head. "What…in the hell…are you *doing*?"

"I must get the poison out."

"And I need…to be naked…for that?"

"I have to see how far the poison has gone up your leg." His voice was authoritative.

I pried my eyes open as he moved forward, balancing on the balls of his bare feet. I spotted my dagger sticking out of his waistband. "Mine," I mumbled. "Give it back. Then I can…get to Ingrid. She can…help…"

"There's no time," he said. "Tell me where you feel no pain. Hurry."

I lifted my head, which took an incredible amount of effort. For the first time since I'd been bitten, I saw my ankle. There were thick, dark holes where Sharky's teeth had punctured the skin. The blood was a dark, muddy red, half dried, half leaking. I wasn't glowing, thank goodness. The pain had risen to the top of my thigh.

I brought my arm down weakly, slapping it against the top of my thigh in a halfhearted karate chop. "It's here...the fire stops here."

He met my eyes for a brief moment and then grabbed on to my waist, sliding me so I was positioned flat in front of him. Then he ripped the rest of my tights off and discarded them impatiently, at the same time pulling up my skirt to expose my bare thigh all the way to the top. I wore underwear, so I was still covered.

But, at this moment, I couldn't have cared less.

Just stop the pain, Tarzan. That's all I ask.

Until he pulled Gram out of his pants.

Then I cared a lot. "Please, what are you doing—" I gasped as all my brain pistons re-fired at once. I started to scream and kick when he angled the dagger down toward my leg, which sent shooting stars skyrocketing through my eyes as my ankle hit the ground over and over.

This strange, half-dressed man was going to cut me with my own dagger!

"Relax, Valkyrie, this blade has more uses than just opening portals. Odin made sure of that when he had it crafted."

"Are you going to cut me with it?"

"Yes, but as I cut, the blade will sear the flesh. I only have to make a small incision above the poison line."

A small incision?

"*Argh!*" I tried to buck up, but his large hand splayed over my stomach, pressing me to the ground, forcing me to keep still. I glanced down and saw the dagger was embedded in my leg. I didn't think that was at all necessary.

I wailed until my voice was hoarse. The fire I'd felt from the bite was nothing compared to what was charging through me now. A volcano of heat cooked my thigh. Smoke and lava should've been pouring out of my leg. I thrashed my head back and forth.

"Only a few seconds more," he said gruffly. "I can see the poison under your skin. The trail beneath is now blue. The dagger has done its job well."

"I can't," I panted. "I can't do this...not...strong... enough."

He chuckled, his voice warming up for the first time. "A lesser beast would have lost consciousness. This is no small task." He finally eased his hand off my stomach as he pulled the dagger out.

I screamed.

When I was done cursing the entire world, I lay there trying to catch my breath.

"Valkyrie, I'm curious. How did you find your way here?" He rocked back on his heels and cleaned the dagger on his filthy pants like I wasn't splayed right in front of him writhing in agony. My blood streaked the fabric red.

I may have lost consciousness for a few moments.

When my vision slowly ebbed back, I spotted him perched on a rock nearby, still waiting for me to answer.

"What did you ask me?" I mumbled.

"How did you land here? And where are your weapons?"

"Um, my weapon is currently resting in your waistband." I glanced around the dismal cave. "And I don't know how I got here. The tree didn't ask me where I wanted to go. It just decided."

He got off his rock and paced over, bending down to inspect my wound. I was happy I was lying down and couldn't see the carnage. "No, I mean where is your battle armor? Your shield and your weapon of choice—your spear, ax, or sword? Shieldmaidens are not seen without their full regalia often. If you meant to hunt me, you came ill-prepared." He ended with a little snarl. "Odin's favorite dagger will only get you so far."

"Hunt you?" I asked, confused. "Why would I want to hunt you?"

"For the reward and glory."

"Huh? I think you've mistaken me for someone else. The only reward I seek is finding my way back to New York." For good measure, I added, "Without any creepy monster following me. I just want to be left alone."

"This is perplexing indeed." His eyebrows locked into concentration. Honestly, his face was incredible. Now that I could focus on it without pain addling my brain, he looked like he'd been carved out of stone, not born. His skin was a deep caramel color and flawless. He could be a Greek statue. And those tattoos and the blond hair. *Holy moly.* "The only shieldmaidens who have tried to reach me here have come through Surtr's lair, paying a hefty toll for their entry. This portal was sealed long ago by the gods." He gestured to the wall behind my head. Then he glanced down with an arched brow, like I kept vital information from him that might have something to do with the unsealing of the portal.

"Honestly, I'm not lying. I have no idea how I got here," I insisted. "Verdandi was trying to kill me, and I pierced the tree with Gram and fell through. Actually, it was more like I was sucked inside after I rammed the dagger into the bark, but whatever, it wasn't my choice. I wanted to return to New York, not come here."

He sat back. "You were in the presence of the Norn Verdandi?"

"Yes, and it wasn't great. She's pretty horrifying."

"Very few escape their lair. The three fates are... powerful beings."

I thought of the big, brave Junnal. "I know."

"My judgment is that you cannot harm me." He stood up. "If I thought you capable, I would have left you here to fend for yourself."

"Left me to die, you mean," I corrected, wondering if I should try to get up or just lie here for a while. Getting up seemed like a lot of effort.

"Wrong, Valkyrie. You would not have died. I simply saved you from a fortnight of agony." He stood, making the decision for me, as he bent over and scooped me up like I weighed nothing.

The pain from the dagger wound had subsided to a dull ache. "Who are you?" I asked as he turned and headed deeper into the cavern.

"I am Fenrir the Wolf."

"I'm sorry, did you say you're a *wolf*?"

8

"Yes, I said wolf. My father is the god Loki, and my mother the giantess Angrboda. I am considered a demigod to some, a monster to others, but my true form is a wolf." He carried me easily, shifting me in his arms as the path became narrower. "My siblings are very different than I, even though we share the same sires. We've each arrived in these worlds for different purposes and must accept what has been bestowed upon us. None can fight their destiny." I heard a hint of a growl. "But I can fight my circumstance, which is what I am forced to do here daily."

"How can you understand me so easily?" I asked. "English can't possibly be your first language." Why that was the most important thing to lead with was beyond me, but I had to start somewhere. "You're from an entirely different realm of reality than me. We shouldn't be able to communicate at all."

"Gods—even demigods—are born knowing all Midgard languages. Without that knowledge, we would be severely weakened."

"Midgard?"

"The human realm, Valkyrie." He glanced at me like I was an idiot. "It was apparent where you hailed from when I heard you speak the first time. If you had spoken another language, I would have responded in kind."

"Why do you keep calling me 'Valkyrie'?" I asked as we emerged into a smaller cave. He came to a stop in front of a dark pool of water. The light in this cave was equally as dim as the other, fueled, as far as I could see, by a small fire pit situated on a higher plateau than where we stood. The ceiling here was taller than the bigger cavern we'd been in, but this room was skinnier, with rock closing in steeply on both sides. "I'm not a Valkyrie." I glanced down at the water, waiting for Fenrir to answer me.

It looked deathly black in the low light, steam rising in wispy tendrils. For steam to be rising in this heat zone, it had to be burning hot in there.

He set me down on a small boulder beside the pool. My leg banged the rock, and I cried out, gritting my teeth. I shifted my weight, and I could feel the blood begin to flow in earnest from the cut Fen had made on my thigh. My skirt was pulled down, so I couldn't see the damage. I pressed my hand through the cloth to try to staunch the bleeding.

There wasn't much else I could do.

Fen backed up a few paces and peered down at me strangely. "I call you Valkyrie because that's what you are."

"I'm *human*," I responded firmly. "I was born in Midgard, as you refer to it. I'm not a Valkyrie. I don't even know what that is. I promise you, there's nothing special about me. If I was something else, I would know it."

Fen took a seat opposite me. "That may be very true, since you are innocent on many levels, but I've never seen a human being *glow* before. My contact with your kind is lacking, as it's been many centuries since I've ventured to Midgard, but to my knowledge, mankind's ability to kindle magic is all but gone. It died out thousands of years ago, when our kind stepped back. We were ordered to never interfere with humans again. For the most part, we've upheld our end of the bargain, but only someone fueled by Asgard blood could have burned as brightly as you did when I first saw you."

"I was glowing because of the tree," I grumbled defensively, rubbing my arms. "When I stood next to it, it infused its stuff into me. I'm not glowing now, see?" I held up a hand.

He nodded. "Indeed, you are not. But trust me, I've come across many shieldmaidens in my lifetime, most of them hunting me, but none has ever shone as brilliantly as you did when you emerged from that portal. Your essence was blinding. Yet you seem to know nothing of your kind." He shook his head. "It's a mystery."

"It's no mystery. It was just the tree." I winced as I tried to reposition myself on the unforgiving hard surface. "It's obviously magical, or I wouldn't have been able to ride around in it like a magical dryer. It gave me its juice, and now it's gone, so no more glow."

Fen tipped his head back and laughed. The sound was a nice break from his hard edge. "Its juice, as you refer to it, is your *sustenance* now. You light up because your body drinks its energy for fuel. Valkyries cannot live far from Yggdrasil. They can find energy in other places, of course, but long bouts without drinking from the tree will lessen them, threatening their very existence. Your glow, as well as your smell, marks you unmistakably as a Valkyrie."

Could that be right?

My brain wasn't comprehending this conversation right

now. Too much had happened, and I needed time to recover before I could figure everything out. Things were changing too quickly. "Once I take a shower, I'm sure I'll smell human again."

Fen chuckled as he stood up. "It seems you have a lot to learn. Why they sent an innocent into my den is still unclear, but you will do well to consider yourself lucky to be alive. It was within my rights to leave you to suffer in agony with ettin poison running through your veins. I do not take kindly to violations of my lair."

"I didn't violate anything," I huffed, hugging myself. "Honestly, I just want to go home." My eyes landed below. My blood had fully coated the rock and was dripping slowly onto the dirt floor. My head spun, my brain feeling light and funny. "Fen, I'm going to—"

I slid off the rock, and everything went black.

I coughed, spitting putrid water out of my mouth. "*Gah!*" I gagged. "Why...*why* am I in the water?" I shook my head to clear the liquid out of my eyes, only to have more flow over my head.

Calling this water was a stretch. It was more like sewage.

"I have no bandages, and these waters are healing. It's all this wretched place has to offer, so that's why I took them over for myself." Fen stood chest-deep in the small pool we'd been sitting next to, his arms supporting me, holding me afloat.

My jacket, blouse, tights, and one lone boot were gone, and I was pressed up against his chest in only my skirt, panties, bra, and the white camisole I'd worn under my work shirt. At least he'd left some of my clothes on.

"What do you mean 'taken them over for yourself'?" I brought my hand up and wiped the smelly liquid off my face. "This water is gross." I spit out more. "It's burning my throat." But as I moved my toes, testing my ankle and my leg, they actually felt good. It must be working. It wasn't nearly as warm as I'd thought it would be either.

It was hot, but not melt-your-skin-off hot.

"These caverns are the most valued in all of Muspelheim, as they contain ninety-five percent of the water found in this realm. But these pools, in this particular cave, are the only waters that contain *solay*, a sacred healing element, so they are revered."

"*Solay* smells like fishy-mud mixed with rotten eggs topped with stinky garbage." Vapors from the steam burned my eyes. The water was like a seltzer bath giving off a putrid effervescence.

"Yes, the smell is very potent. The healing elements are a combination of crystal salt and other compounds found only in these caves. One long soak can heal serious injuries. The salt finds its way into the body and fuses to your internal cells, mending you. Your neck wound is already healed."

I brought my hand up to where Verdandi had slashed me with her nails. He was right. The skin was perfectly smooth. "And they—the people here—just allow you to live here in their sacred place?"

"No, they don't allow me anything." He chuckled, causing my body to shake and the pool to ripple. I lifted my head up a bit so the water didn't splash in my face. "When I was banished here, it didn't take me long to find these caves. I needed water to survive." He shrugged. "So I commandeered them."

"Huh," I replied. "So I take it they're not too happy about that."

"No." He laughed. It was a rich, dark sound. It was the first time he sounded completely relaxed. "They are not. They attack quite often, in fact."

"How many?"

"Fifty to sixty."

I'd just lowered my head, and I jerked it up. "Did you say fifty? As in five-oh?" I immediately envisioned a legion of ettinlike creatures swarming into the tunnels. My arms snaked around Fen's shoulders without my permission. "Can they get in here right now? And by the way, what are *they* exactly?"

"They are called fire demons, and they aren't very big or strong, but they are tenacious." He walked me over to a set of crude steps and set me down. The rocks were smooth and slippery. As my legs took my weight for the first time, I realized the pain was nearly all gone.

"There is only one way in, Valkyrie," he answered. "If they trigger the alarms, I will know."

"Then what?" I stood, making my way along the edge of the pool, testing my leg while trying to get a feel for the small cave. It was too dark to see anything very well.

"Then I fight."

I turned to this man—no, not a man, a *demigod*—and watched as he dipped beneath the surface and came up again, his hair slicked back, water rushing in torrents off his broad shoulders, trailing down his massive chest, his tattoos barely visible in the murky water.

He was a predator, there was no doubt.

A very powerful one.

But I didn't feel scared of him. If I was smart, I should've been. But so far everything else I'd encountered in this strange place had been horrid and hateful. Fen didn't give off that vibe. He wasn't a direct threat.

I wasn't so sure how he'd be when I stole my dagger back. Maybe I'd change my tune. But for now, I had to play nice with the big, bad wolf. That was the totality of my genius plan. "Do you always win when you fight?" I asked curiously.

"Yes."

"Well…that's good, I guess." It was a big, fat relief, is what that was.

He eased over to where I rested with my back against the edge of the pool. I'd found a large rock underneath the surface, and sat half perched in the water.

"Valkyrie"—he brought his huge biceps out of the water and crossed his arms—"you still confuse me. You came here unarmed, you wear no armor, you ask me if I fight well, you are unaware that an ettin bite will not kill you, and you know nothing of this realm. I know not what to think. Your kind fear me, they hunt me. Yet you do not provoke me. Please explain."

"It's easy," I replied. "It's because I don't have a kind or an agenda. I'm not here to kill you or to hunt you. I landed here by mistake, pure and simple. I'd never even heard of you, an ettin, a Norn, or any of this, before a few hours ago." Geez, it felt like a lifetime already. Had it really been only a few hours? "This is not where I want to be. I just want to go home."

"I cannot help you get back to Midgard." His voice held a note of sadness.

"Yes, you can. You have my dagger," I helpfully pointed out. "Just give it to me, and I can stick it into the rock and go home."

"You misunderstand." He shook his head. "The dagger works in Yggdrasil, yes, but you crossed a boundary when you came here. This cavern is not directly tied to the sacred tree. The portal you emerged through is what we call a cillar. It's an offshoot portal, not a true link to Yggdrasil."

"I didn't come out of the tree? It's not behind the wall?"

"No, it's not near here. The tree has many facets. Everything in our world is intrinsically connected to it. It's our most sacred thing. It keeps us rooted together across all worlds. But, not everything touches it directly. That would be impossible to manage, even for gods. The tree itself has capabilities to reach out to things not directly in its path when it decrees it so, but it doesn't work the other way around. You cannot create energy and space, even with the dagger."

"So you mean I came through a tree-made wormhole?"

He frowned. "I'm not familiar with that reference."

"Like a secret tunnel or a trapdoor."

He nodded. "In a sense, yes. But what is still unexplained is how you arrived *here*, in this exact cave. You are not supposed to be able to access this place. No one is. It's an impossible 'wormhole'. The gods destroyed the path of energy through that portal to the tree years ago. Even the tree should have found a different route."

"Why did they destroy it?"

He shrugged. "Because I escaped by it once already."

I got excited, sitting up straighter. "Maybe my landing here opened it back up again!" I rose out of the water. "Let's go check. If you know how to access the portal already, maybe I can open it with the dagger, and we can both escape!"

Fen's face took on a strange look, like he was thinking I'd lost my mind, and something else I couldn't decipher. Finally, he shook his head. "I've already tried, Valkyrie. It was the first thing I did once you landed. I held my hand to it, and the path was cold before you even stopped rolling. No energy, no life. It seems a great impossibility that you were able to come through at all." He looked at me quizzically. "If I hadn't witnessed it myself, I would think such a thing unfeasible."

Of course he would've checked it first. He didn't owe me anything! I sat back down with a thump, the stinky water splashing all over. I swiped it off my face with my hand, more than a little disheartened.

If Fen could've, he would've popped out through the portal and left me there to suffer in ettin-poison agony with no means to defend myself, to eventually be eaten by whatever creatures lived here. Especially since they wanted their prized caverns back yesterday. "Are the fire demons people like us?" I asked hopefully.

Fen hoisted himself out of the pool in one fluid motion, turning to situate himself on the ledge surrounding it. He moved with the grace of a dancer, which belied his bulky frame. He was still wearing his shorts, which seemed like it should be a relief. I hadn't had the courage to look before. They clung to every single inch of him, his powerful thighs outlined in stark definition. They were utterly breathtaking. I'd never seen muscles stand out like that before. As he began to address me, I had to tear my eyes away from the spectacle of them and focus on his face, which was not much of a hardship either. "No, Valkyrie, they are in no way humanlike. Humans resemble gods because they were created in the same likeness long ago. Here in Muspelheim, nothing human would survive for very long."

That didn't bode well for me. "What do they look like?"

"Fire demons."

"Um, can you be more specific?" I slid off the rock and rose out of the water, finding my way to the edge of the pool. It took me two tries to make it onto the ledge and another blundering turn to sit.

Fen had me beat in the grace department by a long shot.

"They are skeletal thin, with skin as dark as night. Their eyes burn brightly, and their bodies are feverish to the touch. They have forked tongues, and their teeth are sharp, like bits of coal made to points."

Water dripped down my body, settling in my skirt. "They sound...delightful."

"They are not powerful beings, but their blood is acid and can devour skin. They lack any real battle skills and can be killed in numerous ways, unlike the ettins you've already encountered. In the scope of our worlds, a fire demon is among the least fearsome."

"Good to know, even though they sound fearsome enough to me. And, in case you've forgotten, I have nothing to defend myself with, thanks to you. So their sharp teeth might be enough to kill me if they get a good hold."

"You will not need to defend yourself. They will not get past me."

Absentmindedly, I pulled my skirt up, hoping to get the water to run out, and ran a hand over the dagger wound Fen had just given me. It was sealed, but tender. Then I brought my ankle up and crossed it over my knee so I could investigate the bite marks. The numerous punctures from Bragnon's hateful incisors were gone, and the skin had fully knitted back together. I reached up and caressed my neck where Verdandi had gouged me, and felt only smooth skin. This really was a miracle healing pool.

I glanced up to find Fen staring at me. I cleared my throat. "Listen, I can't hide out in this tiny cave forever," I told him as I uncrossed my legs. "Like you said, this world is no place for a human. It's already inhospitable to me. It pushes down like a heavy weight on my chest, making it hard to breathe. It's like being forced to live in a stinky sauna. I

77

don't stand a chance of surviving for any length of time. I'm going to need to find a way to get out of here."

"You are no human." He jumped off the ledge and walked toward me. "You will find that you can survive in a lot worse places." He was still wet, but less so than I.

"That's where you're wrong." I swung my legs around, dangling them off the edge. "I'm not who you think I am, and there's no way I will last here. I need to get home." I eased myself down and went to pick up my discarded clothing, which I spotted by the bloodstained rock I'd passed out on.

"No, shieldmaiden, I think you are possibly much more than even I anticipated."

I turned toward him, totally ticked off. "How many Valkyries do you know who've passed out recently from blood loss? If Ingrid is any indication, Valkyries are strong and noble. It doesn't seem likely that they'd faint unless someone had a sword wedged between their ribs." I gathered up my clothing and errant boot, spinning to face him again. "I hardly think I fit the bill of a woman warrior. One bite of poison, and I was ready to throw in the towel."

"Say what you will." Fen stood his ground, crossing his arms. "But I know what I saw to be true. No human could glow as brightly as you did. You are going to have to dig deeply, Valkyrie, because at some point you will be forced to live up to your fate. No human could land in this world. No human could traverse a dead *cillar*. You are *no* human."

"I don't have to do any digging," I grumbled. "I just have to make sure I get out of here before the fire demons flay me open or melt me with their acid blood. I don't care if you believe me. If you're not going to help me, I'll do it myself." I made my way around him, toward the fire burning in the small alcove above the pool. That must be where he lived, and I was tired.

I would plan my brilliant escape tomorrow.

As I took the few steps up the makeshift stairway, I heard what sounded like a flare gun, followed by the sound of a hollow firecracker.

There were two more in quick succession.

Pop...pop, pop.

I spun around. "What was that?"

Fen was a few paces behind me. His face said it all. "They are here."

9

"What do you mean *they are here*?" I cried. "The fire demons? Already?" There was another hollow popping sound. "That sounds like a flare gun shooting off a firecracker."

"They've tripped my wires." Fen bounded up the stairs past me, flinging himself into his living area, grabbing a loose shirt, and scooping up several weapons from the floor all in one motion. "I have rigged lines throughout the cave entrance that are attached to small explosives. It will keep them busy for a few moments."

I rushed to the other side of the cave, following him, tossing my clothes to the floor. I plucked up my shirt and pulled it on. It stuck to my still wet body, making it harder to put on than it should be. Once I was done, I spun around and took a good look around. Fen's makeshift house was rough, to say the least. There were a few cobbled together places to sit and eat, all chunked out of rock. A very crude-looking fire pit sat in the middle with a bedroll to one side.

What I was really looking for was Gram.

It was nowhere to be seen.

"Where's my dagger!" I yelled, fear seeping into every word. "Give it back. I need something to protect myself with in this horrible place. That's what Ingrid told me when she gave it to me."

"Valkyrie, you are to stay here," Fen ordered as he ran down the steps, shirt on, weapons at the ready. "Do not follow me out of this cavern. You will be safe here. I'll be back as soon as I am able."

"What if you don't come back?" I called, fisting my hands at my sides. "I have no way to defend myself. You're leaving me here to die again!"

"I will return, shieldmaiden," he said simply as he leaped onto a small raised platform, then jumped, landing gracefully by the tunnel opening. He turned toward me, his body looking powerful and ready. "They will not best me. I will always come back."

"Don't you dare leave me here with nothing!" My voice sounded hoarse in my own ears. "I swear I will lose my mind, Fen. I will not stay in this wretched world without protection!" Gram had been my only sanity and lifeline since I'd been separated from Ingrid. Without it, panic would settle over me quickly.

He paused at the tunnel opening. "There are a few iron rods buried under those stones." He gestured somewhere behind me. "If the demons manage to get back here, which is highly unlikely, use iron on them. They wither and die if you hit a vital organ."

Then he was gone.

I raced over to the stone pile he'd pointed to and fell to my knees. There was a small recessed area under one side. I used my hands to dig under it like a dog uncovering the best, most rewarding bone of its life.

There, lying under a coating of sand and dirt, were two small iron rods, both honed to crude points. They each measured about as long as my arm. I got up, clutching them, one in each hand. They weren't samurai swords, but I guess they'd have to do.

I glanced around the small cavern.

Now what?

A loud screech rent the air, and my head snapped to the mouth of the tunnel Fen had just disappeared through. It sounded like something awful had just died a horrifying death.

It was followed by a bellow of rage.

The roar sounded like Fen, but it was a much rougher version, more primal.

I searched frantically for a place to hide. There was nothing in Fen's lair, so I ran down the steps and scoured the cave. There was absolutely no cover to be had in this tiny place. The walls were all smoothed out. There were lots of boulders scattered around, but nothing that could hide a body completely. I ran by the pool, hoping there would be something there, and found nothing.

Crap!

Another horrid screech hit my ears. Then another. Followed by a bigger sound from Fen.

Victory didn't sound like a sure thing.

What if there were a hundred this time, instead of just fifty? Or two hundred? If there were enough of them, couldn't they overpower him and swarm the caves? I was trapped back here like a rat. That feeling was getting old fast.

I spun, searching for another way out, an offshoot tunnel or something. But the only exit I could see was the tunnel Fen had taken to the larger cavern.

If the demons rushed back, I was toast, with nowhere to

run. I couldn't stay here. If I made it out to the bigger cavern, where the portal was, I could at least try to find a place to hide. There were tons of dark, recessed areas I could conceal myself in until Fen was done fighting. If the demons could smell me, I'd be out of luck, but it was worth the risk.

I hadn't gone through everything to end up dead, skewered through the heart by a fire demon with burning blood! I wanted to go home, and to do that I had to stay alive.

Holding on to that thought, I ran toward the mouth of the tunnel, gripping the iron rods tightly in both hands. They felt warm and secure.

Not like Gram, but good enough.

I stopped at the opening, cocking my head to listen. I heard screeches, but my best guess was they were coming from farther over than just the next cavern. This cave network had to boast a lot of different rooms.

Now was my chance. I had to make a break for it.

I crept into the tunnel. It was a long one, and after one turn, it got darker. I reached up and placed a hand along the wall, running my knuckles over the bumpy rock as a guide. The skin was going to get torn up, but there was no way I was letting go of either of my rods.

After a few more turns, I stopped and crouched down to listen.

It wasn't easy to move stealthily in a skirt. Why did I have to pick a skirt to wear today? I owned a total of only three. Without hesitating, I stood, tracing my fingers along the seam on the side. Then I took the point of one of the rods and slashed it into the cloth and ripped down, tearing open the seam. Then I did the other side. *Voilà*.

Now it was an oversize loincloth—a skirt I could actually move in.

A loud snarl brought my head up.

Fen sounded angry.

What if he was in trouble? Was I going to stand by and let him get killed? If he died, I would die. If I joined him, wouldn't two of us against the hordes be better odds? But I wasn't ready to fight. I'd never done it before.

I'd likely be a nuisance, rather than a help.

I inched forward. I'd decide when I had to, not before.

One more curve, and a faint glimmer of light hit the walls, casting flickering shadows and giving the tunnel a reddish glow. The big cavern I'd first landed in was straight ahead.

Very slowly, I halted in front of the opening. With relief, I could see the noises weren't coming from this cavern. Tentatively, I placed a foot into the room.

Something jumped in front of me.

It took me completely off guard. All I saw were red, glowing eyes, and I screamed.

It must've been perched up on a boulder waiting. In the low light it looked like a specter—a mere shadow of a thing. Thin didn't quite cover it. The demon was literally a bag of bones. Black, charred skin covered nothing more than a skeleton.

A pair of hot, fiery eyes peered at me fiercely. It stood right in front of me, reaching out its dark digits, trying to snare me in its clutches, its forked tongue spitting disgustingly out of its mouth.

I reacted instinctively, bringing up both weapons. I thrust once without thinking, and the weapon landed with a *thunk* in something solid.

The thing in front of me let out a loud screech.

The iron rod hadn't struck anything vital, but I'd hit it! It wasn't a total fail.

A second later, the demon wrapped its skinny talons around my rod and tried to yank it out of its body. To stop it from succeeding, I pushed my weight against it, keeping it pinned in place while I swung my other arm around and plunged the crude weapon into its neck. It made a gross suction sound, and I choked back the rising vomit.

Killing things was not for the faint of heart, but I had to survive.

I kept that mantra running over and over again in my mind.

The creature's blood splattered my arm. The acid was painful, but I kept my hold.

The thing fell to its knees.

I was forced to relinquish my hold on the rod in its neck so I could swipe my arm down the front of my shirt. I had to get the blood off. It was eating away at my skin, burning me. Open sores bloomed along my arm, the flesh hollowed out like a bunch of bloody potholes. I would need Fen's miracle waters to heal me up later.

My other hand gripped the rod in its side like my life depended on it. I wasn't about to let go of that one.

The demon was almost dead, gasping for its last breath. Its blood was churning and bubbling, reacting with the iron. When it finally fell backward, I stumbled forward, my grip still firm.

I stood over it, investigating. It wasn't quite dead yet. Its eyes unleashed a volley of hatred at me as it struggled one last time, gasping and reaching out its skeletal fingers to no avail.

Finally, after what felt like an eternity, its red orbs began to fade as the lights went totally out, dimming to a dead, jet-black.

It went still.

"Holy mother of gods! That was horrible." I ran the back of my non-bloodied forearm over my mouth. I needed a drink. This one didn't have to have an umbrella.

I waited a few more moments to be absolutely sure, and then tugged the rod out of its body, using my foot as a brace, careful not to get any more blood on me. It took some effort.

When I was done, I side-stepped the body and bent down, yanking the other rod out of its neck. Both rods were dripping with toxic blood. The dead demon wore clothing that resembled a burlap sack—if burlap sacks were made out of dirty, soiled, smelly material. I rubbed the blood from the rods on it the best I could.

The fabric didn't react, unlike my shirt, which was now shredded where the spatters had landed.

Good to know.

I poked the little devil just to make sure it was absolutely dead. It didn't move. I was being paranoid, but this was the first thing I'd ever killed, and I didn't want to have to kill it again.

A roar rent the air.

My head came up.

Fen was hurt. Nothing made that kind of a sound—a growly, angry howl mixed with pissed-off grizzly bear—when they were doing fantastic or winning an epic battle.

That was a cry of agony.

Those little bastards were getting the best of him. I had to go at least *see* if I could help. Fear of being alone in this hellhole propelled me toward the only light filtering into the cavern. As I passed by the portal I'd been ejected out of mere hours ago, I stared at it longingly. I wanted nothing more than to change course and jump back through it, making it to New York by bedtime.

But it wasn't going to happen, at least not right now.

I stopped short of entering a new tunnel. I noticed immediately where the light was coming from in this cavern. Two bright pools of bubbling hot lava lined the sides of the tunnel. No wonder it was so hot and smelly in these caves! I wrinkled my nose, breathing through my mouth.

Ten paces in, I rounded a curve, right as another dark stick figure lurched into view.

The demon and I stared at each other for a few moments, both of us surprised to find the other, its eyes firing red.

Gross.

Luckily, I'd already seen one of these little monsters before, so setting eyes on this one didn't paralyze me with fear.

It grinned at me.

Like it knew I was its prize.

I backed up a few paces to give myself room and brought the irons out in front of me. The last fire demon had been surprisingly easy to defeat, but I wasn't banking on that this time. My best bet would be to get the thing into the churning lava flow. Unless they were used to bathing in hot lava? How could any living thing withstand magma? I wouldn't know until I tried. I didn't want more blood on me, so that was the cleanest option I had.

I sized up my competition.

Its creepy eyes sparked at me. These things were at least two feet shorter than I was, and it didn't weigh very much because it was nothing but bones. What did bones weigh anyway? Forty pounds? As an athlete, I excelled at swimming, but my family had always been big on fun family picnics involving highly competitive softball tournaments.

I could swing a mean bat.

The demon made its way toward me, and I readied my stance. It angled its hands like a praying mantis, clawlike fingers snapping. It opened its mouth, and something that sounded like *greeza* hummed out of its throat.

It certainly wasn't English, and its voice sounded like rocks tumbling around in a blender, but it had been a word nonetheless. The fact that these things could talk was unsettling. I'd already filed them away in my brain as creatures who did lots of heavy breathing but had no real means of communication with regular folk.

It pointed at me, clasping and unclasping its phalanges, and said the word again.

"I'm a greeza, huh?" I said. "Well, why don't you come over here and find out for yourself?"

Its lips opened—if you could call them lips. They were more like two thin lines stuck together. And sure enough, its horrid mouth was lined with a solid row of sharp, black nubbins, just as Fen had described. They looked like shards of black tar. What was it with things down here and their hideous teeth? What could it possibly eat here? They must snack on yummy lava rock for fun.

"Greeza." It kept coming.

"Yep, that's what you keep telling me." I stood completely still. It took everything I had not to turn tail and run.

The thing took its time getting to me.

I didn't react, not even a flinch. I had to take it by surprise. Make it think I was weak and unwilling to fight. I'm sure it thought a greeza would be an easy enough catch.

When it was about a foot from me, stretching out its dead, skinny fingers, I tossed one rod down and whipped the other behind my head, swinging it around as fast as I could.

There was a loud, satisfying crack.

I should've been a softball player instead of a swimmer.

The demon lurched a few feet off kilter, swaying and disoriented, but didn't fall.

I took full advantage of its backward momentum and kicked my leg out, solidly landing a bare foot against its bony hip.

It stumbled to one knee.

I was doing this. I was defeating these things!

Fen had been right. The fire demons weren't overly threatening, or too hard to handle. Not like having to duel Bragnon or coming face-to-face with another giant troll who didn't care if I lived or died.

"Who's the *greeza* now?" I yelled, flooded with a rush of accomplishment. I let it flow over me like a blanket of wondrous relief. Maybe I would be able to survive in this world after all.

If I could do that, it meant I could eventually find a way out.

The demon snarled up at me from its compromised position on bended knee. Its red eyes blazed, sparking furiously, like two hot embers banked in a fire.

Then, lightning fast, it sprang up in front of me.

Well, damn.

10

Its shriveled hand latched on to my shoulder quicker than I could blink. The inky, black nails bit deeply into my flesh. I pivoted away. Its hold broke, tearing my skin.

I turned in a circle, swinging my leg in an arc, tripping the demon. It sprawled to the ground.

This time I wasn't going to risk letting it get back up.

I thrust my rod into it, puncturing its fleshy side. The thing howled and rolled away from me, taking my rod with it.

Hitting a vital organ was harder than it looked.

Luckily, the motion forced the iron rod in deeper. These things were not too smart. The gunk spilling out of it didn't resemble anything like blood—in fact, it looked like bubbly syrup. The iron rod was reacting with the blood, making it sudsy.

The entire thing was ridiculous to watch.

My arm still stung and my wounds were increasingly worse with each passing minute. Blood leaked from welts that still festered. Nothing was healing over. I could see why, looking at the syrupy mess coming out of that thing.

I wasn't interested in getting any more of that on me, so I stepped back, watching to see what it was going to do.

In its frenzy, the demon had rolled toward the edge of the lapping lava stream. It tried to stand, staggering back and forth like a drunk. I knew I had to take my advantage while I had the chance. I ran toward it with my arms locked in front of me, and with everything I could, I rammed it, making sure to avoid the bubbly acid.

The contact reverberated through me, but I'd hit the thing hard enough to toss it off-balance. It wobbled for a few seconds at the precipice of the lava field. For good measure, I slammed my shoulder into its bony back.

The thing toppled, screeching as it fell. Once it hit the lava, the demon began to burn up immediately.

Thank goodness!

It would've been awful if those things could swim around in there like it was a spa. The unfortunate part was it had taken one of my precious rods with it, and there was no way to get it back.

The fire demons were definitely quicker than they looked when motivated. I'd have to be more careful next time. Now that I was alone, I could focus on the sounds issuing from the next cavern. The entrance was about ten feet away.

Fen was snarling and shouting.

He was keeping them busy, but obviously not busy enough if two of them had slipped by him.

They couldn't possibly know I was here.

Or could they?

The first two had appeared to be scouting and had been mildly surprised to see me. That was not a promising thought. Maybe the Norns had rung the alarm once I'd been sucked into the tree? It wasn't out of the realm of possibilities that they'd sent out an all-points bulletin. Or possibly just offered free dental care for life to anyone who could successfully hunt me down. That would be a significant motivator for over half of the beasties I'd seen so far.

The demon had called me a greeza.

It sounded sort of like *girl* or *get her*, but there was no way to be sure, as I didn't speak evil demon.

I crept to the edge of the tunnel, hugging close to one side so I could peek out and see what was happening while hopefully staying hidden. I wasn't anxious to fight any more of those things.

The scene before me made me stifle a gasp.

This particular cavern angled downhill, so I could see most of the action laid out before me. There were fire demons littered everywhere, their piled bodies resembling burnt twigs. And yet dozens upon dozens more were flooding in from the entrance like a swarm of locusts on a mission.

It appeared they would never stop.

Fen was keeping them back, but just barely.

He was positioned on a small dais where the cave necked down. He was bleeding from numerous places on his body, and as he moved, I could see blood streaming down his face.

He fought with an intensity I'd never seen before.

I hadn't witnessed many professional fights in my life, but the way Fen moved was truly incredible. His body was fluid as he flung the demons back, one after another, sometimes multiple demons at once. He alternately struck out with a sword in one hand and a spear in the other, each hand indistinguishable from the other, full of liquid grace and incredible speed.

But there were too many demons.

There was no way he could possibly stop them all. There were hundreds, and more streamed in as I watched. That was a huge difference from fifty or sixty.

I spotted movement high up, out of Fen's reach.

Demons were beginning to scale the cave wall. Once they were over his head, they would land behind him. They weren't trying to fight Fen this time.

They were coming after me!

There was no doubt those little inky bastards knew I was here. I watched as two of them scaled the wall, all the way up to the ceiling. Once they were past their mark, they dropped to the cave floor and ran directly toward the tunnel I was currently hiding in, completely ignoring Fen.

He let out a howl of rage.

Crap!

I couldn't take on two of them next to the bubbling lava brooks. It was too risky. I had no other choice but to meet them head on, hoping I could best them, all the while praying no more came while I was doing it.

Raising my lone iron rod in a defensive position in front of me, I raced into the cavern. "I'm right here!" I yelled. "But I'm not going down without a fight!"

Not only did the two take notice, but the rest of the demon masses heard me, and the entire cave erupted in kinetic demon language. It sounded like a symphony of martini shakers full of ice being rattled simultaneously. I recognized the word *greeza*, but nothing else.

The two demons coming at me wore wicked grins on their ugly, charred faces.

Wrong move, Phoebe! You should've been quiet about it.

"Valkyrie!" Fen shouted, his anger palpable. "Get back! What are you doing in here? I told you to stay put."

"Don't worry, I've got this," I called as calmly as I could manage. I didn't want to take anything away from his focus and risk the horde breaking through his line of defense. I also didn't point out that he hardly had it handled, as if he wasn't covered in blood and close to being overrun.

I leaped in the air and brought the rod around, connecting it with one demon's head as hard as I could. It went down, and I wasted no time thrusting the rod into the stomach of the next forked-tongued beastie five paces behind the first.

We collided hard, the rod going in so far my fist smashed into its chest.

The demon howled as its mercurial blood covered my hand.

"Ow!" I hissed, yanking the rod back out completely. That was going to sting. I'd purposefully angled the strike up, hoping to hit its heart under the ribs—if it even had one. I quickly wiped as much blood as I could on my skirt.

I got lucky, because the demon in front of me fell to its knees.

But I didn't have time to enjoy it, because a nasty snarling came from behind me.

"Valkyrie," Fen yelled. "Watch your back!" I whipped around, still running my burning hand along my makeshift loincloth to get the acid blood off. "Don't try to fight them. Get back to the caves!" Fen roared. "You cannot stay out here. It's too dangerous."

"I can handle this!" *I had to, right?*

The one I had knocked in the head walked back and forth, its forked tongue lashing in and out of its gross slit of a mouth. It looked pissed that I had knocked it down.

"Braza," it rumbled, blinking dark eyelids over its glowing orbs.

"Greeza, braza," I shot back. "It's all the same to me."

It paced in a slow circle, so I followed it. I felt like a sumo wrestler poised at the ready with my comically small rod thrust out. When I circled back around to Fen's direction, I was relieved to see he was still holding down the fort and no other devils were shimmying up the rocks.

"It seems they are after you!" Fen shouted. "They've never attacked on such a level, and they aren't interested in me like they usually are."

"How did they know I was here?" I yelled back. "I just arrived!"

I didn't want to believe it, but I knew it was true. The Norns had indeed rung the alarms.

"Energy is released," Fen growled, dispersing a group of demons with one slice of his blade, "when someone arrives in a world." He grunted as he shot a few more off the dais with a kick from his powerful leg. "The Norns must have sent…a message to watch…for it." He ended with a long swipe of his spear that sent ten demons soaring through the air.

He was something to behold. If I hadn't been so freaked out, I would've enjoyed watching him. Snarling brought me back to the land of the living, where demons were after me.

"Braza benna lai, Surtr," the thing rattled.

"Sorry, buddy, but I don't speak Evil Demon," I said as I lurched forward, trying to surprise it.

The demon dodged to the side and waggled its serpent tongue.

It was on to me.

I had to think of something else. I had no training in this sort of thing, so surprise was my only real tactic. It was an asset I could think quickly on my feet.

"Braza benna lai," it garbled again, and then spat, "Surtr."

"Fen!" I shouted. "Do you know what this thing is saying?"

"It's telling you"—Fen smashed his fist into the side of a

demon head—"by the orders of their ruler, Surtr, you must go with them now. There is no other choice for you." He whipped his sword up and over, decapitating a dozen at once. "Do not go with them, Valkyrie, whatever you do. We will prevail." His voice was firm.

I found it hard to believe that we would prevail with seven hundred fire demons gunning for my blood. But I wasn't going to give up either. I wasn't a quitter.

"Okay, I'll go with you," I told the demon as I lowered the iron rod to my side and assumed a non-threatening stance. "I'll even go quietly."

"Valkyrie, no!" Fen roared with such force the room echoed with his power. I saw more than one demon flinch back. "You will not go with them! I will not allow it. Their method of torture surpasses all others. You will not be safe at their hands, no matter what they tell you! Surtr is evil. He will not trade you to the Norns for anything until he is done. His pleasure will be to break you by taking your flesh."

Break me? Take my flesh? That didn't sound at all good.

But I couldn't tell Fen it was a trick. It would ruin the surprise.

I continued with my submissive posture, while trying not to think about torture and flesh tearing. "Do you understand me, Demon Breath? I said I'd go with you."

The thing glanced at me uncertainly.

I shrugged my shoulders in a what-are-you-waiting-for gesture. My hand and arm were still burning from the demon acid. The skin literally kept peeling off as blood ran down my arm, hitting the ground. It made my grip on the rod slippery, so I had to factor that in.

The demon pointed at my weapon and said, "Wata-ju."

"You want me to put this down?"

The thing snarled, which I took for a yes.

"Okay." I bent at the knee, setting the rod down next to my foot, as close as I could to my body, balancing it slyly on a small rock. "Satisfied now? It's down."

It started for me.

This plan had better work, Phoebe, or you're in a whole lot of trouble.

I stilled myself, as I'd done before, and let the thing get within two feet of me. Just as it came close enough, I slid a toe under the iron. Right at that moment, Fen rent the air with another terrifying howl and yelled, "Valkyrie, you cannot do this!"

My foot connected with the iron rod, launching it up into my waiting hand.

It was just like I'd done over and over in junior high with my baton at band practice. I wasn't a talented musician, I'd given up on that dream early on, but I could wield a mean baton.

The demon grabbed my upper arm and wrenched me forward. I used the momentum to launch myself into it, thrusting the rod into its neck, straight up at an angle, piercing its brain.

Fen broke his stance on the dais and raced toward me.

I yelled, "No, Fen! Get back there. I told you I had this!"

The demon dropped instantly. No screeching, no grabbing.

It was stone-cold dead.

Fen slid to a stop in front of us, his mouth open. "Why didn't you tell me you could fight, shieldmaiden?"

"Um?" *Because I had no idea? This is my very first time?* Demons rushed into the cave in earnest now that Fen had left his perch. There seemed to be no end in sight. We were not going to win this one. "Fen, they're coming."

He whirled around, spreading his arms wide, charging

the incoming mob of forked-tongued beasties like they were a swarm of flies and nothing more.

I stood behind him, hands fisted around my lone rod, skin peeling off my hand and arm. There wasn't enough money in all the worlds to pay me to charge into the demon mass. There was nothing I could help Fen with in there. I would be overwhelmed in a moment.

"Valkyrie, go back to my den...there is a way ou—" He leaped into the air and, right before my eyes, changed fluidly into his wolf form before he hit the ground.

It was seamless and graceful, a beautiful metamorphosis— because this man was a *demigod*. He was no human.

His animal form was unbelievably breathtaking, and truly frightening.

He was the biggest wolf I'd ever seen in my life, at least six feet tall at the shoulders. He had brilliant, gleaming dark fur with streaks of silver flowing through it.

He barreled straight into the demons, his powerful jaws snapping them in half like toothpicks, his enormous body sideswiping them into cavern walls, where they landed on the floor like broken matchsticks. He let out a roar that shook the cave, the rocks actually raining down from the ceiling.

Stunned, I realized he'd just been toying with them before.

Like they were sport. Maybe his only real distraction in this dismal place was a good fight?

If he'd shifted earlier, this cave would've been cleared of them already. It didn't matter if there were hundreds, nothing would've gotten by him on the dais if he'd been in his wolf form.

I should've trusted him.

He was a *demigod*, and I was so very...*stupid*.

Because Fen had left his position to help me, some of the fire demons had spread to the sides, and now that he was occupied, they scooted out of the shadows and made their way toward me. There were too many.

I turned and ran.

It was all I could do.

11

Fen's fierce snarls echoed behind me as I booked through the tunnel back the way I'd come. My only chance was to make it to his lair before they got to me. He'd been in the process of telling me there was a way out, even though I hadn't seen one.

I had to trust him as I raced between the lava fields as fast as my feet could propel me. I sprinted into the original tunnel, hazarding a glance over my shoulder and gasped. There had to be at least twenty demons trailing me, and they were gaining with each step.

They were certainly speedy when they wanted to be.

Instead of heading back toward Fen's den, which would be a dead end unless I could find the exit quickly, which I wasn't hopeful about, I veered and ran toward the portal.

It was only a few feet away, and in the scope of my current situation, it was my only real option. I wasn't making it back to his lair before they caught up to me, even though I was running faster than what I thought was normal.

Maybe, just maybe, the portal would open if I begged and pleaded.

Whatever had tossed me here, whether it had been the tree or interference by another force, might still be awake in there. I had plenty of blood gushing from my arm to offer as payment. I'd give it just about anything it wanted.

I might even promise it my firstborn.

I bounded up to the smooth stone and pounded a single bloody fist against it in a flurry of movement. "Open up! Please. I need a ride! Take me *home*!" Absolutely nothing happened, except my blood was now smeared all over the surface and my hand ached more.

No glow kindled. Not even a flicker.

I kicked it in frustration. "Damn it!"

"Greeza," several gravelly voices rumbled from behind me. "Braza, Surtr."

I slid around slowly, my heart pounding so hard it felt like it was going to thump out of my chest. I made sure my hand stayed on the rock, keeping it pressed hard against the surface, just in case.

The other hand held my only iron rod, but what good was it going to do me now? I couldn't gouge out twenty necks in one swipe. I wasn't Fen.

"Greeza."

"I'm not your greeza!" I shouted in what I hoped was a menacing tone. "I'm not even supposed to be here! This has all been a huge mistake. If you let me go, I promise to never come back. You have my absolute word on that. Tell your leader I want no trouble."

They formed a semicircle around me.

One of the demons stepped forward. They all looked the same—black, charred skin with forked tongues slithering in and out of their awful, thin, dark mouths.

101

This one looked no different.

I thrust my rod up and swung it in front of me. The beastie just stared, blinking its black eyelids over its red orbs.

"Stay back! Or I'll kill you like I did your friends!" My voice was rough and dry.

The thing chortled.

The sound resembled a fork stuck in a garbage disposal, but it was a laugh nonetheless. This demon thought I was weak, even after what I'd done to its pals. I bet they all thought this was going to be a walk down easy street. Just plop me over their bony shoulders and carry me away like the ettins did.

"I will kill you all," I raged. I was *not* going to give up. If Verdandi and Bragnon couldn't get me, I wasn't going to let these guys win. "I swear, I will kill each and every one of you."

Then, without a warning or a signal, they all stepped forward as one, like someone had issued an invisible order.

The leader spoke. "Braza benna lai, Surtr."

"Yeah, I know." I affected a bored tone. "You already said that. I have no choice but to come with you. But listen, buddy, where I come from there is *always* a choice." I didn't wait for a response.

I sprang forward, surprising myself as well as the demon.

Before it had time to react, I'd already sunk my rod deeply into its chest.

These guys were not overly bright on tactics, which definitely worked in my favor. I hadn't premeditated my moves, and I'd trusted my gut. Now I could only hope the rest of the demons, which had just witnessed me brazenly taking out the guy in charge, would see me as a threat and back off.

The demon dropped to its knees.

Yes.

My rod was still lodged in its chest.

I gripped the end tightly, letting out a war whoop as I pulled it back out in one motion. I couldn't help myself. The adrenaline was flowing freely. My skin prickled with it. My heart pumped swiftly, running at what felt like a hundred miles an hour.

The demon stayed on the ground. I wasn't sure if I'd pierced a vital organ or not, but it was down. I darted a glance around the semicircle in front of me. All the demons had their eyes pinned on their fallen leader, then one by one—*to a demon*—they lifted their burning red eyes to mine.

I watched in mild fascination as their irises dimmed and, a moment later, lit up like a new match had been ignited inside their depths. All their eyes re-fired at the same time and were now a blur of swirling bronze.

Heating up to the color of pissed-off orange.

No, no!

A hand hit my leg. My eyes ripped back to the demon on the ground. It was staring intently at me. A grotesque grin flashed across its charred face. The beastie's diabolical tar-filled mouth looked so wrong as the ends turned up, producing more of a crazed grimace than an actual smile.

A small bead of dark acid-blood bloomed out of its mouth and slid down the side of its chin. I watched, horrifyingly riveted, as its forked tongue shot out and lapped it off as it growled, "Teka lai rada, greeza."

No translation needed for that one. Its smug face said it all.

It's all over for you, sweetheart.

Without thinking, I stamped my foot into its thigh and plunged the rod back into its chest, tearing a larger hole as I went. The iron had already reacted with its blood, and now its insides leaked through the bigger hole, gushing out in an oozing mass of bubbling, putrid molasses.

The demon rolled to its side, twitching once before going completely still.

Take that! Yeehaw!

There was no time to be satisfied. I glanced up and all the minions stepped forward at once, each of them emitting a low hissing noise. What was happening? There had been some kind of a shift in them that I didn't understand. They all started garbling at once, each of them grating and screeching something different.

It sounded like a million marbles dropping onto the floor at the same time.

"Stay back," I shouted, my body now flush against the inactive portal. I had absolutely nowhere to go and was fresh out of options. The beasties had their newly orange eyes lit on me. I could see them pulsing. Someone else was in charge.

Someone a heck of a lot smarter.

A long bellow echoed through the room, shaking the rocks from the ceiling and sending them tumbling to the floor.

Fen was in the tunnel.

Help was coming!

The demons snapped their heads toward the sound in unison, like a mass of cyborg robots from every sci-fi movie I'd ever seen. Their togetherness was downright creepy. Having this many demons under the control of one unified brain was *not* going to end well.

I really didn't want to meet the brain behind this operation.

I stood on tiptoes, frantically trying to get a glimpse of Fen, but the stick figures gathered in front of me effectively blocked my view.

Another demon separated itself from the others and

marched toward me, stepping over its fallen friend like it wasn't even there. This one looked angrier, and its eyes flickered in agitation. It stopped a few paces short of me and turned its head, issuing a few sharp, barking orders to the group.

The demon beasties reacted swiftly.

Half of them turned and ran toward Fen, while the other half came at me in a speedy blur of black limbs.

There was nothing I could do to protect myself.

Bony hands grabbed on to me and pulled, yanking me forward, their fingers jabbing painfully into my skin.

"No," I screamed, trying to resist. "Fen!"

He roared, still in his wolf form, but the other demons had swarmed him. It would take him a moment to break free.

Suddenly, I was off my feet.

These things were carrying me, just like the ettins had, their skeletal hands a lot stronger now that they had me in their tight grips. I twisted and turned, bucking like crazy. "Let go of me!"

They headed back toward Fen's lair. They were moving quickly, and it was pitch dark once we hit the tunnel. I kicked my legs out. "Let me go! I'm not going with you!"

We emerged into the smaller cave, and the demons below me ran straight for a small pile of rocks just past the pool. The new leader extended its hand and said something, scrabbling at the first stone. It was a big boulder, but it rolled it away with little effort.

A pinpoint of red light shot into the room from the now exposed hole in the wall.

There'd been an exit in here all along.

I rocked my body with renewed vigor. They were *not* taking me out of here. I channeled all my strength into freeing the hand that still held the rod. They had taken me while I'd still been clutching it. I yanked it up, feeling sharp nails bite into me, but finally tore free. I swung the iron down in anger, screaming at the top of my lungs, "Get away from me!"

My rod connected with the demon next to me as a pulse of energy raced through my battered arm and into the rod. The demon flew away from me like I'd shot it with a high-powered rifle.

There was a smoking hole where his shoulder used to be.

He was dead where he landed.

Holy crap!

The demons stopped in their tracks, pausing uncertainly, talking loudly, until their leader stepped forward and yelled something garbled.

It walked over and laid a hand on me. "Dona tagit rue."

Some kind of pulse shot through me, and I was paralyzed. I couldn't move.

The demon had spelled me with something!

My precious iron rod dropped to the cave floor with a clatter as the leader gave another command. A few of the demons went to work on the rock pile. In no time, they created a small body-sized opening.

A red, hazy glow permeated the room.

This world was more than just creepy—it was downright hellish. And from the looks of the light outside, it was getting worse by the second. "Fen!" I screamed as the minions bent down and began to squeeze through the hole. The ones left tossed me on the ground. One grabbed on to my ankles and began dragging me through like a sack of meat, cackling as it went. I still couldn't move.

"Phoebe!" Fen called from somewhere behind me. He was human again. "I'm almost to you. Hold on!"

I heard a loud scuffle and another shout. He was still fighting them off. The ones in the main cavern must have caught up to him.

The demon yanked me farther through the hole. Others helped by shoving at my shoulders. Their voices and shouts had become frantic, their movements jerky and impatient.

They knew they were running out of time.

Fen wasn't going to make it in time. "It's too late! I can't move!" I yelled. "They're taking me away." I was fully ensconced in the hole now, closer to the outside than in, my feet feeling a major increase in temperature.

There was a hoarse growl behind me, and Fen came into view, his body battered and bloody. He crouched down, tossing away the remaining demons, and extended his arm into the hole, but I was out of reach.

"Valkyrie, grab my hand!" Fen shouted. "Grab it now!"

"I can't. They spelled me!" I cried as I slid a few more feet out of reach. "Fen, I can't break free! They're going to take me. Please help me!"

Fen cursed as he started to tear at the rocks around the opening. He was much too big to fit in the tunnel. His strong arms ripped at the hole, trying to make the opening wider, but it was going to take too long.

Full heat hit my legs.

"Valkyrie! I will come for you!"

It was the last thing I heard as the demons yanked me into the red, reedy glow of their world.

12

I inhaled and choked. The air outside was thick and dense, much more so than inside the caves. It coated my throat. The demons wasted no time hoisting me in the air again, and this time I had no weapon to aid me.

But even if I had, it wouldn't have helped. I still couldn't move.

As they ran, I coughed, my eyes watering. I struggled to take in the landscape around me as we passed by. A thick, hazy smog floated around us. It was tinted scarlet and hung in the air like a cartoon. It had to be well over a hundred degrees. Sweat beaded on my brow and tumbled down the side of my face as the demons jostled me along.

We descended a mountainous slope at a quick clip. By the light, I couldn't tell if it was day or night. There was no orb hanging in the sky to gauge any kind of time. I had the sinking feeling it was perpetually dusk here.

Their world was a sullen, ugly place that reeked of despair.

I gave a halfhearted attempt to rotate my body, but it was

no use. Nothing cooperated. Blood still leaked from my arm and hand. My camisole and ripped skirt were saturated with my own sweat and blood and covered with holes where the demon blood had eaten through the fabric.

All the wetness should have made me slippery in their grasps, but their skin was bumpy and abrasive, and they had no problem holding on tight.

At the bottom of the slope, the beasties set off at a run, full speed across the red moonscape. There was no cover that I could see, other than a few scattered boulders here and there. The horizon was peppered with what appeared to be deep, dark craters. I did not want to know what lurked in those holes.

There were no trees, no greenery, no life.

It was a world devoid of any hope.

My head started to spin in earnest after a half hour of being tossed around on the shoulders of the minions. The blood loss made me light-headed, and the pain, which had thankfully held off under the adrenaline of fighting back in the caves, had come rushing back with a vengeance. My body pulsed in tandem to the pounding of the demons' feet hitting the ground mile after mile.

I struggled to keep conscious.

Abruptly, after what seemed like several hours, most of which I'd spent blacked out, the demons slowed. I was half delirious but managed to open my eyes and hold my head up a few inches to try to see what was happening. A thin crust of dust had hardened along my eyelashes, and it took me several tries to get them all the way open.

Spread out in front of us was a wasteland of broken, dead trees. It resembled a petrified forest from this vantage point. As the demons moved closer, I discovered it wasn't a forest of trees at all. It was a forest of dead bodies!

All different kinds.

As the beasties wove through it, I could only recognize the ones shaped like ettins. The rest of the monsters were unfamiliar. The wicked forest boasted a variety of strange creatures, each hanging limply from long sticks, arms spread. The sticks had been driven into the ground. None of the bodies looked remotely human.

Small relief.

Most were burnt and charred beyond all recognition. As the demons ran, the bodies swayed from their repulsive sticks like brittle leaves in the hot, dusky, red-tinted air. Every mouth I gazed upon was frozen open in pitiful agony. It was hard to feel sorry for an ettin, but I came close.

Bile rose in my throat for the seventy-fifth time. I struggled to keep some kind of containment cap on my ever-leaking sanity. I knew I wasn't going to survive whatever was coming, and a wave of sorrow took hold of me, rocking me to the core with blinding emotion.

I didn't want to die!

I half cried, half gasped in the putrid air, my face wet with tears, my mind numb with memories. I tried to focus on what was happening around me, but I couldn't see anything clearly anymore. Thoughts rushed through my brain, but nothing was coherent, nothing seemed to matter. Instinct and pure determination had saved me thus far, and I had to grasp on to that. I desperately wanted to live! I had so much more to experience.

I yelled in agony, my teeth clenched as I struggled to hold my fracturing mind together. With new resolution, I yanked fiercely at the hands restraining me, the ones hurting me, and thrashed my body. The demons growled, flashing their jagged, coal-stubbed teeth and snarling their nonexistent lips.

It took me a second to realize I was animated.

I could move again!

Just barely, but that meant the spell must've been wearing off. It gave me a small nugget of sunshine in this sad, desolate landscape. I forced my eyes open and made myself *see*.

If you give in to the darkness, you may as well roll over and die, Phoebe. You're going to have to keep fighting. Ingrid's voice was in my ear, urging me on. She was right.

The demons neared the end of the forest of death, approaching a short, fenced enclosure, possibly a barricade. It extended as far as I could see on either side and seemed to be made out of the same black tree branches that held the bodies aloft. And to make it more designer fabulous, on the sharp, pointed tips of the fence rested more charred heads, haphazardly hooked through empty eye sockets or gaping maws.

The demons stopped before a large gate.

In moments it swung open, and the demons hurried through.

Inside the enclosure was row after row of rickety stone or stick hovels cobbled together like no thought had been given to longevity. *They must not have a long life-span.* The entire area resembled a living ghost town that was still somehow thriving against all odds.

As we passed, more beasties stuck their heads out of the shacks, and even more followed us.

Every muscle in my body tightened, screaming to escape, to lose consciousness, to claw out my own eyes—*anything* to make this all disappear.

Please, please, make this go away!

I willed myself not to cry, swallowing back the stinging tears again and again, forcing myself to keep seeing. *Make yourself live, Phoebe. You have to do this!*

The demons brought me into a large arena separated

from the rest of the living quarters by a huge circle of smooth, onyx stones. The rocks were perfectly round and sat aligned, one about every two feet, like evil sentinels. As we passed through the boundary, I shivered and my reflexes convulsed uncontrollably.

A large lava pit churned in the middle of it all, with several contraptions rigged beside it.

Nothing good will happen here.

A huge throne, carved out of the same black onyx stone, sat with malice to one side. Just beyond the large chair lay several boulders with smooth tops, like long tables.

Or altars.

The beasties marched over and threw me down onto the smooth boulder closest to the bubbling pit of lava.

It was stained with a sticky, dark residue and smelled like death.

More bile.

Four minions held my arms and legs steady, while others brought up some material hanging from the sides and proceeded to restrain my wrists and ankles. The cloth was the same burlap mesh they all wore. When they were done, I was immobile. The fabric was harsh and unforgiving, scraping against my already sensitive skin.

Even though I was restrained, I struggled. "You bastards, let me go!" My movements were getting stronger and stronger by the moment. The spell was definitely waning.

Too little, too late.

Then, without warning, the demons parted like water as something lumbered toward me, its footfalls vibrating the ground.

I spotted its terrible sword first.

The blade was curved and at least three feet long. But it wasn't metal.

STRUCK

It was made completely of flames.

Orange flickers lashed out of it, dancing along the invisible edge, jumping with a fiendish intensity. The color of the licking heat matched the color of all the demons' eyes as they peered at me, awaiting my death, yearning for it.

The thing coming was as big as Junnal, but that was where the similarities ended. Its skin was charred black, like the rest of the minions, but its face was more human-shaped—oblong rather than round. Its eyes blazed a hideous, deep red, but the very worst was its nose. In place of a normal nose were three terrifying slits. It opened its maw, and not one, but two forked tongues lashed out as it spoke.

"You. Human girl," it rumbled. "Trespass. My land." It slapped its chest, in case I wasn't sure whose land it was talking about.

It spoke English? *Please tell me this isn't a demigod!*

I blinked. It was all I could do. This beast was the most terrifying thing I'd ever set eyes on in my entire life.

The demons gathered closer, crowding toward me, not wanting to miss any of the impending action. They were more aggressive now that their boss-man was here, and they wrestled each other for a prime viewing spot.

"Me. Surtr," he boomed in a gravelly tone, which sounded less like rocks in a blender and more like his tongues regularly got stuck in the back of his throat.

He didn't wait for me to answer before arcing his fiery sword down on me, sweeping it along the length of my body.

I screamed as my skin bubbled and burned.

The flames licking me were hotter than anything I'd ever felt before. My skin steamed, blisters and blood erupted. The pain was overwhelming. My eyes rolled back in my head. I was one breath away from passing out.

"Weak. Not Valkyrie," Surtr bellowed.

"Please!" I cried, forcing myself to stay awake, to *endure*. "Please, let me go. I didn't come here on purpose, I swear. I wasn't trying to trespass. I just want to go home. If you let me go, I'll leave this place and never come back!"

"No." He paced menacingly in front of me, swinging his awful, flaming sword of doom too close for comfort. "Price for you. Too high."

"I have money," I pleaded. "I'll give you anything you want."

"Verdandi will have…when I finish."

"Don't do this. If you torture me, I won't survive!"

"Silence!" Surtr commanded. He raised his hand aloft, and his beasties flooded around him, cheering, shaking their stick fists in the air. He peered at me, his tongues grotesque as they alternated in and out of his mouth—a mouth filled with razor-sharp black teeth. "Human blood…is *good*. We take flesh…before deliver to hag."

"No, please, *no*," I moaned while squirming in earnest, the fabric chafing deep bloody furrows into my wrists and ankles. "If you do, I swear I won't make it. If I die, Verdandi will be angry." She probably didn't care one iota if these demons killed me. They would've done her job for her. "I've seen her wrath, and it's terrible. You don't want to get close to that! I'm human, like you said. I won't survive!"

Surtr shot his head back, and something close to laughter boiled out. "You will…thank us…human." He sounded like death. "We will not…roast you…like others. Close to death…but not dead."

There would be no thanking going on.

He meant to torture me, just like Fen said.

Surtr turned and issued commands in his language. The demons sprang into action.

"No," I whispered, crying to myself. "Oh my gods, *no*."

As the demons flittered away, busy with their new errand, Surtr stalked toward the lava pit and took a seat on his big, black, shiny throne.

I closed my eyes.

Convincing myself to rally wasn't anywhere in my mind.

Instead, my thoughts went to my mother and father, my friends, my life. It all flickered before me in sharp detail. Christmas morning the year I got my first bike, the red one I had asked for. Splashing in the lake near our home on a warm summer day. My father's infectious laugh. The year I made the swim team and broke two longstanding records while my parents proudly looked on. My first, sweaty kiss behind the hardware store and the feeling of the tingles as they shot to my toes.

Too much to lose.

I wasn't sure if I'd blacked out or not, but when I opened my eyes, several demons were leaning over me, each fisting sharp objects that resembled shards of flint. They also carried small bowls chipped out of dark stone. The bowls were gritty and stained, and the smell coming from them was rancid. Like everything else around here.

It felt like hours had passed, but I couldn't be sure.

I wrenched my head in the direction of the throne. It was empty.

Please don't die, I begged myself. *You can do this, Phoebe. You have too much to lose.* My mother's voice floated in my ear, left over from a dream that had just dissipated. One that I'd dreamed many times before in my youth. She was sobbing, clutching me as an infant. She wouldn't let go. *We love you, Phoebe. Please, live.*

The demons began to touch me, and I screamed, "Get away from me, you little creeps!"

"Greeza." They all chortled as they brought the flints down to my exposed skin. "*Hurt.*"

"Oh, now you decide to speak English? It's too late to try to get on my good side. You're all going to pay. Every last one of you! I promise—"

Multiple flint pieces sliced my body at once.

One of the minions raked a piece down my battered arm, tearing a deep, continuous, jagged line from the top of my shoulder to my wrist. The demon's eyes flared hungrily, its mouth greedy, its hateful tongue flashing in and out in delight.

Blood gushed from the wound, and the pain was beyond excruciating. I gasped for air, screaming and shouting in agony. The demons ignored me. Instead, they placed bowls under my body to better catch the gushing blood.

"Please, no," I moaned, shaking my head side to side. A sharpness pierced my thigh. I was going to lose my mind. "*NO!*" My voice hoarse. "You don't understand. I'm not going to survive! Surtr, you will have nothing to give Verdan—"

Agony seared my legs as they gouged and cut, my blood spilling onto the altar, splashing into the bowls.

I opened my mouth to scream, but nothing came out.

The demons paused, and I rushed to catch my breath. My throat thick and raspy. "You're done, right? That's enough. Torture complete." I had no idea why I was still conscious. The pain had eclipsed into something else, something I didn't have a name for. "Please, stop," I whispered, my voice full of pleading. "You're killing me."

"Take her flesh," a voice roared. Surtr's footsteps pounded toward the altar. "Her flesh...with her blood." He spoke something in his language, and the demons jumped at his command. They peered down on me with opened mouths, hovering closer, their faces ablaze with anticipation.

"You don't need my flesh. The blood is enough—"

"*Take it.*"

A demon hungrily lowered his mouth to my side. "No! *NO!* I will pay you whatever you want. My father…he will pay—" Teeth grazed my skin. A forked tongue lapped at my blood. Sharp points sank in, tearing at my flesh. My skin ripped loose in its mouth. "*Arghhhh!*"

Sanity-splitting agony rocked me to the core. Deep down, a current zipped through me. I could sense the energy sparking low. I was furious. I was delirious. I was out of my mind. Something was shifting in my body. Lightning struck above my head. Thunder clapped loudly, sounding terrifying in my ears.

The demon holding my flesh in its mouth, still attached to my side, flew backward.

"See?" I mumbled in a daze, barely conscious. "That's what happens when you mess with me." The hurt raging though my body was moments from overtaking me. The last of my energy was ebbing away, blown out in one last hurrah. I was almost happy to see it go. I couldn't take any more of this, mentally or physically.

I was done.

The last thing I saw was Surtr leaning over me. "Not enough power…little Valkyrie. Still…too human." He laughed. It was an ugly sound. Just before I lost my grip on reality, I heard him utter his last command. "Take…*more.*"

13

Someone was screaming. It wasn't me.

It couldn't be me.

The sound was hideous. It was a high-pitched keening, over and over again. I came to in a rush, my eyes flicking open just in time to see several demons dart away from the altar. Away from me.

That's right, get the hell away from me!

My body throbbed, the pain immeasurable. I couldn't believe I wasn't dead. My entire soul screamed in wretched, numbing agony. The demons had taken flesh from everywhere. The blood loss was too much, the damage too great. I wasn't going to make it. As it was, I was barely cognizant.

Why was I awake?

I couldn't bring myself to gaze down the length of my battered body to see the damage. I was too scared. But I wasn't going to be conscious for very long, so it didn't matter.

Surtr stood over me with his sword raised.

Just end it already.

I tried to focus on him, but my vision swam. He yelled something to his demons, but could they even hear over the horrible screeching?

Someone stop that insufferable noise!

The demons were retreating in droves, some of them running. Surtr was furious. He wasn't paying attention to me.

That's odd, because he's supposed to be killing me, right?

With supreme effort, I turned my head to see what the leader of the demons glared at, snarling with his fiery sword raised for battle.

Fen? Is it Fen?

I'm sorry, Fen. But you're too late. There's nothing left.

Not Fen.

So not Fen.

The thing speeding toward us looked deadly. My adrenaline jumped at the sight, even though my body was too injured to do anything about it. My eyes tightened, forcing the muscles to focus harder.

Its sleek, black body slithered along the ground, up and over obstacles like they weren't there, crushing things in its path, lashing out with its tail, sending demons flying, demolishing shacks with one strike. I blinked.

That can't be right. Why is everything here black? It's a cruel joke.

It slithered closer. It had no fear.

It was the biggest snake I'd ever seen.

Behind it, another one advanced in its wake. Then two more.

No. No. No.

Didn't they understand? There was nothing else they could do to me! They'd done it all. They didn't need to bring in the terrifying snakes. They had broken me fine without them. They had torn and ripped my skin, drank my blood. There was nothing left for Verdandi to crush. I smiled at that. *Nothing left for you, witch.*

"Jondi! Jondi!" the demons screamed in their garbled voices.

Surtr's lofted sword trembled above my head. The serpents were almost to the altar. The keening noise was overpowering. I still didn't know who was making it. I heard a strange pop and felt blood flow out of my ear.

Hurts.

My vision faltered. Sounds around me grew shallow. My heartbeat was the only thing I heard. *Thump…thump…thump.*

"*Releasssse…*her."

I forced my eyes back open. *Was that the snake? Did it just speak? No. Impossible. But, Phoebe, everything can talk here! Even demons!* I tried to laugh. Nothing came out. *Awful place. Nothing should talk.*

Something pressed against my body.

It didn't crush me, but it was rough and it hurt. I called out in pain. Surtr was shouting again. He wasn't next to me anymore.

I tried to focus, but everything in front of me was black. Black with smooth, shimmery scales. Holy crap, the snake was next to me! Actually, it was sort of bowed over me, pressing against my side, its gigantic head towering above the altar.

It had driven Surtr back.

I could feel its malice. Nothing good could come from this.

Are you going to eat me? Please, snake, do it quickly.

"Valkyrie!"

The snake sounds like Fen? That was funny. A small giggle escaped my mouth.

"Valkyrie, I'm here!" A hand landed on the top of my

head, the only place the awful demons hadn't sunk their terrible teeth. *Didn't want to get hair in their precious mouths, too unsuitable to chomp. Must get caught in their throats.*

A soft voice was next to my ear. "I am so sorry, shieldmaiden. I failed you. But I'm here now."

"Snake." The sound was so small, I wondered if I'd spoken it out loud at all.

"Yes, snakes. I made an alliance with the Jondi serpents. It was the only way to gain entrance quickly. They will protect us now."

He was here. *Nice to have someone to hold my hand in the end.*

"Valkyrie, I need to lift you. This is going to hurt." His arms slid underneath my body.

I screamed. *Almost gone.* I struggled. Needed to tell him not to worry. It wasn't his fault. *Don't bother trying to save me. Hurts too much.*

"What is it, Valkyrie? You have to stop struggling." His head hovered above my mouth.

"There's nothing...*left to save.*"

※

It's wet. I can't see. I lash out. It hurts so much.

"Shhh," a voice soothes me. "It will get better. You are healing."

"No," I moaned, thrashing. "Can't."

"Yes, Valkyrie. You can."

Blackness.

※

Water lapped at my neck. I didn't know how long I'd been out. I was on my back. It was warm. It felt good, even though I still hurt.

I opened my eyes.

"Welcome back." Fen grinned above me.

"What?" my voiced croaked, my vocal cords stiff. I swallowed and tried again. "Where am I?"

"We are in the healing pool, shieldmaiden. You've been…mending for a long while." Fen's voice held the hint of a growl. His arms were strong, supporting my weight easily.

I felt a sense of déjà vu.

Had we been in the pool the whole time? Bragnon's bite had to be better by now.

Then it all came rushing back. This horrible world, all the hideous creatures, my capture, my torture, snakes, demons. I splashed and grabbed on to Fen's shoulder, glancing around the cave. "What if they come back?" I craned my head toward the entrance. "Why are we still in here? I can't go through that again! I can't believe I'm not dead already. We have to get away. Right now!" I was babbling like an idiot, but I didn't care. I wanted out of here. *Had* to get out of here.

"It's going to be okay, Valkyrie. Calm yourself. The Jondi serpents patrol the entrances now. We are safe for the time being. You are still weak. Please relax."

I did a solid once-over around the small cave again, still clutching Fen's shoulders, just to make absolute sure, then reluctantly lay back down.

Water lapped over my exposed breasts, my nipples hardening from having been exposed to the cooler air. Cooler should've been an oxymoron in this place, because it was hot or hotter. "Oh my gods, I'm naked! Why am I naked?" I shot out of Fen's arms, searching for footing on the pool floor, and failed badly.

My legs were as weak as a newborn's. The extent of my

injuries seared up my spine, crippling me as I put pressure on the balls of my feet. I flailed, my arms windmilling as I slowly slid under.

Large hands grabbed me and eased me out of the water, cradling me carefully in powerful arms. He clearly knew I was still in pain.

He said nothing.

I coughed, spitting the putrid water out of my mouth. "Ow." I conceded my defeat and stopped fighting. Fen looked mildly amused by my antics. In fact, he was just short of full-on laughing. "Don't snicker at me, wolf. Being naked in your arms..." As I said those words out loud, a kernel of heat seared through me, heat that had nothing at all to do with the scalding temperature of the water. "Well...let's just say it surprised me, okay? I wasn't expecting to be...unclothed or...alive, for that matter."

"Valkyrie, your nakedness does not bother me in the least." Did his eyes just flare a teensy bit? "It would've been counterproductive to heal you with your clothes on. What was left of them, anyway. I figured your life was worth more than your modesty." His lips went up in a cocky grin. "Plus, it kept me quite...focused on my task."

I brought my arms out of the water and settled them over my chest, covering myself. At heart, I was still a small-town girl, and thus far, I'd had limited experience being completely nude with anyone, much less an unbelievably sexy demigod—one who'd just saved my life.

Once my arms were out of the water, I spotted lots of jagged scars, ugly and thick, like a web of horribly tainted skin. "Oh."

"They will heal," Fen said softly.

"How long have I been in...here?"

"Five days."

"*What?*" The wounds the nasty demons gave me were healed over, it was true, but Bragnon's bite and Fen's cut from Gram had healed in mere moments compared to this. "Why...why has it taken so long?" I stammered, the ordeal rushing back through my mind like flickering scenes from a movie. I closed my eyes, a single finger up in the air. I needed a moment. The memory was solid, but my brain had the decency to change it slightly, making it seem like I'd been a spectator instead of re-living the vicious assault again. I was grateful, but it was strange.

Fen stayed quiet, his strong arms supporting me.

Once I was ready, I opened my eyes. I needed to swallow a few times before I spoke. "How come it's taken me so long to mend?"

"The demons used their onyx stones to cut you. They are sacred here because they resist healing. That's why they use them. That way they are able to inflict as much damage as possible. I told you, shieldmaiden, they don't fool around when it comes to torture." I shuddered, the water rippling softly around me. No, no they didn't. "The stone leaves a residue behind that reacts negatively with the solay, these healing waters, so it keeps hurting you instead of healing you."

"But my arms are scarred over." Kind of. "If the onyx keeps your tissue from healing, why are they all closed up?" I was in pain, but it was a lingering ache, not a tissue-shriveling kind of pain.

Fen looked uncomfortable for a moment. "I had no choice but to cut the residue out."

Ohmygods!

"When you say *cut*, what...exactly do you mean?" My stomach lurched. There couldn't have been much to cut. I'd been filleted by those demons, my body bitten, sliced, and consumed. What had been left to slice out?

Fen's eyes darkened with emotion. "I couldn't let you die like that. It was lucky you had the dagger with you, though how you obtained it is still beyond me. Odin guards his treasures well. If it hadn't been here, you wouldn't be alive."

"You used Gram?" I swallowed. "To slice and dice me?"

"I had no other choice, Valkyrie," he replied quietly. "It was either that, or let you perish."

I glanced away.

How hard could that have been for him? I wasn't sure I could even do such a thing if he needed the same from me. It must have been awful. Thank goodness I'd stayed unconscious. Small favors, and all that.

By my count, he'd saved my life three times already.

Without thinking, I brought a hand up to his face, forgetting my nakedness for a moment. My fingers connected with his smooth skin, and energy rushed out to greet me. I brushed an errant piece of hair off his forehead, and he closed his eyes. I murmured, "It must have been horrible for you. But thank you. I'm happy to be alive, but I'm sorry you had to do such a hard thing."

Fen's eyes flew open. He looked slightly appalled by my words. "You're *sorry*? Valkyrie, I diced you up. You shouldn't thank me just yet." His voice was rough. "It was hard to see where to cut, even with the aid of the dagger. There are no guarantees that you will be completely whole again." He cleared his throat and glanced away. "But I did it to the best of my ability."

"I don't care if I'm scarred." I really didn't. "I'm lucky to be alive. And I have only you to thank for that. And, by the way, my name is Phoebe."

"What?" Fen looked a little flustered at the change of topic, his gaze intense on mine.

"You always refer to me as Valkyrie or shieldmaiden, and

125

I just realized I never properly introduced myself. My name is Phoebe Meadows." I covered my nakedness again with my arms. "I know it's a little late for this, since I'm currently lying butt naked in your arms, and you've already saved my life three times, but now is better than never. You can call me Phoebe if you'd like."

Fen did that grin thing with his mouth again, where it just went up on one side. Another spike of heat hit me. "Thank you...Phoebe, for your introduction. I will keep that in mind. You've taken to calling me Fen, which none has ever done before. You may continue. It pleases me."

I arched a brow.

He was right. I'd shortened his name without really realizing it. *Fen* just made sense. *Fenrir* was a mouthful. I paused and considered how to phrase my next question.

Now that I was alive, I wanted to make sure I stayed that way. If this Valkyrie stuff was real, and I was one, I had to find out more. "Can I ask you something? When I was fighting against the demons, right before they took me out of this cave and after I was cut for the first time, some strange stuff happened. There was lightning and thunder. And I think I might have...released some energy? Demons flew in different directions." I took a deep breath and kept right on going. "I really don't know what to think. And honestly, I don't know if I'm fully capable of handling the news if I am a Valkyrie or not, but I can't ignore it any longer. I have to be able to defend myself next time..." I trailed off not knowing what else to add, except, man, I hoped there wasn't a next time.

Fen's face held a look of wonder. He shook his head slowly. "Phoebe, you really and truly don't know what you are?"

"I really, truly don't," I grumbled. "It would be nice if you laid it on me."

14

When Fen had said my name, my arms had erupted in goose bumps. I was distracted, but listening. "There is no doubt you are a shieldmaiden. Ever since you came tumbling through my portal," he told me, "I've had my suspicions about you. That's why I didn't kill you immediately. A normal Valkyrie, armed with a powerful weapon forged for a god, wouldn't make it far into my lair. I can assure you. But"—he stopped, consternation showing on his face— "there was something different about you from the very start. And even though you shone brighter than any Valkyrie I'd ever seen, you didn't threaten me. Instead, it was the opposite. I've been trying to puzzle it out ever since. Your humanness is at the forefront, that much is clear. You are young, just struck, correct?"

"I guess so." I shrugged, causing my head to bob down into the water. "I didn't realize anything important had happened. I mean, yes, I woke up in a pile of shoes, but we all thought it was faulty lighting. So, yes, I was just…*struck*. What does that actually mean?"

"Valkyries come into their immortality in their twenties, I believe. In order to achieve this, they are struck with an energy charge that changes their body chemistry drastically. The strike is sent by Odin himself to those he deems worthy. Not every child born of a Valkyrie becomes immortal, and Odin can choose any female from any race, in any world, and grant her the gift of immortality if he sees fit. After her strike, her human body begins to change as her Valkyrie powers rise to the forefront."

"Okay, now wait just a goldarn minute." I splashed my arms and tried to sit up, forgetting my nudity for the moment. I could not have this conversation lying down. Fen obliged by gliding me over to a submerged boulder. He set me down gently and moved to the other edge of the pool, crossing his arms, amusement in his eyes. "Let me get this straight," I said once I was settled securely on the rock. "I was struck by some kind of magical energy sent from Odin that shot out of the lights in the storeroom at Macy's, hitting me and knocking me into a pile of shoes? And because of that, I'm now *immortal?*"

"On your way to being immortal, Valkyrie. You are not there just yet."

"How long does it take?"

He shrugged. "I don't know for sure, not being a Valkyrie myself. But I do know that your body will need to consume energy on a regular basis to help the metamorphosis. It's how you will survive and thrive. Without it, especially since you're an infant, you will wither and die. You've been vastly depleted these last five days because of your recent…trauma. You will need to feed very soon."

Feed? It sounded like strapping a bag on a horse. But I was hungry. Strange hungry, like my cells were starving. "How do I…feed?"

"Um…" Fen cleared his throat as he repositioned himself, crossing his legs at his ankles. "There are several ways for a Valkyrie to consume minor energy, but your main sustenance must come from Yggdrasil itself. The life force of the tree is inherent to your very creation. There will be nothing else of its likeness that will keep you alive forever. You must always be near it."

"I didn't see the tree the entire time the demons were ferrying me across the plane. You'd think, because of its size, it would be a hard thing to miss." The tree had made me glow, so therefore it gave me sustenance? Totally weird. Thinking of myself as anything but Phoebe Meadows from Wisconsin was surreal. But if what Fen was saying was true, and I was a shieldmaiden, and there were more creatures like these in the worlds, I had to learn how to fight them. I didn't want to be a victim again.

I thought of Ingrid and smiled. She would be proud. After what happened with the demons, I couldn't risk feeling that vulnerable again. My sanity wouldn't be up for grabs a second time. My mind skipped to the memory of the demons slicing me up, their skeletal hands brandishing the onyx against my skin, and I gagged.

Never again!

"The fire demons guard Yggdrasil fiercely," Fen said. "There is a vast crater to the east of their kingdom. The trunk is shown only partially there. The tree manifests itself differently on every plane and has the ability to move freely when it wants to. But for as long as I've been here, the tree has stayed in that same location."

"How long have you been here?" I asked hesitantly.

"Many years, Valkyrie. Too many to count."

"Oh," I answered. What a horrible fate to be tossed in this unforgiving world. I wanted to know why he'd been cast here, but the closed look on his face redirected my next question. "You said there are other ways for me to get small bits of food?" My stomach wasn't grumbling, but I was weary and fatigued in a way I'd never been before. If I truly wanted to heal, I knew he was right. I'd have to eat, and the sooner the better. "I think my body is really hungry, but not for food." Consuming energy actually sounded appealing to me.

"There are a few ways you can get it." Fen ran his hand over his face, appearing a little unnerved. He rearranged his body, and the water lapped against his abs. "In Midgard, human-generated electricity can keep you fueled for a time. On other planes, there are energy sources you can draw from. But here, I know of only one place you can get energy other than Yggdrasil."

"Well, I don't have a return ticket to Midgard, and the tree is far away, so how do I get it here?"

"As a demigod"—Fen cleared his throat—"I am flush with power. My power can be transformed into the kind of energy you need to feed." As he spoke, his eyes sparked with something feral that sent shivers racing down my spine. "It can happen from touch, kissing, but the greatest source is during the act of…"

Ohmygodsinheaven.

"*Sex?* Are you referring to sex?" My voice ended an octave higher, and I gaped, my eyes losing focus for a good, solid moment. I almost slid off my rock. I gripped the slippery surface like my life depended on it to keep from tumbling under. "Why…why on earth does it have to be…sex?" *Maybe because you're not on* earth, *Phoebe.* My hand slipped again, and I had to regroup. I wasn't a prude—and truth be told, the thought of sleeping with Fen made my libido skyrocket and my legs quake—but I'd never had a one-night stand before. Sex to me had always been a commitment, something you did with a lover. "You said touch and kissing. Does that give enough?" I asked hopefully.

"Valkyrie, know this," Fen said, his voice stony. "I will never force myself upon you. There is no need to look so horrified. I did not know that you would be...so averse to our coupling. Touching and kissing, although nice, will not provide you with enough food, but will give you some. During the act of copulation, there are a few other...factors involved." He brought an arm up and rubbed the back of his neck, his bicep jumping. "My power becomes concentrated for...a very brief moment. It's all about the transfer of energy from one body to another." He looked wildly uncomfortable. "All who live in Asgard know this already. I've never had to explain it to someone."

His semen packs a punch?

Is that what he's talking about?

Why did I find that more surprising than a huge, talking snake? Or fire demons with acid blood? Or a witch out to kill me?

"I'm...I'm not horrified"—I was kind of horrified—"or...averse." I definitely wasn't averse. "I just...need time to digest this." *Yikes, not digest, Phoebe! Ick.*

"Valkyrie, I will leave you to your thoughts. I am going to check in with the Jondi." Fen hoisted himself out of the pool. He wore the same pant-shorts, but the way they clung to his muscular legs made me tingly inside this time. Having sex with him would not be a hardship. It would just be strange and awkward. He turned back to me, and I had to look away, pretending to fix my hair so he couldn't read my face. "When I get back, we must formulate a plan. We need to get to Yggdrasil, and it will be a dangerous journey."

He walked away before I could reply.

Fen had been gone a long time, and I was sleepy. I'd hooked my ankles on the edge of the pool and had managed to keep floating without much effort, but I was in danger of falling asleep.

While he'd been gone, my mind whirled. I kept trying to wrap my brain around the crazy idea that I might, in fact, be immortal, but then just as quickly dismissing it. It was too strange.

On one hand, with everything I'd experienced in the last few days, it seemed feasible. But on the other, when I thought of my normal human life in New York, and of growing up in a small town with two human parents, there was no part of me that could match the two together.

Instead of forcing the issue, I floated in the warmth, doing my best to ignore the stinky *solay*, and tried to clear my head of all thoughts. Meditation didn't come easy to me, but in college I'd learned to do it out of necessity. It was either get a handle on my stress, or let it eat me up. It was going pretty well, but the problem was, with each growing hour, I felt more depleted, my movements more sluggish.

I yawned.

My body was threatening to shut down whether I wanted it to or not. The damage done to me by the demons and not eating had taken a hefty toll. Emotionally and physically.

Where was Fen, anyway?

I hadn't asked him anything about the deal he'd made with the snakes and why he hadn't forged an alliance before today. If he'd been here for years, it seemed like making a deal with the serpents would've made his life a lot easier in this dark place.

Unless the snakes had demanded something from him that was too big?

Something he hadn't been willing to give before.

Oh, no.

A bad feeling whispered through me. What if Fen had agreed to give the monsters something he didn't want to part with? What if the price had been too high?

My ankles splashed into the water as I struggled to stand, my arms doggie paddling. I'd moved around the pool in the last few hours and had taken some tentative steps that hadn't ached too badly, but the sudden strain on my body sent new shock waves burning up my legs.

"Ugh. I'm getting sick of this." I slapped the water in frustration, instantly regretting it when a spray of water shot up my nose. Then my arms started to ache with all the sudden motion. "Damn."

I was ready to exit this pool.

Fen had said my clothes were toast. Maybe he'd set something to wear by the pool? Very carefully, I maneuvered along the edge, checking hopefully for any clothes lying around. There were none. With effort, I hoisted my upper body out of the water, panting as I pulled one leg over the side. I was forced to leave this pool like an old lady after a water aerobics class. If this didn't mark me as a big, strong immortal, I didn't know what would. Once I had both legs out, I lay on my stomach, panting like a dog after a long walk in one-hundred-and-twenty-degree heat.

Two down, one to go.

I inhaled and shifted my body so my legs dangled off the side. Then I slid down the wall until my feet hit the dirt floor. I stood slowly. My legs shook like leaves in high wind as hundreds of needles of pain rushed upward from my feet.

But I managed to stay upright.

After a few minutes, the pinpricks receded to a dull throb. *I can do this.*

I took one step forward, and then another. I was wobbly and weak, but I was moving on my own. I passed the tunnel opening to the larger cavern on my way to Fen's lair. Right as I stepped in front of it, I heard a noise.

It was an unmistakable slithering sound.

Ssssssssssssss.

Before I had a chance to react, a giant black, scaly head emerged, not ten feet from where I stood.

I screamed and fell backward, hitting the ground. The thing was massive up close. As it came nearer, I saw its eyes were a violent shade of amethyst. I scooted back as fast as I could, ignoring the pain, my palms scraping as they maneuvered over the rocky terrain. "What do you want?" I yelled. "Get away from me!" I searched for something to defend myself with. There was nothing around me but small rocks. I picked one up, fisted it, and launched it at the giant snake, which had no qualms about coming closer and closer.

"Valkyrie!" Fen shouted from somewhere in the tunnel. "Do not fear! The serpent is just coming to get your scent."

The snake angled its neck toward Fen, and then back at me.

I froze as it extended its huge head over me menacingly. It had to be enjoying this. I watched in horror as its long, forked tongue unrolled out of its mouth soundlessly.

It must be mandatory to have a forked tongue in this world.

A low hiss emitted from its throat as its barbed tongue slowly whipped back and forth just short of my face. I closed my eyes, but didn't flinch. I wasn't going to let this serpent have any more of my fear. I'd given it away too many times already.

After a few moments, I opened my eyes, ready to heave

another rock, or grab on to its tongue, or do *something* to make it go away, just in time to see it fly backward.

It smashed into the cavern wall with a clamorous boom, rocks exploding and dirt and sand raining down. I brought my arms up to shield my head from the falling debris.

"This is not how we agreed to do business, Jondi!" Fen raged. The snake had bounced once, but sustained little damage. It recovered in moments, hissing like a madman, advancing on Fen so fast I couldn't track it. Fen swung his powerful fist, and the serpent went flying again. "You were to wait for me to enter first. *That* was our agreement."

15

I scuttled out of the way, wedging myself into the shelter of a midsize boulder. My adrenaline had kicked in, so I felt no pain. I was grateful, as it infused me with hyperenergy as I watched the fight unfold. I needed all the energy I could get.

The serpent was three times as big as Fen. Its black scales glittered iridescent in the low lighting. But this was not a fair fight. Fen's arms bulged with power. His tapered waist swung to the side, his abdomen flexing as his fist shot out again, connecting squarely with the serpent.

But this time the beast didn't fly backward. It was ready. It absorbed the impact, ripples streaming through it like quaking Jell-O. It immediately lunged forward, its horrid serpent face stopping inches from Fen, the barbs on its tongue wagging, ready to strike.

The standoff was intense. Neither of them backed down.

My heart began to race. If the snake monster won, I was dead. It would gobble me up in one bite or sell me back to the demons. I had just vowed not to be a victim. I had to *do* something.

I made up my mind. No more weakness.

I would survive.

But before I could make a move, Fen yelled, "Get the hell out of my domain, Jondi! Or else you die here. You know you cannot best me. This is your last chance."

"You would go against us *soooo* quickly? You risk much, dog." The serpent's voice sounded like a long, creepy whisper coming from somewhere deep inside its throat. "Your word *issss* binding. Do not forget yourself. We are your *masterssss* now."

"That was not our bargain. I agreed to free you, but you do not rule me. I am no one's slave. *Never* a slave," Fen snarled.

The thing let out what sounded like huffs of air all in a row. "Take heed. If you break your vow, your life is *ourssss.*"

"I don't intend to break my vow, serpent. You have her scent, now get out." He leaned into the snake, his biceps jumping, one step away from throttling it again.

The serpent angled its huge head at me, its deep purple eyes swirling. "*Yessss*, and she smells *delicioussss.*" Its tongue snapped out so fast I almost didn't see it.

You won't be getting a piece of me, buddy.

Seemingly satisfied, it turned and slithered out, its massive body fluidly crossing the rocky floor.

Fen rushed forward, bending over and scooping me up. I didn't protest. "Valkyrie, I apologize. That was not my intention. The Jondi have agreed to get us to the crater that holds Yggdrasil, but in case the demons attack, they need your scent among them to track you. Are you hurt? Did it harm you?"

Instinct shot up inside me.

Survive.

I wrapped my arms around Fen's big shoulders, my hands winding around his neck, running through his long, silky hair. I prodded the back of his head gently with the tips of my fingers, while leaning forward, licking my lips. Lust shot through me.

I wanted to taste him. I *needed* to taste him.

Fen's eyes widened in surprise, and his breath quickened. "What's this?"

Instead of answering, I covered his lips with mine. He responded in kind. The man was magnificent, and I needed energy desperately. My body screamed for it. Need overpowered my rational mind, and I let it.

The moment our lips met, his firm to my soft, sparks of energy leaped between us so powerfully my body sizzled from head to toe. I jerked back, regretfully breaking the connection. Fen's gaze was pinned on mine, blazing with need. "That...that..." I stammered, my breath coming in quick bursts, "was a transfer of energy. I...feel it running through my body." I ran the tip of my tongue over my prickling lips, enjoying the sensation, yearning for more.

My body felt alive.

I need more.

"Valkyrie," Fen growled, eyes locked on my mouth. "Put your lips back on mine, and I will give you what you crave."

I dove up to him, my fingers fisting in his hair, pulling him roughly to me. His mouth met mine fiercely. My lips parted, welcoming him in, seeking what he had to offer. He turned his head, deepening the kiss, exploring, searching.

I wanted to cry.

The intensity was so sweet.

After all the heartache and pain, my body felt alive, buzzing, sensitive to his every touch as a tidal wave of delicious current raged through me. "How long has it been since you've been with a woman?" I breathed, my hands enjoying the feeling of him all over.

"Too long, maiden…far too long." His gaze was combustible.

"You taste so…*good*." I licked my lips.

"I need to touch you." He turned me effortlessly in his arms and slowly guided me down the length of his body. He took my lips again, ravaging me with another long kiss as I inched down his hard frame. His strong forearm stayed locked around me, so no space separated us.

When my toes hit the ground, he slid his thigh smoothly between my legs, supporting my weight, knowing I was still unsteady on my feet, splaying his other hand hard against my back.

All the new sensations made my head spin.

His hardness was pressed against my stomach, his leg tight against my core, and I instinctively rocked my hips against him, enjoying all the feelings. The buildup of pleasure inside me was spiraling quickly. I broke the kiss, arching my body back, locked in a mindless rhythm.

Yes, yes, I need this. Have to have it.

"My gods, Valkyrie. If you keep this up, this will not be a lasting encounter," Fen said roughly as he bent over and latched on to a nipple, taking me deeply.

"*Oh.*" The sensation of his mouth around me almost sent me over the edge right then and there. "Fen, please forgive me," I panted, leaning up to face him. "I don't know what's happening. I just know I need…*more.*"

He placed his hands on my hips, gripping my backside and guiding me back and forth, helping me achieve my pleasure. Then he hoisted me up in his arms.

I wrapped my legs around his strong body, locking myself to him, running my hands over his chest, relishing in the dampness of his skin. I raked my nails along his pecs, up to his neck, and into his silky hair. I would never get sick of his hair. It was thick and soft and perfect.

The current of energy that ran between us was palpable. Electricity shot into my body in tantalizing waves from all over. I drank it in as fast as I could. Each lave of his tongue filled me with more. He was full of so much power. The aura of it cracked and sizzled around us.

Give me more, wolf.

Fen found my breast again and teased the sensitive peak, twirling his tongue around it. I threw my head back, arching until I thought my back would break as a stab of lightning shot around us, followed by a clap of thunder so loud it rocked the cavern, sending rocks tumbling to the ground.

"Valkyrie...you must...slow down," Fen groaned, his voice low and husky. "I want to give you what you need, but at this rate, I will spend my seed before we are finished, and therefore help you none. You are too...exquisite."

I mewled at the loss of contact. I tried to find my brain, so I could answer him coherently. "Yes," was the only word I could find.

Fen shifted position, sliding me farther down his body so I sat lodged at his waist, my legs still locked tightly around him. I brought my hands up and cupped his face, leaning in, lightly skimming my lips over his, craving his touch like a drug.

I knew I was drunk on the power he was transferring to me, but I didn't want to stop.

Invisible jets of electricity flew from his mouth to mine. I licked his lips greedily, running my tongue all over them, tasting him, lapping up his power.

"Valkyrie, you are driving me mad," he growled, swinging me around and stalking to a large boulder. The stone had a smooth top, just big enough for the both of us. He backed me up against it.

I unlocked my legs and sat, shifting to rise up on my knees, pressing my fingers into his massive chest. "I want...you," I ordered, pointing to the smooth top of the rock, "to lie down."

My words sounded strange in my own ears, slurred and bold.

I shook my head.

Now that we were fully separated, everything began to dim, and my brain began to clear. As our gazes locked, light speared through Fen's eyes, his wolf just behind them, raking me with his intensity. It sent chills racing up my spine.

Gods, he's beautiful.

I brought my fingertips back to his chest and traced the contours. His body shivered, quaking under my touch as beads of energy jumped to greet my waiting fingertips.

He shed his shorts and moved up onto the boulder next to me.

"Oh," I breathed.

He was magnificent. I hadn't expected less, but he was truly incredible, his body glossy with sweat and fully primed for me.

Suddenly, I didn't know what to do. I felt completely overwhelmed and out of my league. The more time we spent separated, the more I came back down from the energy high. I was torn. This was both me and not me. The new me wanted him unequivocally, but the old Phoebe was embarrassed by her brazenness.

"Is this what you want, Valkyrie?" Fen asked. His face seemed sculpted of stone, yet his eyes were soft, pleading.

"I think so," I answered honestly. "But, I'm not sure." I tore my gaze off him so I could think, my thoughts swirling.

"My body is sort of acting on its own. It's literally begging me to take your energy however I can get it. It wants to survive and is blinding me with need. I want it, I know I need it, but I feel…" *We hardly know each other, I don't usually act like this, I can't believe I'm doing this.* "This is very intimate."

He nodded, his face pensive. "Indeed. However, if it eases you, not all realms act alike. In my world, Asgard, the one I occupied before I was banished here, we sought pleasure freely. Coupling is looked upon as a way to enjoy pleasure to its fullest. It is not considered shameful."

I bit my lip. "I can understand that. But that's not how it works in my world—especially for me. I was raised to honor a…coupling between a man and a woman. Sex is not a sport to me." If I was intimate with this man, there were bound to be feelings wrapped up in it. I wasn't ready for that. I hardly knew him.

"We need not continue." He gave me a smile. "I will get you to Yggdrasil so you may feed. Consider it done."

I nodded my agreement, but it felt hollow.

My body ached for his, even now.

I glanced down the length of him as he moved off the boulder, and shuddered inwardly. I reached out instinctively, stopping him from leaving. My palm boldly settled over his abdomen.

He drew in a sharp breath.

Energy raced out to greet my hand. I blinked, gazing up at him. "I'd like to get to know you. I mean…I hope you're not too disappointed. I'm happy to start slowly. Maybe we can…sleep next to each other?" I was bumbling this badly. All I really wanted to do was take his mouth again and ravage him, seeking only pleasure like they did in Asgard. But the real Phoebe was going to have her say. I needed time. And a clear head. This was all new to me—the feelings, the cravings, the power. It was overwhelming.

If I was going to be with Fen, it was going to be a clear choice, not a survival instinct.

Fen studied me for a long moment, his face impassive. "Okay, Valkyrie. As you wish. You need rest, and it's late. We can…embrace while we sleep." He slid off the boulder, grabbing his shorts. After he donned them, he turned. "Would you like assistance upstairs?"

I shook my head. "No, I need a moment to gather my thoughts."

He nodded, and I watched him walk up the steps. Emotion flooded through me. As he left, it felt like I'd lost something vital.

I spent time thinking about everything, my brain whirling as I lay back on the warm stone. My body felt so much better. The energy Fen had given me, even though it'd been a small amount in the scope of things, had revived me. My scars had healed over even more, and oddly, it had begun to heal me emotionally as well.

My body knew what was good for me, better than I did.

After a while, I was done thinking and ready to sleep. I ran my hands through my hair readying myself to see Fen again. I moved off the boulder, standing on weak legs, and wobbled up the steps. I was still naked, so I covered myself in an effort to maintain some kind of dignity.

Once I arrived, I found Fen awake, waiting for me on his pallet. He scooted back, patting the place in front of him.

I took a massive breath and doggedly moved forward.

16

Fen's living quarters were rustic at best. He'd managed to create a sleeping area out of a pile of dirt that had been formed into a misshapen pallet, topping it with scraps of burlap fabric he'd no doubt stolen from the demons.

"You don't, by any chance, have any clothing I could borrow?" I asked, standing in front of him, trying not to be too self-conscious. My jacket was here, but it would be too hot to wear, but later I could tear it up and try to make something work.

"I have a few garments under that ledge. You are free to use them." He gestured across the room to what resembled a sitting area with a long, rocky bench.

I walked over to where he'd indicated and found a few items. I turned back to him. "Are these your clothes? It looks like you're trying to keep them preserved for a rainy day." If they were his, they'd never fit me.

"They are mine, but they are not for a rainy day. It never rains here, and it's too hot here to wear anything other than what I have on. There is a tunic in the pile. Long ago it was white, but it should be large enough to amply cover you. I'm not going anywhere that I will need it."

I took the tunic out. It was more gray than white and visibly marked with age and wear. It had long sleeves, a curved hem, and white leather V-neck ties. It was a quality shirt, likely expensive. I shrugged it on. The arms were comically long, but the hem hit mid-thigh, perfectly covering all my vital areas. I rolled up the sleeves and tugged my hair out of the collar as I walked back toward him. The lighting in this cavern was low, casting shadows all over. "Where does the light come from?" I sat on the edge of his pallet, not sure what to do. "And how do you know if it's night or day?"

"The light comes from the lava. It bubbles under various parts of the floor. The cracks emit the red glow you see, as well as the heat. I know it's night because my body is well attuned to the climate. There is no orb in the sky. It's perpetually dusk. But this realm has its own rhythms. Come and lie down." He patted the uninviting burlap in front of him. "We must sleep to gather our strength. It's a long journey to Yggdrasil, and it will be fraught with peril."

I crawled in next to him. It was too hot for blankets.

After a few moments, he wrapped an arm around my waist and I scooted back against his chest. Energy immediately began to seep into me. It wasn't a big current like before, when we had been intimate, but it was there. I hoped, after hours of sleeping this close to an energy source, I'd wake up feeling even better.

We lay together for a while in silence, but I was too curious to go to sleep. "How did you arrive here?" I finally asked. "You said you used to live in Asgard and you were banished. But why?"

"Ah, Valkyrie, that is a long story indeed." He stretched, repositioning himself, settling his arm over me once again.

Having him this close relaxed me. I could get used to this peaceful feeling, like nothing bad could happen if we just lay together like this. "I'm not going anywhere for a while, so feel free to make the story long, chock full of good, quality details."

Fen chuckled, and his arm tightened around my waist. "I will answer your questions, but in return you must answer mine."

"Deal," I said eagerly. I had nothing to hide.

"My story starts many years ago. As a young wolf, I could not control myself. A single year after I was born, my mother was no longer able to care for me. My father, the god Loki, was not a part of my life in any way. I was brought to Asgard so the gods could watch over me. One god in particular, Tyr, son of Odin, was designated my keeper. Tyr is the god of war. He was the only god right for the job, strong in both body and mind."

"Did you become friends?"

"In a way. It was more a pupil-to-master relationship, but I grudgingly learned to respect him over time. Without his guidance, I realize now, I would've been left unable to function as a man. His methods might have been considered harsh to some, but they were what I required."

"How long did you stay under his tutelage?"

"Just short of three hundred years."

I gasped. "You're kidding me!" I tried to turn, but I was locked in Fen's embrace, enjoying the slow current of energy trickling in, and he held me steady.

Fen laughed, his chest rumbling, causing my body to shake and more energy to filter in. "No, Valkyrie, I'm not. Midgard operates very differently than the other realms. Humans have a life-span that seems only a moment to us."

Sadness washed over me as I thought about my family

and friends. If I really was a Valkyrie, they would be gone much too soon. "So what changed for you? Something had to have happened to land you here in this wretched place."

"The Norns happened," he replied, his jaw tight. I could detect the strain in his voice. This wasn't going to be an easy story to relay, and I appreciated that he was going to tell it anyway. "It was their custom to journey to Asgard once a year for the Celestial Festival, our biggest celebration. It's akin to your Christmas holiday, but lasts for a solid month. During their time there, they made predictions, scribed the future, told tall tales, and generally wreaked havoc. It is against the law to harm them in any way, and they are left to do as they please."

"Verdandi was awful. I saw the other two for only a moment. One was beautiful. The other looked like a witch."

"Urd is the witch. She deals in the past. Skuld is beautiful, but it's deceiving. Her true form is that of a hag, like her sisters, but she is gifted with glamour, and she uses it mercilessly to bewitch others. She sees the future and is the prime reason why I find myself here. Verdandi deals in the present. She has the ability to see only what's about to happen, a few minutes before and a few after. Together they are a great force and are fearsome if crossed. This particular festival, they were asked to predict events of Ragnarok, which they did happily before a large crowd."

"Ragnarok?"

"It puzzles me, Valkyrie, how you can be so ignorant of our ways. Even if you were raised on Midgard, you should have had some instruction. Children of Asgard are told the story of Ragnarok almost at birth."

I shook my head. "Believe me, I was raised human and only human. I'm still unsure if I'm actually a Valkyrie, but if I am, I'm a very ignorant one."

Fen's chest rose and fell against my back. I wasn't sure if he was going to continue, but he did. "Ragnarok is our fated battle, the one that pits gods against gods. It is our final day of reckoning, as well as the end of the cosmos as we know it. Most will die, but some will live on for the rebirth. No one knows when it will occur, but the Norns know who will fight whom to the death."

I stiffened beside him. "Do you die?" My heart began to beat faster.

"Indeed. But not before I kill a great leader, perhaps the greatest god of all."

I exhaled slowly. This was not happy news. "Is that why they sent you here? Because you have to kill a god?"

"It is. On that fateful night, the Norns gleefully stirred their bubbling pot and Skuld foretold that I was destined to kill Odin in the battle of Ragnarok. After that, my life became a living chaos."

My breath stuck in my throat, and I rose up on an elbow, turning to face him, his features serene in the low light. "Odin? You're supposed to kill Odin?" Why couldn't it be any other god? "Isn't it hard to kill a powerful immortal? And if you know you're supposed to do this horrible deed ahead of time, can't you change your mind or something?"

"In our world, there is no escaping your destiny, shieldmaiden. Ragnarok has been foretold for thousands upon thousands of years, new details emerging as the hags see fit. The only exception is that no one knows when it will happen. It could be in a millennia, or it could be tomorrow."

I settled back down, contemplating, inching my back closer to his chest, my body seeking his energy and comfort. I wasn't ready to confess what Ingrid had told me about Odin being my father, because I had no idea if it was true or not.

That was something I needed to figure out on my own first. "Did Odin banish you here himself?"

"He had a hand in it. But it was Tyr who ultimately tricked me."

"Tricked you?"

"Valkyrie, my history is a very long saga, but boiled down, yes. I was fooled like a child. The day after the Norns' prediction, they chained me up. But it didn't last long. I broke every restraint with which they bound me. Over time, they had a special rope made, crafted by the dark elves. I did not know it was magical. Had I known, I would not have been hoodwinked so easily. Alas, my ego was inflated from all that I had bested. So when Tyr wagered me I could not break this new chain, I scoffed." He growled. "When they showed me Gleipnir, the rope the elves had crafted, it looked as fine as silk. Nothing more than a wool spinner's yarn. Of course I could break it! I was a demigod. So they bound me with it." His voice dropped. "It was my undoing. I could not break it, no matter how hard I tried. The wager was set. If the rope held, I would be cast to another realm to live out my days. If it broke, I would be free."

My heart ached for him. What a sad fate. He'd had to endure so much pain in his lifetime. "So they tossed you here just like that?"

"Not at first," he answered after a moment. "The bet was that I would be banished, but it said nothing about escaping. I broke out of every realm they placed me in, and came back with a fury, trying to exact my vengeance on those who I felt had wronged me. I was feral, out of control. Muspelheim, this realm, was their final straw. I broke out once, and that's when they sealed up all the portals. So you landing here was a shock indeed. It should not have been so."

"Fen, I don't know what to say." It all seemed too severe,

but what did I know about gods and their ways? "That's...a horrible story. I'm sorry it happened to you."

He chuckled. "A Valkyrie who feels for the rabid wolf. It is nothing short of a miracle." His arm tightened around me. "I would almost think Ragnarok was upon us now, as it seems worlds have collided. But then I would be free of this place, yet here I languish."

"That makes no sense whatsoever," I said, my voice rising in anger. "If you're going to be free *anyway* so you can fight in Ragnarok, why keep you here all these years? What a waste."

"After the Norns' prophecy was heard by all, the gods could not trust me any longer. They thought I would strike sooner than later. I was a threat in the face of their well-being."

I shook my head adamantly, which rolled and bumped against Fen's rigid chest. "Nope. Because if no one can escape their destiny, like you said, then you couldn't have harmed Odin before Ragnarok began. Odin is *fated* to die at Ragnarok, not before."

"It's a mystery, I will give you that." Fen's chest rumbled. "But gods act in fear when they are threatened, as do humans. We are not so far apart in that respect. We want to protect ourselves against all odds, to live, to thrive. I didn't...control myself well the times I escaped. I was beyond all reasoning, lost in a red rage. Therefore, each time I arrived back in Asgard, the gods were justified that they had made the right decision by banishing me. I was dangerous, a threat to everyone. So in a way, I helped seal my own fate."

"Don't say that!" I was truly angry now. "You were only acting like anyone would if they were banished from the home they loved. I would've been angry, too."

"No, Valkyrie. I was *blind* to my anger. I would've killed

anything that stood in my way, and did. My wolf form is fierce. It took an army to subdue me each time."

"I saw you in your wolf form." He had been beautiful and terrifying.

It was Fen's turn to shake his head. "No. I rein myself in to fight the demons. They are a nuisance for me, not a true threat. If I truly let my beast out, the entire mountain would've been destroyed."

"Oh," was all I could say. Fen bigger and fiercer than what I'd seen would be overwhelming.

"Now it's my turn to ask the questions."

"Okay, but I don't have that much to share. Like I said, I was born and raised a human and have led a boring life." Up until now.

"Where do you hail from?" he asked.

"In Midgard? Wisconsin. It's one of the fifty states in the United States of America."

"How old are you?"

"I'm twenty-four." I had to have turned twenty-four by now, but maybe my birthday was today? Hard to know. But snuggling next to Fen was as good a present as any. Getting back to New York would be even better. "I've lost track of time, but my birthday was a week after I was first struck." I assumed my birth certificate had been faked, so it would be impossible for my parents to know my true birth date, but it couldn't be off by that much. I had pictures of myself as a newborn.

"Have you ever witnessed strange things during your time in Midgard?"

"Yes." I paused. "But not really until I hit New York. Then things got strange fast."

"As one nears immortality, they have a heightened sense of the world around them. Many species from other realms visit Midgard. They are glamoured while they are there, as is mandatory, but you would have seen through some."

I thought back to the man on the subway stairs and shivered. He had told me to get away. He had been trying to give me a warning. How had he known who I was?

"Do you know anything about your real parents or your lineage?" Fen asked.

"Not really," I hedged. "I was kidnapped by the ettins an hour after my friend Ingrid told me I was in danger. She mentioned my mother was a shieldmaiden, as well as her sister. That would make Ingrid my aunt. That's all I know, but it's all still hard for me to believe it's all true."

"And your mother's name?"

"Leela."

"I'm not familiar with that moniker, though that's not saying much. I have been far removed for a long time."

"How long?"

"Six hundred years."

"Oh…" I couldn't fathom what he'd been through and how long it had been.

"We must rest, Valkyrie. There will be time to answer more questions tomorrow."

My eyes slid shut, almost at his command. I was weary, but comfortable, my body taking as much as it could from my willing host. I knew my dreams would be filled with Fen and what had almost happened between us…and what still might be.

17

I'd found a pair of linen pants, which Fen had likely been saving, as there were no clothing stores down here in the pit of despair. After much discussion—me declining and him insisting—he'd cut them off to fit my height, and I'd donned them. I was in the process of threading an old rope through the pant loops as a makeshift belt when Fen came into the cave.

"The serpents say the pathway is clear. We will leave shortly." Fen came up the stairs and gathered up his weapons, sticking them in a sheath he wore around his waist.

I nodded. I'd awoken feeling more refreshed, but still weak. I'd spent the morning soaking in the pool. My scars had healed even more, and I was in very little pain, which was nothing short of amazing considering what damage there had been. The energy I'd taken from Fen throughout the night had certainly given me some strength, but I needed more.

My dreams had been outrageous, as predicted. I'd dreamed of Fen and little else, tossing and turning throughout the night. Feeling his body electric next to mine this morning as I woke had almost taken me over the edge. The Valkyrie part of me wanted to devour him immediately and take everything I knew he was willing to offer. It'd taken everything I had to keep my hands to myself. I'd practically leaped from the pallet to get away. Fen hadn't commented on my strange behavior, which was a relief, and had left me alone.

Now as he walked over, I turned away, flustered, remembering intimate details about my brazen dreams—including but not limited to—straddling his beautiful tapered waist and having my way with him. I tried to appear busy getting ready for our journey, but there wasn't a lot for me to do other than finish making my belt.

I hoped he couldn't read thoughts, because if he could, I might not be able to show my face in these caves again.

He smiled, seemingly unfazed by my dirty mind, handing me an iron rod. Apparently, he had plenty of these lying around. I took it, but voiced my displeasure. "I want Gram, not this stick." I shook the weapon. "It's my dagger, and it's time you gave it back."

"I'm sorry, shieldmaiden. But it's far too precious for me to give up."

"Are you going to try it in the tree?" I asked curiously. That's what I would do.

"Of course. I would not waste this opportunity." He'd answered me like I'd been daft to even ask.

"What about me?" I cried. "You can't leave! I wouldn't survive here alone. We saw how swimmingly that went already."

"It's not an issue," he answered. "The dagger will not work, but on the rare chance it does, rest assured that I will take you with me."

"And how are you going do that?" I crossed my arms, huffing indignantly.

He gave me a lopsided smile. "I reach out my hand to you, and you clasp it."

I dropped my arms, looking incredulous. "That's it? That's how you take someone with you?"

He shrugged. "Most of the time. Sometimes the tree rejects the second traveler, but it's rare."

"Then what if I'm rejected?" I wailed. "Fen, you have to let me try first! There's no way I can survive here, and you've lasted for six hundred years. I wouldn't make it a month. Please, let me go first!"

He shook his head. "No, Valkyrie. On the off chance the tree rejects you, once I get out, I will come for you. The serpents will keep you safe until I return."

"The serpents!" I sputtered. "Like...like they did yesterday? I'll be snake dinner by the time you land elsewhere."

"They are bound by an oath. They cannot hurt you."

"That's not at all comforting!" I yelled. "This is not a 'let's go help Phoebe so she can eat' trip to the tree. This is a 'Fen trying to escape' trip! With *my* dagger."

Fen stopped two feet from me. My eyes were directly in line with his chest, and I refused to meet his gaze. The double-crosser. "Make no mistake, Valkyrie, I will not let an opportunity like this pass me by. I've waited hundreds of years to be rid of this place. I will come back for you. You have my word. But there is no sense in arguing about this, as the chances the dagger will work are close to zero. We are wasting our time and our breath discussing this." He turned abruptly and returned to gathering things and sticking them in his waist.

I was far from mollified. "Why don't you think the dagger

will work? You told me, right when I landed, that Gram could provide passage. It's already worked for me once. I'm living proof."

"Yes, but you're not me. The gods do not leave things undone. They will have made the journey impossible for me, even with the dagger."

I rushed up to him, my hand animated in front of me. "That's why *I* should be the one to put it in the tree." I grasped on to his forearm. "They don't know I exist. Well, most of them don't, so they haven't had time to ring the alarms." Possibly Verdandi had, but I couldn't worry about that. "I can get it to work, then I'll grab for you and you can hitch a ride with *me*." It was a perfect, sound plan.

Fen shook his head. "No. I will not give it up."

"That makes no sense!" I stomped my foot.

He took me by the shoulders gently, his face set. He leaned down so he spoke directly at my level. "If the dagger does not work for me, it will not let me 'hitch a ride' either."

"Okay," I said slowly, thinking fast. "Then we can find another way."

I met his gaze, and he looked away, his hands still braced on my shoulders. "There is no other way." Currents rushed in from his touch, infusing me with energy. It was the only reason I hadn't stepped back. "If the tree takes you, you will not have the means to return, Valkyrie. You are too young. You have no knowledge of our worlds. Getting anyone to aid you to help me will be impossible. I'm known as a terror far and wide."

"Fen, I promise to come back—"

"No."

"But..." He didn't want me to leave. "That means you're willing to keep me as your prisoner here, when I could use this journey to escape."

He dropped his arms, defeated. He wouldn't meet my eyes this time. "For a time, I guess you are correct. Though, you are no prisoner." He turned and walked away.

"Why would you possibly want to keep me here against my will?" I called to his retreating back, my voice angry. I wasn't done with this conversation.

He glanced over his shoulder. "You are the first person I have had a conversation with in six hundred years. I cannot go back to the way things were. I will not survive. I will lose my mind within a fortnight. As it was, you arrived at a critical time. There will be no going back to what was."

I pondered that. "What do you mean by 'critical'? Are you talking about ending your own life? Please tell me that wasn't it."

"I would've tried, but likely not succeeded…for long. I would be forced to do the deed again and again and again, for all eternity, to find any peace."

"Until Ragnarok."

"Yes."

He walked down the stairs and out of the cave.

I sat down with a thump on a crude bench, trying to process what had just happened. My brain couldn't fathom what it would be like to live alone for six hundred years. I didn't have the capacity to fully grasp it. Fen's reasoning was sound—he wanted to keep me here so he didn't lose his mind. I could understand that. I would feel the same way. But holding me here against my will, and denying me the opportunity to escape, wasn't the answer either.

Both of us would suffer.

He had to know that if I escaped, I'd find my way back somehow. I'd get Ingrid to help me, or Huggie.

But what if that didn't work? And he was trapped here alone for another six hundred years?

I would never forgive myself.

I rubbed my temples.

The only option I had was to convince him to trust me on the journey. Trust that I would come back for him. Fen said it was a long trip to the tree, so I'd have ample time to make him see my side. I couldn't stay here. I would eventually die. Plus, we'd have to take a trip to the tree every week so I could feed. That wasn't going to work. The serpents hadn't agreed to be our bodyguards for life. The demons would catch on.

Fen wasn't thinking clearly.

I stood, turning in a circle, feeling discombobulated. "He's going to have to find a way to believe in me," I said. "Once I escape, I'll convince everyone he's no longer a threat. That he's changed. Then I can free him."

"Valkyrie!" Fen's voice carried through the caverns. "It's time to go."

"Coming," I called, picking up the iron rod I'd dropped. My pitiful weapon against demon kings who wielded flaming swords and giant snakes with forked tongues bigger than my entire body. If Fen disappeared through the tree and left me, this tiny weapon would be no match for any of them.

I found Fen in the third cavern over, past the lava streams. He paced by the entrance to another tunnel. "Once we leave here," he told me, "you must listen to me above all else. The demons fear the Jondi, so they will stay back, for the most part."

"The most part?"

"They might launch a firefight."

"What exactly is a firefight?"

"They will shoot flaming arrows at us, among other things." His face remained impassive.

What other things? I didn't want to know. "I will follow your lead."

"Good." He turned and walked into the narrow tunnel, and I trailed behind. "The serpents are at the entrance. They have positioned scouts along the way. They communicate by vibration, so we should have ample warning beforehand. If things go awry, you must take shelter, possibly in the folds of one of the serpents."

I stopped walking.

Hell to the no. I wasn't cozying up to one of those giant snakes! Much less getting into its *folds*. "Fen, you can't be serious—"

"I am. You will die if you don't do as I say. I will be fighting. I cannot protect you at the same time." He raised an eyebrow, as if to say, *Look what happened last time.*

"We'll see," I hedged as I began to walk again. "I'm not promising anything. Those things are beyond creepy." I stopped just in time to prevent myself from crashing into Fen's broad back.

He'd come to a halt abruptly at what looked like the opening to outside.

I peered around his shoulder.

We were situated high up on a precipice, the valley spread out below us. The entire realm was layered in varying shades of reds and oranges, covered in dark shadows. There was no orb in the sky. It looked like Earth an hour after sunset, except redder and more brutal. "It feels like we're on another planet," I murmured. I'd seen outside before, but not like this. Being on the ground in the hands of the demons had been a much different experience than seeing miles out into this vista. "The heat hits you immediately."

"Yes, it is oppressive," Fen agreed.

There was movement to the right as we stepped out. A massive serpent was positioned there. It spoke to Fen. "We are ready. Remain *clossse*." It began to slither down the path in front of us.

We followed.

I clutched my iron rod with all my might. At the bottom of the hill, six more serpents lingered. They all looked vaguely the same—each had dark scales the size of two of my hands put together, hauntingly violet eyes, huge forked tongues. Some were taller, some shorter, but in essence they were all the same.

One slinked forward.

I was fairly sure it was the same one that had harassed me in the cave. Only because this one had a small divot missing from the side of its head, something I'd noticed earlier. It must be their leader. "The *coassst* is clear. We will *sssset* a *vigoroussss* pace. You must keep up. It *issss* not *sssssafe* to linger."

"I know that, Jondi. We will keep up. Worry about the demons, not us," Fen told the snake in short, clipped tones.

Three snakes took the lead, then Fen and me, then three snakes behind. It was a motley crew by anyone's standards.

We'd gone about a mile when tremors hit underneath my feet. All the snakes froze immediately. Fen shoved me behind him as he scanned the desolate area surrounding us for a threat.

I couldn't sense or see anything.

"That was a Jondi signal," Fen whispered to me. "The serpents will interpret it and let us know."

Once the vibrations died down, the snake leader slithered up to us. "They have *ssspotted* a group of *demonssss* to the north. They are *clossssing* in quickly. They are armed with fire. We must double our time to outrun them."

I was already tired. The heat was more than oppressive— it was hateful. I was sapped of energy.

"We will ride on your backs," Fen announced.

Say...what?

"That will *cosssst* you more." The snake grinned in an ugly way, its mouth turning up at the ends in a cruel, macabre grimace.

"You forget yourself, Jondi. Part of our bargain is for you to get us to the tree safely, whatever it takes," Fen retorted. "And if carrying us as passengers is what it takes, then so it shall be."

While they argued about the particulars, I scanned the horizon. I spotted movement up ahead and pulled on Fen's arm. He ignored me. I yanked it down, and words tumbled out of my mouth. "Something is up ahead, and it doesn't look friendly."

18

Fen's head wrenched toward where I was gesturing, and he yelled, "Did you not send scouts up ahead?" He turned to a towering serpent. "If you are double-crossing me, our bargain ends now. In *death*."

The snake appeared furious. It slithered up to another one of its brethren and began to hiss at it in a language I couldn't come close to understanding.

Immediately, two snakes took off in the direction I'd seen movement.

Fen pulled me aside. "The Jondi are notorious for ill dealing. We must be on our guard."

"Then why would you choose to trust them in the first place?" I had trouble keeping my voice lowered.

"Because I had no other choice. We must get you to the sacred tree. There are too many demons on this plane— literally thousands—and they are all mind-controlled by Surtr. They are not strong on their own, but if enough swarm at once out in the open, they have the potential to overpower us. The serpents are the only other creatures that inhabit this plane, and they have a long-standing truce with the demons. If Surtr attacks the snakes, he runs the risk of breaking their alliance, which will cause him hundreds of years of aggravation and a possible eventual extinction of his race."

"If the snakes can help you, why have you waited this long to form an alliance with them?"

Fen's face darkened. "I had a previous alliance with them long ago, when I was new here. In the end, the deal turned disastrous. They tried to take me prisoner instead of honoring the deal we had agreed upon. They intended to ransom me for their release."

Why would anyone think Fen wouldn't retaliate? "Exactly how disastrous are we talking?"

"When they crossed me, I decimated them. I left a few females and some young males alive and told them to remember what had happened that day and to pass the story on. If I ever came calling again, they were to honor our dealings or face my wrath. I have not needed them until now. These serpents remember." He gestured to where the snakes were congregated, still hissing and huffing. "They will think twice before crossing me, but I must remain vigilant."

"What's in it for them? Why are they helping us?" I asked.

"They crave freedom. This is not their realm of origin. They were cast here, as I was, and seek their homeland above all else."

That was an interesting tidbit. "Which realm are they from?"

"Jotunheim, land of the giants. Their natural habitat is mountainous and green, nothing like this wasteland here." He swept his arm out. "This landscape pains them as much as it does us."

"Wow," I said. "They must have done something really bad to be sent here."

Fen shrugged. "Not really. Mimir, the seer who guards the sacred well on Jotunheim, foresaw an uprising between the serpents and the giants. To ensure it never happened, the giants cast them here."

I couldn't even begin to understand the logic of these worlds. It all seemed counterintuitive. "That goes against the whole destiny thing you keep bringing up. If the snakes are supposed to rise up, won't it happen eventually anyway? Even if they are cast here?"

"Likely," he replied. "But as I've explained before, that is how we do things. If we get word of a threat, we eliminate it, much like humans. It's intrinsic to our nature."

I pondered that. Without the serpents' help, we wouldn't be able to get to the tree. "Maybe the snakes are meant for another purpose—" I was cut off as the Jondi leader slithered over to us.

"We *sssstay* here until we get word."

Fen stalked forward. "If this is a trap, you will find your death in my jaws."

"It *issss* no trap. *Jusssst* an *oversssssight*. The threat ahead is likely a few demon *ssssscouts*. They will be taken care of momentarily. I *sssent* other troops to take care of the north. When word *comessss* back, we will carry on."

The snake wound its huge head toward me, and I cringed back. It smiled and hissed before moving off to join the others.

A few moments later, vibrations ran underfoot. The leader seemed satisfied and ordered us to move on. We started again, this time with one snake in front, Fen and me, and two in the back. There were some shouts up ahead, and then silence. The two other serpents rejoined us without comment.

Apparently, both threats had been eliminated. For now.

We walked for a few hours, talking only sporadically, the heat oppressive and the topography changing little. It was how I imagined the Sahara Desert to be, but hotter and yuckier. As we passed crater after crater, I glanced in, imagining fire-breathing dragons nesting at the bottom. I was certain this would be their habitat if they existed. I decided to ask Fen once I caught up. "Do dragons exist in these realms?" I asked.

He slowed. "Yes. But they do not live here, and there are only a few in existence. Nidhogg is the most fearsome. That dragon resides at the base of Yggdrasil and is said to chew on its roots for sustenance. Though no one I know has ever witnessed the dragon in the flesh. During Ragnarok, Nidhogg is supposed to rise, bringing its curses with it. After Ragnarok, the dragon will spend eternity guarding the bodies of the fallen at the Shore of Corpses."

"That sounds downright…jolly." Everything about these worlds was doom and gloom. "Is there anything wonderful in these realms? All the stories you've told me so far are about death and destruction. Why would anyone choose to be here when Midgard holds such beauty?"

Fen cocked his head at me strangely. "Our worlds hold vast beauty, Valkyrie. Unparalleled to anything you've ever seen on Midgard. Asgard, home of the gods, is the most breathtaking of them all. The city's walls are carved of ivory and stand nine stories tall. Windows as vast as you can imagine gaze out on spectacular views of crystalline rivers and mountains so massive their peaks touch the sky. There are lakes and waterfalls as far as the eye can see. Pathways paved in marble wind through the realm. The homes are lavish, gilded in gold and silver." He sounded wistful. "Everything has harmony in my world, unlike Midgard,

AMANDA CARLSON

where everything seems on the verge of chaos." New York City did court some chaos. My hometown was lovely, however. No chaos there. "There are other realms full of beauty as well. Jotunheim, where the serpents hail from, appears like Midgard's mountainous West, except everything is bigger, grander, and far greener. Alfheim, where the elves reside, is mystical, full of twining forests and lush valleys."

That did sound nice. "So it was just dumb chance I landed here? On hot, scalding Mars, instead of one of those beautiful places?" I shook my head as we trudged through a small crater. "Some girls have all the luck."

Fen reached out a hand to aid me. I grabbed on, enjoying the feeling of the current as it leaped from his body to mine. "I think it was more than luck you landed here," he finally answered. "The elves or giants would've bargained with your life freely, not caring if you lived or died, as is their way. Feelings do not factor in with outsiders."

"Because Surtr is so kind and gentle?" I replied. "I'm thinking anything would've been better than what I went through here. The elves could've tied me up under a waterfall, and that would've been a thousand times better than what happened on Surtr's altar." Calling up the memories made me feel like vomiting. I pinned my eyes on the distant horizon so I could keep moving forward without breaking down. It was still too fresh.

"The elves would've subjected you to far worse. They deal in psychological warfare, burrowing inside your brain, teasing you with cruel imaginings until you feel your brain will explode. You would go insane from the false memories. The giants, on the other hand, are fascinated with sexual exploration. If you get my drift. You would not have survived their...proddings."

Did he mean sexual...warfare? I'd had no idea there was

even such a thing. "Honestly, I don't even want to know what that means, and please don't tell me."

"What it means is beyond the physical wounds you sustained on this plane. You will heal in time, but the emotional wounds you would've endured in another realm would've debilitated you completely. Someone must be looking out for you. Someone very powerful."

"Oh." Before I had a chance to reply with more, the serpents in front slowed.

The leader made its way to us. "The crater of *Yggdrassssil* is up ahead. If the demons are going to attack, it will be *ssssoon*."

"I can't see any crater." I went up on my tiptoes. Not that I could see a crater very easily, since it was *in* the ground.

"The serpent means in an hour or two," Fen said, turning to the snake. "You will have contingents joining us well before then?"

"*Yessss*. We will be ready."

Fen nodded and the snake left. We resumed our slog through the wastelands. "Why would it say it was up ahead if it's an hour or two away?" I questioned. "That's a long time from now."

"In these realms, high alert is the only thing that keeps you alive. The snake was only indicating that Yggdrasil is within our reach, so we must double our guard."

"M'kay." I pondered. "But I thought we'd been on high alert...the entire time."

Fen chuckled. "The chances we would've been ambushed by demons back there were one in several thousand. The chances we *will* be attacked now move up to one in five."

We walked another half hour in silence.

I was drenched in sweat and feeling light-headed. My stomach wasn't growling—not sure if that was ever going to happen again—but it craved sustenance. It was a deep, instinctual feeling. I knew that once I fed from the tree, I would feel amazing in a way no regular meal could satisfy me.

Idly, I wondered if I could ever eat food again. Or enjoy it?

Thinking back, Ingrid would eat popcorn and drink soda with me on movie nights. I had no idea if she did it for show or not. I'd fallen behind, so I hurried up to Fen. "You seem to know a lot about Valkyries," I said as a segue. "Can I ask you something? Do you know if they eat regular food? I'm not a vampire now, am I? If I eat something, will I puke it up?"

He tossed a glance over his shoulder, grinning. "I've seen Valkyries partake in meals in my time. I have no idea how food tastes for them. They don't need it to survive, but they seem to enjoy a good feast with gusto."

Relief swept through me. It would be hard to participate in life on Midgard without eating meals. "Okay, thanks. I'll have to ask Ingrid when I get back." If I got back. This was my opportunity to convince Fen to let me go through the tree. I cleared my throat, keeping pace with him. "I have some powerful friends back on Midgard who can help me get back here, you know, if the dagger doesn't work for you. If you let me go, I can come back and free you. You'd just have to stay close by and wait for me."

"What friends?" he scoffed. "The lone shieldmaiden, Ingrid? That is hardly a powerful ally. And, I can assure you, no Valkyrie will help free me."

"She will if I ask her to!" I insisted. "If I tell her you saved my life and you're imprisoned here unfairly, I'm sure she will help. She's honorable. She will do the right thing."

Fen's laugh was a deep baritone. "Shieldmaidens are

honorable…to Odin alone. They are slaves who rarely think for themselves. They follow his cause blindly. In case you've forgotten, he is the reason I'm stuck on this plane. Each time I escaped, he sent his loyal Valkyries to hunt me down with orders to bring me back, dead or alive. Dead would've been preferable, though unlikely. They enjoyed their sport immensely, and I tell you they will not help you."

I was at a loss and wondered if Ingrid had ever hunted Fen. "She's not my only ally…I have more." The raven kind of liked me. Ingrid had said the raven was old and powerful.

Fen raised his eyebrow. "Who do you have, little Valkyrie, to help me escape?"

"Huggie?" I'd phrased it like a question on accident. I'd meant to come off sounding confident, but I really had no idea if the bird would help me.

"Who is Huggie? He doesn't sound all that powerful."

Ingrid had told me the raven's real name was Hugin, so I tried that. "I mean, Hugin?" Still a question. "Hugin is a raven—"

Fen stopped so abruptly I crashed into his back, bouncing off like I'd hit a wall. He spun around, grabbing me by the shoulders, his grip painful. To say his reaction surprised me was an understatement. "Who are you?" He shook me. And none too gently. "You have ties to the raven Hugin? The bird is Odin's chief informant!" He let go, pushing me away as he spun around, his hands lofted in the air. "I should've known. I have been so stupid." The snakes stopped, curious about Fen's sudden behavior, and slowly formed a circle around us. "You had Gram in your possession. A weapon crafted for Odin alone. You glowed too brightly, yet you had no knowledge of our world. You reeled me in perfectly." He turned and faced me, his voice low, his face furious. He stalked toward me. "I will ask you only one more time. *Who* are you?"

I took a few inadvertent steps backward.

Fen's voice had boomed loudly, scaring me, but when a hiss sounded over my shoulder, I came to a halt. I picked the angry demigod over the snakes.

I'd made a huge mistake, and it was too late to take it back. "I'm no one! I told you the truth before. I'm not lying," I cried. "Huggie...I mean, Hugin...showed up in my apartment unannounced the day I was struck. I'd never set eyes on the raven before. Then Ingrid came in, and everything went to hell! The ettins kidnapped me, tossed me in the tree, and you know the rest. I only met Hugin that one time. But he seemed to want to help me! So I figured if I got back to New York, I could find him. Ingrid said he was powerful..." I ended lamely, "So I thought the bird could help me get back to you."

Fen shook his head. "I do not accept that answer. Odin does not lend his favorite possessions freely to just *anyone*. Who are you to him? Answer me!"

"I don't know! You have to believe me! I don't know Odin. I've never even met him." Fen was far too angry for me to confess things I only partially knew to be true. I didn't have the answers he wanted. Ingrid had told me Odin was my father, but I had no proof. If I told Fen that now, he'd toss me to the serpents as a mealtime snack and walk away.

He was in no frame of mind to listen to reason.

"Valkyrie, you are testing me to my very limits—"

A sound whizzed overhead, and a whoosh of flames erupted next to us.

"The *demonssss* are here," a snake hissed. "We must alert the *otherssss*."

Fen grabbed me, pressing me tightly against his stomach as he turned in a slow circle. "This is not over," he ground in my ear. "Stay close to me, or you die."

19

Demons had surrounded us. We'd let down our guard, because of me, for only a few moments. But that's all it had taken.

We were situated in a small valley with large boulders flanking either side. Fen was dangerously on edge. "How could you let us be surrounded, Jondi!" he yelled. "Where are the others?"

"They are coming. We have *ssssounded* the alarm."

"We are too close to the tree to turn back now," Fen fumed. "You will get us there, as agreed, or die."

More flaming arrows whizzed by.

"We will honor our bargain, have no fear." The snake turned and spat orders at the remaining serpents. They fanned out around us. They were the bigger targets, but as an arrow zoomed down, it bounced off one of the snake's big scales and dropped harmlessly to the ground.

Their scales must be tough as steel. I hoped they were fireproof, too.

"It seems only a small contingent," Fen said, still holding me. "My guess is there are only seventy to eighty."

"That's considered a small group?" I said. "Seems like a lot to me." I ducked as another arrow whooshed over our heads.

Fen let me go, giving me a look before he turned to the leader. "We are wasting our time waiting for the others. You can move faster than the demons can run, Jondi. We will ride on your back to the rendezvous place. Once there, we will reevaluate."

The main serpent angled its head toward us, seeming bored. "Fine. We will *transssssport* you."

Fen wasted no time leaping onto the leader's back, gesturing to me to get on the one next to him.

"Um." I paused, hoping he was kidding as I eyed the huge beast in front of me.

"There is no time to ponder this, Valkyrie. Jump on or face the demons alone!" Fen's face was set.

I examined the snake. Its back was taller than any horse I'd ever seen by quite a few feet. The scales appeared slick. I wasn't a demigod, so I couldn't just *hop on*. I tentatively reached a hand out to touch a scale and recoiled at the feeling. It was hot. It felt pliable, yet hard like metal, which was strange. The scale left a slimy residue on my fingers, but it wasn't sticky. So strange.

"Get on!" Fen ordered. "We must move now."

The demons had ramped up their arrow attack, and fiery sticks shot past me on all sides. "I can't just jump on!" I cried. "I'm not tall enough, and the scales are slippery." I sounded like a child to my own ears and cringed.

Fen's nostrils flared once as he leaped off his ride and stalked toward me. "You are a *Valkyrie*," he intoned. "You can indeed just *hop on*." His hands pivoted around my waist, and the next thing I knew, I was flying through the air.

He'd literally tossed me onto the snake's back, and once I landed, the big serpent swiveled its head and hissed, its giant fork coming within inches of my face. Its breath smelled like putrid waste, and its eyes were hard. I'm sure it hoped I would fall off so it could eat me.

Lovely.

We started moving immediately.

I had no idea where to grab on. My hands kept slipping as I tried to find a good hold. There was none. Finally, I pried my fingernails between the scales. When the thing began to rock faster, I was certain I would fall off.

"Use your legs!" Fen roared.

In a very unladylike—un-Valkyrielike?—gesture, I bent over and wrapped my arms around the snake's neck column and pinned my legs around its back as tightly as I could and closed my eyes, holding on for dear life.

The arrows stopped within the first few minutes, so it hadn't taken much time to clear the demon area, which was a positive. I hoped at this rate it wouldn't take much time to get to the tree. I clung to the snake's back like a scared cowgirl for about fifteen minutes more, when thankfully we came to a stop.

I glanced up, hoping to see the tree, only to find we'd stopped in front of a large barricade.

On top stood Surtr with his awful, flaming sword.

I didn't want to immediately start panicking, but brutal images of what he'd done bombarded me, and I began to feel woozy, my body threatening to pass out.

"Valkyrie!" Fen shouted. "He cannot hurt you. He is no match for the Jondi. He is here for show only."

I nodded lamely. Fen must've seen my face. "How are we going to get by him?" I gestured at the barricade that seemed to be made from nothing more than a bunch of twigs piled up hastily.

"It is there only to make him seem more eminent. It is not a true barrier."

Surtr didn't seem to enjoy us talking about him.

He brandished his fiery sword over his head and swung it down, pointing it directly at me. He shouted something menacing that thankfully I couldn't hear.

What happened next must have surprised Fen, because his yell sounded deafening in my ears. At Surtr's words, a ball of fire shot out of his sword and headed straight for me.

From there, everything happened fast.

The snake I was on bucked, trying to get out of the way, but it was no use. The flame tore through its neck and landed squarely in my chest, the force launching me backward and to the ground, where the fire began to grow and fester.

Fen shouted something again that I couldn't hear. The next thing I knew he was standing over me as pain rippled through my body. Why was I still awake? I tried to focus on what Fen was saying.

"It's a spell, Valkyrie. Fight it!" Fen's words finally penetrated.

A spell? A flaming, horrible spell? How was I supposed to fight it?

Oddly, the spell hurt, but I didn't feel like I was actually *on fire*.

A big snake head loomed above me. Its words were loud and clear. "She *issss* not *sssstrong*. We should leave her."

I am strong!

How dare that snake pass judgment on me? I'd survived a ton already. If I wasn't strong, I'd already be dead.

Fen got to his knees, placing a hand on my chest. Right

where flames should be sprouting. "You must fight this. Surtr's magic is weak. Spinning spells is not his craft. He is trying to scare you or force us to leave you. He knows he will not win against the united Jondi."

I tried to form words to ask Fen how to fight it, but they wouldn't come. My brain was not on board, because the spell was messing with me.

"Leave her," the snake hissed. "If we do, they will let us *passss* to the tree unharmed. You have the weapon."

"We are not leaving her," Fen stated evenly. "She is malnourished and has little strength. She is new to this world and our ways. It is her dagger that will free us all, lest we forget."

I closed my eyes.

Maybe they should leave me. I wasn't worthy of saving.

A moment later, something soft yet firm landed on my lips, and delicious tingles flowed right after. My eyes flew open. Fen was kissing me, infusing me with his strength. "That's it, shieldmaiden. Drink it in and aim it at the spell."

How?

Energy began to mount inside me the longer his lips touched mine. I could now sense that something was obstructing my body. Fen's tongue lapped at mine, gently at first and then more demanding. I opened myself up to him, forgetting where we were. If I could've lifted my hands, I would've twined them in his hair. More nourishment entered my body.

"That's it," he told me in soothing tones, his voice as breathless as I felt. "Now aim the concentration at the spell."

"Then...what?" I managed, breaking from the kiss, but desperately wanting more.

"Your power alone will disintegrate it. You are stronger than Surtr. Just have faith." I did as he asked...kind of. I envisioned the thing in my chest and how much I wanted it gone. "That's it." His lips touched mine again, and he breathed a soft breath into me. "Keep doing that."

My chest began to feel lighter.

I had no idea what I was doing, other than craving his energy and being pissed off about the spell. It seemed to be enough.

Much too soon, Fen stood up, reaching a hand down.

I blinked. The pain was gone. I took his aid and stood. I was flustered by the sudden intimacy we'd shared, so I tried to look anywhere but at Fen. I was also confused. "Why did you help me?" I had to ask. "You could've just let me die. You think I lied to you, so why let me live?" I brushed myself off, keeping busy.

"You wouldn't have died from that, shieldmaiden. It was just a minor inconvenience."

"Well, you could've left me and gone to the tree on your own. It would've taken me some time to overcome it on my own. Only one rickety barricade stands in your way to freedom. I'm sure Surtr could find a way to do me in if given half a chance."

When I finally glanced up, Fen's eyes pierced me with intensity. "I spared you because you are still a mystery to me. That is all. Once the mystery is revealed, then we shall see if you live or die. If I find you are an agent of Odin, you will feel my wrath." He turned and walked away, dismissing me.

I shook myself. His words had been harsh. If Odin was truly my father, explaining it to Fen in a way that would make him understand I had no ties to the god, other than genetics, would be extremely difficult, if not impossible.

I couldn't think about that.

Surtr's booming voice echoed around us. It was garbled,

half in English and half demonish. I made out, "Surrender…
will die…punish."

There would be no surrendering.

Fen strode to the edge of the wall of serpents. More
snakes had joined the group, but I didn't know when they'd
arrived. There were at least fifty in attendance. It was quite a
showing.

I could see why Surtr was thinking twice about charging
us or sending out any more spells.

"You will comply with our wishes, demon king," Fen
addressed Surtr. "Have no fear. We will make a deal to your
liking."

"I will not make bargains with you," Surtr cried, his voice
strained.

"Yes, you will," Fen finished. "If you do not, the
consequences will be far too grave."

"Give me the girl, and you can have the tree. That is the
only deal I will broker."

"The girl is not an option. Let us access the tree, and we
will spare your world and your demons," Fen said. "After we
have gone, we will agree to pay damages in a worthy amount
you choose, to be delivered by an agent within one season.
That is my final offer."

Surtr's roar was devastatingly loud. He was not happy
with the deal.

Verdandi must've offered him much more to deliver me,
battered, bruised, and almost dead, to her door.

"Then we will fight!" Surtr boomed, hoisting his flaming
sword in the air, swinging it overhead.

"As you wish," Fen said, his jaw tight. He turned to the
snakes. "How many demons are we dealing with?"

A new serpent I hadn't seen before answered him. "Two
thoussssand. More to come."

Fen cursed. "We must not diverge from the mission. It is simple. We clear a path to Yggdrasil, and the Valkyrie and I go down. Once we are through, the fighting stops."

"You *musssst* honor your agreement with us."

"Of course I will, there is no question. But we are not all going through the tree now. I will return with the key you will need for your passage back to Jotunheim as time allows."

"How do we know we can *trusssst* you?" The serpent narrowed its eyes. This must be their military leader. It was bigger than the other snakes and so dark it was almost hard to see in the low light. It bent down and bared its gigantic fangs at Fen.

Fen wasn't fazed. He crossed his arms and stood his ground. "Now you choose not to trust me? I will do as agreed, upon my honor. We are both prisoners of this realm, do not forget. We were tossed here against our will. I will get the key to you in due time. I have no reason to back out of our agreement."

"If you do, we will put a price on your head."

Fen scoffed. "Serpent, there is already a price on my head. Once I escape from here, every creature in all the realms will be hunting me."

"How will you evade them?" the snake asked.

Fen shrugged. "I plan to lose myself in Midgard. There are many places to hide there."

"After you get *ussss* the key."

"Of course. Do not fear that I will break my word. I am not the one who backed out of our last agreement."

I had no idea what the key would look like to get the serpents out, but I assumed it was something big. I hadn't thought about where Fen would go once he escaped, but Midgard seemed logical. My world was big, with lots of hiding spots and lots of people.

STRUCK

Fen drew Gram out of his belt, slashing his palm quickly. He brought the hand up to the snake and placed it on one of its scales. After a moment, the big beast nodded. Fen turned to me. "Get ready to run."

20

Run? Run where? Before I could figure out where we were going, the snakes all lunged forward at the same time. Fen grabbed my hand, and we took off after them, more serpents bringing up the rear.

"This is your plan?" I shouted. "Just run at the man with the flaming sword?"

"Relax, Valkyrie. We will be past his barricade in less than one—"

Suddenly, we were flying through the air. Fen had literally leaped over the barricade, dragging me with him, the demons and Surtr distracted by the army of Jondi bent on attacking.

We dropped into a huge trench. The crater below was larger than I'd imagined it would be. It was at least fifty feet deep.

Fen was slightly ahead of me and let go of my hand a moment before he landed. Faster than I could blink, he hit the ground, pivoted, and caught me up in his arms.

The impact sent us both spinning, crashing to the ground.

It was hardly a smooth landing, but it was better than hitting with no cushion at all. We both lay sprawled on the ground, breathing hard.

Once I gathered myself, I glanced around. At the far end of the crater, a massive amount of bark protruded. The tree didn't go up through the surface. It was contained inside.

It was almost like it had been stuck here for safe keeping.

I crawled to my knees excitedly. "I don't understand how this works, but I've never been happier to see anything in my entire life!" I began to move toward it. "We can finally leave this place." I glanced back, elated.

"Wait, shieldmaiden! It's not safe yet," Fen called, starting after me.

I stopped. "What do you mean? I don't see anything." I searched around for trouble, baffled, and as I watched, one by one, demons crawled out from behind rocks and out of holes, completely surrounding us.

I took a few steps back as Fen closed the gap.

"We will fight these here and hope the snakes keep more from descending," he whispered in my ear, holding me steady, hands braced on my shoulders.

"Okay." What else was I going to say? I reached for the iron rod I'd stuck in the loophole of my pants, but it was gone. I hadn't even realized I'd been without it.

Fen withdrew something and handed it to me. It was my rod. "You left this behind."

I palmed it. "Yeah, I'm sure I'll be a force to be reckoned with now that I have it back."

Fen lunged forward, slicing a demon that had ventured too close in half with his sword. "Better than with your hands alone."

"I'm not so sure." I brandished the rod in front of me, trying to appear more menacing. I hoped I never set foot in this realm again. Once was too many times.

A demon came toward me, its mouth curved up into a grotesque smile. "Greeza."

"Yeah, I've heard that one before, but you're not getting me this time, stick man. I'd rather die than be your *greeza*." I stabbed my iron rod into its chest. The tip penetrated, then stopped with a loud *thunk*.

I'd hit its sternum.

"Valkyrie, you'll have to do better than that," Fen tossed over his shoulder, his voice full of smirk. He'd already taken out ten demons.

More surrounded us with each passing moment.

"Very funny," I grumbled, yanking the rod back. The demon came with it, unimpressed with my efforts to kill it. I repositioned the rod like a bat and swung it at its chest. The thing broke in half like a brittle matchstick.

As we fought, Fen and I edged closer to the tree. It was radiant, the bark glimmering in the low light. The energy it stored inside called to me like a siren. I needed its sustenance. Having been gone from it for a while, it was clear to me now how much the tree meant to me.

If this didn't work, and we were forced to leave this crater, I would die. The conditions in this land were too harsh, and it was clear, if given the chance, Surtr would take me back to the torture table. I'd save him the trouble and use the iron rod on myself before I'd let him harm me again.

I swung at another demon, taking it down, and the one behind it.

They kept coming. "Did they camp here waiting for us?" I called. "Where did they all come from?"

"These demons are the guardians of the tree. They live here. They likely have tunnels and homes below ground."

"Now is not the time to tell me that!" I cried. "We

willingly jumped into a fifty-foot crevasse full of demons? Again, this was your plan?"

"We were limited in our options, Valkyrie. If we had not partnered with the serpents, we would've fought them up there, and then again down here. This way we have only this lot to deal with."

"That's reassuring, except *this lot* is growing by twenty demons every time I blink. Why can't you just turn into your wolf and be done with it?" I swiped at another demon. "I'm not sure we're going to get ahead otherwise." As we inched forward, more demons gathered between us and the tree.

"Not an option. I wouldn't be able to use the dagger with my paws."

"That's exactly why you should give Gram to me," I insisted. "You take out the demons as a wolf, I run to the tree, you change back, grab my hand, and we're out of this hellish place forever."

"No."

Stubborn demigod.

I slashed at more demons, Fen's back to mine. We were moving at a snail's pace. "Where are the snakes?" I asked. "Why aren't some of them here to help us? One swish of their tails, and this place would be cleared out."

"The serpents can't get out of this crater without assistance. It's too deep and the walls too steep. We are on our own here. Their job is to make sure no more enter and Surtr is well occupied."

"Oh."

"Let me take the lead," he ordered.

I edged around. He immediately increased our pace. "I think the demons have tripled, and I see more coming up from the holes from below," I said. I was barely able to keep back the ones advancing on me. They seemed leery of Fen, so they weren't all charging at once, which seemed like the only reason we hadn't been overrun.

Two came at me at once.

I swung at the one closest to me as the other reached out its skeletal hands and raked its bony fingers across my forearm. "*Ow!*" Blood spurted from the gouges. In retaliation, I pierced it through the eye with my rod. There was a resounding squishing noise. "Gross." I covered my mouth with one hand while I yanked the rod out with the other.

"Go for the neck," Fen said. He swung his sword perfectly and cut three demons down at once. "It's much more efficient."

Show-off.

"There are too many to aim properly," I answered testily. "And it's tricky because I'm trying to keep their acid blood from burning a hole through me."

"Don't worry about their blood. Once you get into the tree, it will heal you."

"What if we don't get to the tree?"

"We will." With a yell and a charge, Fen barreled forward, and I followed. It looked like we were going to make it after all. The demons were no match for Fen's strength. "We are within paces of it, Valkyrie. Get ready. I'm going to pull out Gram. You hold them back while I place the dagger—"

There was a violent shout, followed by a loud thump that shook the ground.

Demons screeched around us, moving every which way. Surtr's voice preceded him as he rose to his full height, his flaming sword already lofted high above his head. He truly loved that thing.

I didn't want to be hit with another spell, so I crouched

down. Then I realized it was a stupid move, because he could hit me if he wanted to no matter where I was—he could still *see* me—but I didn't know what else to do.

Fen took me by the arm and dragged me behind him, brandishing his own sword. "You are too late, demon king," he announced. "We made you a nice deal, and you frittered it away. Now you'll be left with nothing."

I peeked out from behind Fen's broad back.

I'd seen Surtr when I had been dazed and lying on the altar, and again on top of the barricade. He'd looked tall then, of course, but standing here I realized he was truly a giant. He had to be over eight feet tall. His face was cruel, misshapen, and bulgy, his teeth awful and sharp. His nose, with its three slits, was still the worst thing I'd ever laid eyes on. He wore a dirty loincloth and a furious expression. "You will pay with your life, son of Loki." Surtr stormed forward. "You have meddled in business…that is not yours." His voice sounded rough and harsh. English was definitely not his first language.

Fen began to walk backward, forcing me along, too. He was trying to get us to the tree. The only good thing to happen since Surtr's arrival was that the demons had scuttled away, moving in reverence to their master.

I glanced behind me.

The tree was only about ten feet away. It beckoned me. I reached out a hand, yearning to touch it. My pulse jumped in anticipation, and tingles shot up my arm.

"Valkyrie, be ready. Surtr's sword has the power to rend us in half if he so wishes. It's a powerful weapon crafted by the dark elves. It's the only thing on this pitiful realm that can truly harm me."

"Okay," I answered. "You plunge the dagger in the tree and we go? We're only going to get one chance."

"Yes," he replied. "We are—how do you say on Midgard—between a hard place and a tree."

"That's not it exactly, but I get your drift." I tried not to sigh too loudly. Fen getting us out of here had to work. If not, that flaming sword was going to do some serious damage.

"You cannot escape," Surtr growled. "The paths have been sealed. The Norns are awaiting you. If you enter…alarms will ring. Your fate is with me." He cackled. "I will enjoy your torture." He swung his sword down in a large arc. He'd gotten dangerously close.

My back hit the tree.

Hallelujah!

My fingernails raked the bark, and a low moan issued from my throat.

The tree immediately infused me with energy, then all too quickly, Fen twirled me around, handing me his sword. "Look menacing," he ordered, pulling Gram out. "This should only take a moment."

I needed two hands to lift the large broadsword, so I dropped my rod and managed to hike the sword above my head. "Stop!" I ordered Surtr.

The giant stopped, but looked puzzled as to why. "You cannot defeat me, little *human*."

I didn't want to point out that he had indeed stopped. "Um, I'm not trying to defeat you?" I had no idea what to say, but confusion could only help. As Surtr had moved forward, an army of his demons had lined up behind him.

Behind me, Fen cursed.

Not a good sign.

Fen shouted a rush of words in a language I didn't understand. I heard Gram strike the bark again and again, to no avail.

Surtr chuckled. If you could call it that. It was more like rocks rolling around in a pail. "I told you. You will not leave here."

Fen snarled, turning. "That's what you think, demon. I will leave this plane, either through this tree or by my death."

"Fen, give me the dagger," I urged in a low voice. "Let me try." He ignored me, instead taking the sword from me. He was livid. "Don't do this," I begged. "I might be able to help us! We can't win this battle, we have to escape. *Please*."

"You heard him," Fen answered stonily. "The way is locked to us. We must fight."

"It might be locked to you, but maybe not to me!" I cried. "I won't survive this fight. Do you see those demons? We are trapped in a hole with an army of things bent on killing us. This is so not the time to be stubborn."

Surtr took one giant step forward and aimed his sword straight at us. Fen raged, using his own weapon against the demon king, swinging his broadsword up at Surtr's lofted arm. The demon king turned at the last moment, dodging Fen and whipping his hand around, crushing the base of his sword against Fen's shoulder.

The impact sent Fen reeling away from me.

I was backed up against the tree, arms splayed behind me, fingernails embedded in the bark.

A cruel grin broke over Surtr's nasty face. He knew he had me, and he was going to enjoy it. Ever so slowly, he brought the flaming sword in front of me. I closed my eyes, frantically drawing more energy from the tree, begging it in my mind to open up. Flames licked at my chest, my tunic catching fire as the point broke the skin. "*Argh!*" I gasped as blood began to flow. "Just kill me already! I've had enough of this world, this hate, this *inhumanity*!" Energy poured into me from the tree as lightning shot overhead. Thunder rumbled soon after. I couldn't see where the lightning had struck, because Surtr's sword was lodged in my body.

I was losing consciousness.

"Valkyrie!" Fen shouted.

I forced my eyes open in time to see Gram arcing through the air as Fen tackled Surtr. I caught the blade by the handle as the horrid sword dislodged from my body. I screamed, falling to my knees. But my scream had been muffled by the sound of something else.

CAW-CAW. CAW-CAW.

21

Huggie appearing was the most welcome thing to happen in a very long time. I squinted up to the sky, one hand trying to staunch the blood gushing from my wound.

The bird circled above us, gliding effortlessly in the air.

Put the dagger in the tree.

I wasn't going to argue. I scrabbled to my knees, bracing my shoulder against the bark, ramming the tip of the blade into the tree.

Light swirled at the tip immediately.

Relief flooded through me, and I almost fell over. The tree began to tug on the dagger, welcoming me into its embrace. I sighed, resting my head against the bark, just wanting this to finally be over.

I was about to let it draw me inside when I heard a shout, bringing me back to reality.

Fen was still fighting Surtr.

The demon king had the advantage and was about to slice Fen in half, his mighty arms up, the fiery blade whooshing down.

"No!" I screamed, jumping to my feet, ignoring the pain in my chest. "Fen, take my hand!" Fen leaped out of the way right as Surtr's sword crashed down millimeters from where his body had just been, sticking in the rocky ground.

Fen extended his arm and grasped my hand.

Surtr gave out an angry wail.

Fen's face was grim. "This is not going to work, Valkyrie. But I'll let you try."

I clutched the dagger tightly with my other hand, but the pull from the tree was gone, the light already fading. I cried as I let go, pounding a fist against the rough surface. "Let us in! We will die if you don't!"

Huggie flew overhead with a loud flap of his wings.

Fen released my hand. "Your agent is here. The raven will escort you home. Good luck, shieldmaiden." He stepped back.

Surtr yanked his sword out of the ground, but for once he wasn't focused on us. As we watched, Huggie dive-bombed his head, his beak shearing off part of Surtr's scalp.

That had to hurt!

The rage coming off of the demon king was beyond measure. He vibrated with it.

Huggie circled back and flew low.

Leave the wolf behind.

"I'm not leaving him!" I yelled furiously. "He's the only reason I'm still alive. He deserves to come with me!"

He cannot accompany you from this realm.

"That's what you think!" Blood still leaked from my chest, adrenaline the only thing keeping me upright. I was so preoccupied with giving the raven the stink eye, I didn't see Surtr begin to advance.

"Valkyrie!" Fen shouted. "Move!"

Too late.

STRUCK

The flaming blade rushed down quickly.

Searing pain lanced through my body like an arrow. I glanced at my thigh in shock. The sword had rent it open to the bone. Muscle was torn and gaping from the hole. My head swam. I heard Surtr's gleeful howls, but not much more.

"You will not...save her," Surtr boomed to Huggie, his head tilted up at the sky.

Strong arms lifted me off the ground.

Fen had me. "*Shh*, it's okay, Phoebe." He was trying to move me, but my hand was sealed tightly around Gram. I had grabbed on in the chaos, and I wasn't about to let go. It was the only thing keeping me conscious.

If I broke away from this tree, I would forfeit my life. It was crystal clear.

"Don't...move," I whispered on the barest of breaths.

"What did you say?" Fen asked, his voice soft and tender, full of concern. "I have to get you back to the healing waters, shieldmaiden. Or you'll die."

"No," I moaned. "We leave now through here. Together. Or we both die...here."

Leave the wolf. The tree will save you.

Instead of answering the raven out loud, which would've taken more energy than I had, I cried in my head, *I'm not leaving without him. We either both go, or we die. Fen might come back from the dead, but I won't.*

What you ask is forbidden.

This time I yelled out loud, "I don't care! Break the rules." I was done debating this. I met Fen's gaze, his blue eyes radiating something intense. I smiled weakly. "I'm trying to broker a ride for you. I told you I wouldn't leave without you."

"It's okay, Valkyrie. I didn't really expect them to let me leave. I will survive alone." He began to set me down.

I grabbed on to his shoulder with my free hand. "You called me Phoebe."

"What?"

"When you picked me up, you called me Phoebe instead of Valkyrie or shieldmaiden. I liked it." My eyes slid shut, and my head fell back. The pain was too much.

"Raven!" Fen shouted. I could feel his fury. "Take her now!"

Just like that, he was going to let me leave.

Before I could form a rebuttal, Surtr's voice erupted, full of nastiness. "No one is leaving here...without my permission." Huggie cawed loudly overhead. "Stay back, raven. This is my realm. You are not in charge—"

A sickly sound of ripping flesh followed the loud clacking of a beak.

Surtr let out a roar mixed with pain.

Huggie was playing for keeps. That bird had moxie.

"I'm going to set you down now, shieldmaiden," Fen said as he lowered my body to the ground. "I need to take advantage of your agent's distractions to escape. Farewell. I wish you well in your life."

Pain of a different kind rushed through me.

In my haze, I grabbed on to Fen's neck, clutching it for dear life. He was my true lifeline. Without him, I wouldn't be able to cope in the new world that had become my life. "No," I whispered, imploring him. "We go together."

He knelt next to me. His hand touched my cheek. "That's not possible, Phoebe. Maybe we will meet again in the next life."

I squeezed. "No, this is the life we're supposed to meet in," I said stubbornly. "I can't do this without you. Please...*stay*."

Huggie snapped his beak above our heads. I didn't look up.

You must leave.

"I'm happy to go any time you decide to open this up for us," I mumbled. "I'm fading fast, so make up your mind." My hand was still wrapped around Gram, even though it was now awkwardly above my head. "It's now or never. Once I let go, it's all over."

Surtr gave a war whoop. His heavy footsteps vibrated the ground as he neared.

There will be repercussions.

I don't care, I said internally. *Won't there be repercussions if I die? Make up your mind, bird.* One by one, my fingers began to unfurl from Gram. *Please.* I'd uttered the last word in my mind on the thinnest of thoughts.

Huggie didn't answer. Instead, I felt the tree open up, beckoning me once again. I was still holding Fen in a death grip. I heard him gasp.

"That's right," I said, my throat hoarse. "I just finagled us a one-way ticket out of this hellhole. The only thing I ask is please make sure I stay in one piece. I'm about to cash out."

He gathered me in his arms once again. "I will keep you safe. You have my word." His arms tightened around me.

"You will not leave here!" Surtr shouted. "You are my prisoners!"

"It seems you have that wrong," Fen answered. "And if you come any closer, Odin's favorite pet will peck your eyes out. The bird is just waiting for a reason to do so."

The tree ramped up its pull.

We would be off this plane soon. The word *relief* wasn't big enough to describe how I felt, wounds and all. On my last breath, I uttered, "Please, Huggie, tell the tree to take us to Midgard. I want to go home."

It's not safe.

"I'm hurt. I need to heal and find Ingrid. I'm begging

you, just take us home." I had no idea if Huggie was in charge of directions, but since the tree opened only after he'd said so, I was thinking he had some say.

As you wish.

Our bodies tumbled through the void. Fen still held me, and I was grateful. I tried to cry out, but there was no air.

The last thing I heard before I lost consciousness was Surtr's angry howl.

Goodbye, evil. I hope we never meet again.

22

"Phoebe." The voice was low and hushed in my ear. "You must wake."

I was warm and content and just wanted to sleep. "Not now," I mumbled. "I'm so tired." I tried to turn over and burrow deeper into the warmth, but I was stuck.

The voice chuckled, rocking me gently. "If you point me in the right direction, I'll carry you to your bed."

My eyes flew open, my hands clutching on to huge biceps. It was dark. "Fen? Did we make it back?" I sat up, wincing as I glanced around at our surroundings. "My leg still hurts." I brought a hand down and tentatively stroked it through the huge rent in my pants. It was sealed, but the scar was tender. I felt my chest through my barely there tunic, but that seemed fully healed. "I thought the tree was the cure-all. Why am I still sore?"

"My guess is you were too malnourished, and the ride was short." Fen stood easily with me in his arms. "Your leg has mended enough, but you will require another trip to the tree in a day or two."

"Where are we?" I squinted around in the darkness. Trees surrounded us, and we stood on a large rock.

"I believe it's a place you call Central Park, but I'm not certain."

"Where is Yggdrasil?"

"That is another mystery. It seems we took—how did you phrase it—a wormhole?" He chuckled again. "The tree must like you. It tossed us out ahead of the normal pathway."

"Did Huggie come through with us?" I asked as Fen began to walk. All was quiet, which was a hard thing to achieve in New York City. It must be the wee hours of the morning.

"Your agent has not arrived yet."

"He's not my agent!" I huffed. "You can put me down. I can walk on my own. My leg aches, but it's not that bad." Fen was reluctant to comply, but acquiesced, slowly edging me down to the ground. Leaving the warmth of his body was shocking as the cold air whipped through my tattered clothing. Fen's dirty tunic and ripped trousers were no match for freezing temps. "It's still winter! *Brrr*." I don't know why it surprised me. My teeth began to chatter, and I hugged my arms across my body. "I thought time might've sped up while I was gone."

"The realms do have some time changes depending on how far they are from one another, but nothing significant. How long have you been away from Midgard?"

I gazed up at him. He stood close, and I'd forgotten how tall he was. I came eye to eye with his bare chest. "I'm not sure." I started to walk, reaching back to grab his hand. "A week maybe? I lost track. Come on, we have to get to my apartment."

He followed without complaint.

We made our way out of the park, and as I glimpsed the

first street sign, I realized we weren't too terribly far from my building. We couldn't take the subway. It would raise too many eyebrows. Not as many as we would've in my hometown—a half-naked demigod and a rumpled, filthy girl dressed in oversized, tattered clothing would've been stopped and questioned by everyone. People would take notice in New York, but no one would likely corner us. But I didn't want to take the chance.

Plus, I wasn't sure I ever wanted to go down into the subway again after what happened. I wondered if ettins had homes down there. The thought was too horrible.

That left only one mode of transportation: hoofing it. "We're about twelve blocks from my place," I told Fen. "In New York, that's considered close."

"It is of no matter, Valkyrie. I have not enjoyed a different landscape in hundreds of years, and the cold does not bother me." His head tilted upward, and he took in all the buildings as we walked by. "Midgard is not as I remember it. Things have gotten…grand."

"When was the last time you were here?"

"One of the times I broke out. Maybe two hundred years ago?" He shrugged. "It all blurs together."

I hurried us along, and we made good time. When we were two blocks away, I had a sudden panic attack. I stopped, tugging Fen into a recessed doorway. "Are we being stupid going back to my place?" I asked. "What if Verdandi knows where I live? Huggie said it was dangerous to come here."

"It's possible," Fen said, his face thoughtful. "But Skuld will foresee your movements wherever you go, if you are not cloaked, so it's of no use to worry. We will fight if they come."

I bit my lip. That didn't sound good. "How will we know if I'm cloaked or not?"

"They will not come."

"Oh." Duh. "Maybe we should go to Ingrid's first? If she's home, that's great. If not, we can see if she left us a note."

"The shieldmaiden lives nearby?"

"Right across the hallway from me."

"Do you know others in this city?"

I thought about Sam, my only real friend here. She would let us in, no problem, but her questions would be off the hook. She'd be mad I skipped town without telling her. It would take more time than we had to calm her down and answer her questions at the moment, not to mention we looked like beggars and my feet were freezing cold. "I have one good friend, but she lives farther midtown. We can use her as a last resort. I'm sure no one knows about her. I just met her a few months ago."

"Once we get to your building, I will investigate. If there are beings of Asgard nearby, I will know it."

"Um, okay." I stared at him. "That would've been helpful to know beforehand."

"I cannot teach you everything about our world in only days, Valkyrie," he mused. "It will take years."

"Our world?" I commented as we started walking again.

"Of course," he said, giving me a rare upturned smile. "You are a Valkyrie. You are made of Asgard. You may not fully realize it yet, but you are not of this plane, even though it's the only home you've ever known. Your birthright is the land of gods."

I pondered that. "It's strange to think of myself in that way." I wasn't sure it would ever seem normal. "Like it's not real, or somehow a mistake, and someone is going to jump out and tell me it was all an elaborate hoax."

"This is no hoax. You must get over your skepticism and accept your destiny. It will make you stronger."

"How will it make me stronger?"

He quirked a brow. "For one, you will learn to harness the power within you and wield it to much greater strength."

"The power within?" That sounded both ominous and hilarious at the same time.

"Valkyrie, you glow brighter than a star. Where do you think that resides?"

"Inside…me?" I had no earthly idea. "Listen, I'm not even going to pretend to understand how this all works. My brain can't even fathom such things. My life has become a complicated sci-fi movie with a plot twist you have to pay attention to, and even when you're following it, the end doesn't make any sense."

"Every fiber of your being holds energy. It's who you are now. It's what you're made of. When we were leaving Muspelheim, you glowed as brightly as the first time I saw you."

"I did?" We were within fifty feet of my building, and I put a hand out to stop him.

"Yes, you did."

"That's my building. Second from the corner across the street." I gestured, then glanced up to my two tiny windows, one of which Huggie had come through. My apartment was dark. That should be a good sign.

"I will go first," Fen said. "So far, I feel nothing. Stay here and be alert."

I grasped his forearm. "I don't think that's the right thing to do."

"Why not?"

"Because last time the ettins got me. I'd feel much better if we worked as a team. Then, if things hit the fan, we can escape or fight *together*."

Fen inclined his head. "I don't dislike that idea. Your

reasoning is sound. Let's go." He took off across the street.

I followed closely as I continued to glance up at the buildings. I had met some of my neighbors over the last few months and prayed none were looking out the window right this exact moment to witness me trailing a huge shirtless man in dirty cutoffs running toward my building barefoot in the middle of winter.

That required more explanation than I had in me.

I arrived at the front door a moment after Fen. His hands were on the glass, ear pressed against it. "I am picking up nothing. What floor do you live on?"

"The fifth, which is at the top. It's a tiny studio."

Fen turned the door handle. It moved freely. "It's not locked?" he asked.

"Not always," I answered. "Tenants get lazy."

"It's of little consequence. A lock would not keep out what is hunting us."

I shivered. "When you phrase it like that, it sounds awful."

"Make no mistake, Valkyrie. They will come."

"Just the Norns?" I asked.

"All of them. There will be a bounty on my head, set by Odin. They will clamor like flies, each of them wanting the honor of being the one who turns you over and brings me back."

"That sounds...great," I replied in a listless tone. Would we ever be free?

Fen's face was set. "You and I will need to have a long discussion very soon. There is much you haven't told me. If we are to be a team, as you described, there must be transparency. And you can start by explaining why Hugin, the eyes of Odin, is your agent."

"I told you, he's not my agent." Was he my agent? I

really had no clue what an agent did. "What I told you in the cave was the truth. I was born and raised on Midgard. Ingrid came to find me, I got taken, and that's all I know."

"Ah, shieldmaiden, it's the information you haven't divulged that I crave." He edged inside, and I went after.

The man was smart. Relaying what Ingrid had told me about my life was going to be rough. He might choose to leave me, and I wasn't sure how I'd be able to cope in this strange new world without him. If Verdandi arrived with backup, I wouldn't know the first thing to do. There was so much I had to learn.

Fen crept up the stairs on full alert. He didn't make a sound. I came after, trying to be quiet, but managed to sound like a herd of elephants tramping up the steps.

"You might want to tone down the noise." Fen smirked. "I'm having a hard time picking up on the real danger."

"Very funny. I'm trying to be stealthy, but this is all I've got. These stairs are beyond old. How come you're not making them creak?" I took another step, and a board made a loud groan.

"Because I know how to move with grace." He chuckled.

"Grace, my ass," I whispered as we turned down a short hallway and went up another flight. "You're a demigod. You have tricks up your sleeve I wouldn't begin to understand."

"Indeed, I do. But that's for another day, Valkyrie."

We reached the fifth floor, and Fen stopped a few treads from the top. "All seems clear, though I wouldn't advise we linger here too long."

"My studio is down on the right. Ingrid's is on the left. Let's go to Ingrid's and see if she left us any clues to where she went. Then, if the coast is still clear, we can go to mine." I was curious to see if my apartment looked the same or if it had been trashed in my absence.

Fen veered around the banister and went left toward Ingrid's door. He paused in front of it, bringing his hands up to the wood. He waited a few seconds. "No one is here." He tried the knob. It turned.

We both slipped inside.

I knew Ingrid's apartment like my own. Other than Sam, she was my closest friend in New York. We'd alternated movie and popcorn nights in our apartments every Friday. Her studio was set up much the same as mine, but reversed. Her kitchen was on the left, and her sleeping area and small bathroom were on the right. She had a single bed, which gave her more space. Her studio was sparsely decorated, even more so than mine. There was no furniture other than the single bed. Not even a lamp. Her TV sat perched on the windowsill, propped up by a cardboard box.

"The shieldmaiden wasn't intending to stay long," Fen concluded as he opened her closet. There were a few shirts hanging and not much else.

I checked the tabletops and went into the kitchen. No note on the counter tops. I opened the cupboards. They were fairly empty. A few dishes and cups, enough to serve popcorn and soda and no more. I opened the fridge. It was bare, save for a few cans of Coke.

I'd had no idea she had so few things. I'd never opened her closets or cupboards before. She always handled the food and drink when I'd been there.

I walked back into her living area and found Fen tugging on one of her flannel shirts. It barely stretched over his arms, and there was no way he would be able to button it, but it would cover him enough until we could find something better.

"I need clothes, too, and a shower," I told him. "If you think it's safe, let's go over to my place. Then we can figure out what to do next."

Fen nodded. "The Valkyrie has left no weapons here. After we gather suitable clothing, we must find a means to defend ourselves."

"Gram!" I breathed. "Please tell me you have it." I hadn't thought about the trusty dagger since we'd arrived. I'd been too relieved to be home.

He grinned as he pulled it from beneath his waistband. "It was lying right beside us when we landed, even though none of my other weapons came through, which is not unusual. The tree decides what it likes and what it does not." He held Gram in front of me. "After your shower, you're going to tell me how you acquired a possession of this magnitude."

I headed toward the door. "I can tell you right now," I shot over my shoulder. "Ingrid gave it to me, and before you ask, I have no idea where she got it." Out in the hallway, I waited for Fen, and we both made our way across the hallway, him stealthy and me hitting every creaky floorboard.

"There is no one here," he said, his ear to my door. "But I must break the lock."

"That's fine," I said. I didn't lock it, so that meant someone had been here. He popped the lock easily, and cautiously we went in. I flipped on a light. My apartment seemed just as I'd left it, the closet door open from when Ingrid had packed my duffel, the bed rumpled where the bag had lain. I walked into the kitchen. The only thing different was that the window was now shut, but maybe Huggie had shut it on his way out? He was magical after all.

I came back to the sleeping area to find Fen gazing out into the street from my only other window. "I sense danger," he said, glancing at me. "It's coming, but I don't know when." He turned around and gestured toward my tiny bathroom. "Take your shower and get dressed. We have much to talk about."

Hastily, I hurried over to my small bureau and grabbed a pair of jeans and a sweater.

I had to admit I was looking forward to this shower like nothing I'd had in a very, *very* long time.

23

The hot spray felt like the heavens had opened up and were raining down on me. I was finally completely clean and stink-free. I'd stayed in until the hot water ran out, feeling a little guilty I hadn't saved any for Fen. But if he really wanted a hot shower, he could go over to Ingrid's.

I'd used a gallon of shampoo and conditioner, and as I toweled off, I inspected my leg wound. It looked a little grisly, but it was healing. I examined the rest of my skin and could see no remnants of Surtr's torture. Thank goodness. Wearing those scars for an eternity would've been beyond difficult. It was truly miraculous they had all vanished. Even my chest, where I'd taken Surtr's blade right before we left that realm, was totally healed, my skin pristine and smooth, like nothing had ever happened.

I hung the towel up and glanced around the small space. My bathroom wasn't much bigger than a broom closet. I picked up my clean clothes and shook them out. Dang, I'd forgotten to grab a bra and underwear! Since they were vital to the process of re-clothing myself, I grabbed the towel back off the rack and wrapped it around myself, poking my head out the door. "I forgot a few things," I said.

"Don't be shy, shieldmaiden." Fen smiled. "I won't bite."

"I just need some underwear."

Fen lounged on my bed, his hands clasped behind his head, pillows propped. He grinned at me like he didn't have a care in the world.

I stopped at the foot of the bed, my freshly combed hair slicked back and dripping down around my shoulders.

He sat up.

Our gazes locked, and I exhaled a shallow breath.

"Come," he whispered.

Without hesitation, I paced around the side as Fen moved to the edge. He opened his legs, and I stepped between them, my eyes fastened on his. I wanted this.

More than anything.

His fingers undid the towel above my breasts, and it dropped to the ground. I stood before him, naked. But this time I didn't feel vulnerable or uneasy.

I felt *alive*.

His hands slid down my arms. He cleared his throat, his eyes never leaving mine. "You are beautiful, Valkyrie."

I reached up to caress his face. "Thank you for helping me escape. You gave me Gram, even though you didn't know if I could bring you back."

He leaned forward, his full lips brushing mine. Sparks flew as his energy transferred to me. He drew back, his eyes hooded. "I helped you because there was no other option left to me. I could not stand to see you destroyed, even though the selfish part of me wanted to keep you by my side. Giving to another freely is a new experience for me. It is something I'm not familiar with."

I met him halfway, our mouths melding, the kiss deep

and tender. My hands fisted in his hair as he urged me closer, enfolding me in his strong embrace.

I broke the kiss, half panting, half accusing. "You took my heart without asking." Without giving him time to respond, I leaned in, this time running my tongue along his wonderful lips. I could be with him for several lifetimes and would never get tired of those lips.

He moaned as his energy leaped into my mouth at incredible speeds. "The very first time I set eyes on you, I knew you were mine." His voice wasn't above a whisper. He leaned back on the bed and took me with him, our lips fastened together. I crawled on top, enjoying his warmth and giving him my own. "I need you, Phoebe," he murmured into my lips, his arms locked around me. "You have my heart."

"I need you, too," I replied. I'd never meant anything more in my life. I had wanted him before, but I was ready for him now. "Do you think, maybe, I was sent to your cave on purpose? I wouldn't have survived in that realm without you." I needed to feel his lips again and took his mouth softly at first, then more insistently.

"Yes," he said simply, rolling me over, removing his shorts and shirt. He gazed down at me, his arms braced on either side of my head. "Phoebe, once I have you, I'll never have another."

I raised an eyebrow. "Is that a demigod thing?" I ran my hands along his bare chest, my fingers tracing the hard contours. His skin was silky soft, his muscles firm, yet quivering, beneath my touch.

He flashed me a dazzling smile. "No, it's a *me* thing. Never once in my many years has a woman ever come close to capturing my heart. I never expected to give it to anyone. This is something I do not take lightly, so you're stuck with me, shieldmaiden."

"Trust me, I'm not giving you back." My hands slid to his neck.

He bent his head, and I arched up. The kiss was searing. I felt it all the way to my toes. The energy transfer was building with each kiss, and I knew it would culminate in something mind-blowing.

My body ached for it.

He slipped a hand between us, reaching for my core, and I called out. "I have to feel you," I said, not recognizing my own bold voice as I slid my hand down, finding the enormous length of him and stroking it lightly. His entire body pulsed with power. My hand vibrated with it as I discovered him for the first time. New senses came alive in my body, and they sought him like a drug.

I craved every inch of him.

Leaning up, I ran my tongue slowly across his broad chest, and where my wetness hit his skin, power exploded in my mouth in short sparks. It was like licking invisible Pop Rocks.

I ran my hands over him faster.

"Don't," Fen bit out. "Valkyrie, I cannot…hold on for long when you touch me there."

I let go of him reluctantly, prodding him to turn over. If I couldn't touch him there, I would explore him elsewhere.

Once he was on the bottom, I straddled him.

My tongue slid over one of his nipples. I pressed it between my teeth and pulled gently as I sucked. Fen let out a guttural sound, which pleased me. I'd never had a chance to play the temptress before.

I liked it.

I lost myself in his beautiful body, toying with it, licking every inch, enjoying the texture, and drinking in his power.

"Gods!" Fen roared. "I don't know why the fates have

blessed me after so long, but you are absolutely stunning." He ran his hands up my sides, caressing me, tangling in my hair. He leaned up to capture my mouth. After a long, intense kiss, he said, "I give you my power willingly."

I smiled. "Thank you."

Fen scooped me up, settling me firmly on his lap, crushing me with a kiss so deep I couldn't breathe. His hands jutted through my hair, his hardness pressed firmly between us.

I squirmed against him, my legs locking around his waist. "*Yes*," I moaned.

"Valkyrie," Fen groaned, "your wish is my command." His powerful arms threaded under my thighs, lifting me off his lap. Then, very slowly, he slid me back down onto the length of him. As his tip broke through, I yelled his name, grabbing on to his shoulders, wiggling my hips down. "Easy," Fen ground out hoarsely. I gave an impatient cry, my body flaming to be full of him. "*Gods*, you're so *tight*." He tossed his head back, his long hair falling behind his shoulders. He guided me with his hands at my hips, pumping his shaft slowly into me.

"More," I breathed as my body blossomed, opened, expanding for him. My hands gripped him fiercely with each rock of my hips. "Yes. *Yes*." The feeling as I slid down on him was so intense, sparks of light fired behind my eyelids.

Power swirled between us, gathering strength.

There was no way to stop it, even if I wanted to. I was too greedy for him. Fen held me in his arms, our bodies slick with sweat, sparks jumping between us like live wires.

If this is what heaven feels like, I want it all the time.

My core was on fire, hot and tight around him. "Fen!" I gasped. "I can't stop." A small bolt of lightning shot out of me as I began to rock on him harder. With strong, quick motions, I rode him, the tingling reaching new heights with each thrust of my hips.

"You're...glowing..." Fen ground out, "...can't wait...anymore." He grabbed on to my hips, plunging deeply as I quivered around him, my body alight. I was one hairsbreadth away from release. "I need to be in control now, Valkyrie." He turned quickly, spreading me on the bed, grabbing me tightly with both hands as he thrust into me again and again.

"*Oh*!" I thrashed my head from side to side. My body was aflame for him, his power and energy entering me from all over.

"I will...not finish...before you." He lifted my thighs higher, hooking them over his forearms, arching his body over mine. He pumped harder and harder, and my mind was lost to him. He growled, "Come for me, Phoebe."

As the spasms hit me, I shouted his name. A boom of thunder filled the room as wave after wave of sensation washed over me, drowning me completely.

So good.

"Phoebe!" Fen yelled as he released. As he filled me, another orgasm crashed over me, right on the heels of the last. My body vibrated with this new, potent energy, consuming it greedily, sparks crackling above our heads.

"*Fen.*" I held him with both hands, connecting us completely. My body ached for everything he could give me. My head spun.

So much power.

He grasped the back of my neck and took my mouth hungrily, feasting on me as he ground his hips against mine, spending himself dry.

Once the last drop of his luscious energy was gone, Fen lay on the bed, gathering me in his arms. I was exhausted and exhilarated at the same time. "That was...incredible," I whispered as I beamed up at him.

Fen ran a forearm over his mouth, his breath coming in short bursts. "That was more than incredible. It was indescribably good, and you're still glowing."

I lifted my hands in front of my face to see.

They'd taken on a definite sheen, though nothing like the full shimmer when I went through the tree the first time. But I felt rejuvenated for the first time in too long. "I think my leg is healed!" I exclaimed, lifting it up to inspect it. "I can't feel any aching." Happiness threatened to burst through me. "The scar is completely gone. That's incredible. You are a potent demigod." I turned to him, grinning.

I hadn't had much experience with relationships, but Fen was everything I could've hoped for. In this new world I would be forced to navigate, I needed a best friend and ally and couldn't believe I'd gotten both in one man.

One beautiful, incredible man. Life without him now seemed unimaginable.

"Rest now, Phoebe," he chuckled, gathering me in his arms.

I went willingly, feeling content and sleepy. "I love it when you say my name," I murmured into his warm chest.

His chest rose and fell as he laughed. "Then I'll have to use it more often. Sleep now. We will be on the move shortly."

"You said we needed to talk." Sleep filled my voice. "About stuff you think I kept from you."

"In due time." He kissed the top of my head. "Neither of us is going anywhere."

24

*C*AW-CAW. *CAW-CAW.*

I bolted upright, the sheets falling around me. It was still dark. I felt like I'd been asleep for only a moment. I tugged the blankets, bracing them in place with my forearm.

Fen was already up, arms crossed, a scowl on his face. He didn't seem nearly as surprised as I was to see Huggie perched on my bedpost. "Odin's agent, what brings you here so early?" Fen's tone was blunt.

The raven cocked his head, like he was gathering pertinent information about the situation. I could only imagine what the bird was thinking. Phoebe and the wolf in bed together. Oy. Once he was done, he clacked his beak.

"Um," I stammered, pulling the covers up to my chin. "What are you doing here? Are we in trouble? Is Ingrid with you?" I realized now it had been stupid of us to stay in my apartment. We'd both been carried away, and I'd been so, so tired.

The shieldmaiden is at the Valkyrie stronghold. I have sent word.

I glanced over at Fen to see if he'd heard the bird. "Can you hear the raven?" I asked.

He shook his head, his face stoic. "I can only hear him if he so chooses, and as of right now he has not deemed me worthy."

I didn't really want to be the intermediary here, because Huggie would likely reveal important information that we both needed to hear. "Huggie, you're going to have to include Fen in our conversation. If we're in trouble, he has to know about it, even more so than I do."

The bird clacked his beak. *If I talk to the wolf, the information will find its way back to Odin. It is safer this way. You are in danger. You must leave this location as soon as possible.*

"And go where?" I asked. I turned to Fen and said, "The raven said if he talks to you Odin will find out, so it's better he doesn't communicate directly."

Fen leaned forward. He was naked and beautiful, his hair tumbling forward, his gaze intense. "You would keep my location from Odin himself? I don't believe you, raven. You have always been his agent, his eyes and ears to the world. Your purpose is to take information back to your master, not protect his wolf prisoner. You will betray me, it's only a matter of time."

I placed my hand on Fen's arm. In response, he opened his arms and gathered me close, tucking me firmly against his chest. It was a dominant gesture meant to let the raven know where we stood.

I went along with it willingly. "Ingrid told me Huggie does his own thing," I addressed Fen. "She said the raven is tied to Odin, but because he's so old, he has gained his own power. Maybe he's exercising that independence to help me?"

Fen turned to gaze down on me. "And why would he do

that? What does the bird owe you? You claimed to have no ties to Asgard. Why would Odin's henchman, a very powerful creature in his own right, choose to help you of his own accord?"

"Um." I shrugged. "I have no idea. I didn't even know who I was until a few days ago."

"Who are you?" It was a bold question, directed right at me.

The raven became agitated, flapping his wings. *I caution you to not tell the wolf you are Odin's daughter. He will not react to the news well.*

My mouth opened and closed.

I didn't know what to do. Fen waited for my answer. "A Valkyrie?" I hated not confessing, but my bottom line was fear. I was scared of losing, especially after what we'd just shared together. The news could create a huge rift between us that would be too hard to repair. My chest ached.

I wished with all my heart that I had no ties to Odin, the god Fen was slated to kill at Ragnarok. It was all so confusing.

Fen shook his head. "Even after being intimate, you still choose not to trust me?" He disentangled himself from me and slid off the bed, heading toward the bathroom. His backside was incredible from this vantage point. "I am going to shower, shieldmaiden. When I return, I expect you to give me the truth. I expect nothing less." He paused in the doorway, his arms splayed between the two jambs, piercing me with heated eyes. "Without truth we have nothing." He shut the door. The shower turned on a second later.

I slumped back on the bed, crossing my arms. I huffed at the raven, "He's right. Without honesty, we have nothing. I'm going to have to tell him what I know and accept the consequences. Why are you here?"

You are in danger, and your safety is my priority.

I said internally, *Fen's right. Why do you care about me at all? I should mean next to nothing to you, even if I am Odin's daughter. I need to know why you're helping me.*

I made a pledge to your mother.

I sat up straight, clutching the sheets as they threatened to drop. "You know my mother?"

I do. It was to her I made my oath to look out for your safety, not Odin. It was her last wish before she was taken away. When you came of age, I chose to honor it. She is a valiant shieldmaiden, worthy of much respect. The bird flapped his wings, readjusting himself on the post.

I had no idea what to do with that information. I wanted to meet my real mother. "In order to honor her request, are you keeping my whereabouts from Odin?"

In a way.

"In *what* way?"

I have stayed away from Asgard, but I am due to return any day. When I arrive, I will not lie to Odin. He knows you are a Valkyrie. It was he who sent the bolt of lightning that struck you. He wishes you to stay alive.

Tricky bird.

"Will you tell him about Fen?" I asked.

If he asks, I will tell what I know. He knows the wolf has escaped. He will not know all the details.

"How did you find me in Muspelheim?"

I was waiting in the tree for your signature.

"You can wait in the tree indefinitely?"

I can.

I answered internally, *I'm not sure what I'm supposed to do now. Odin kept me a secret, threw my mom in a dark realm, and hoodwinked the Norns for over twenty years. Now that my secret is out, everyone is trying to kill me. How do I make it all stop?*

Your existence has changed vital pathways that connect our worlds.

The Norns despise surprises. If you die quickly, those pathways change back and, for the most part, are not harmed. The longer you live, the more the damage becomes irreversible.

"What does that mean?" I sighed. "It's so complicated. I just want my regular life back." But I was keeping the wolf.

The bird squawked. *You must stay alive. Until killing you no longer changes the outcome.*

"How do I do that?"

Find your mother. She will protect you.

"I'm assuming that's not as easy as it sounds."

You need powerful allies and training. Then you must go to Svartalfheim and retrieve her.

"The land of dark elves?" I shivered.

Yes.

"How do I find powerful allies?"

The shieldmaiden Ingrid is one. She awaits your arrival at the Valkyrie stronghold. But there is another. I will tell you where he will be at midnight tonight, and then I must leave here. The bird flapped his wings. *I have already stayed too long. If I linger, they will track me here.*

"Are you talking about the Norns?"

Yes.

"Why aren't they here now?"

I have cloaked you both.

Trickier bird.

The water in the bathroom shut off. Fen would be out soon, and I was going to have to come clean. I desperately hoped he didn't hold my supposed parentage against me.

If he did, I would have to regroup.

Huggie jumped off the perch onto the mattress, his wings flapping. *To find your ally, you must head to the docks, where you will find a boat hidden from human eyes. You will find who you're looking for there.*

"Which dock? There are quite a few."

The boat location changes. The wolf will know once you are near.

"Then what?"

You must go to the Valkyrie stronghold. There you will find safety and receive training. Once you are ready, find your mother. Only then will your existence solidify enough to change all the pathways permanently.

"Where is the stronghold?"

In a place called New Mexico. The location is in a remote valley, not easily traversed. I must leave. They are scanning for me even now.

"Will I see you again?" I asked.

Yes.

With that, Huggie soared into the air over the partition and out the kitchen window. I could feel the chilly breeze wafting in, so I got out of bed, donned a robe, and went to shut it.

When I came back, Fen stood in the bathroom doorway, one of my tiny towels cinched around his waist. Water beaded down his chest.

He was truly magnificent.

"Has the raven gone?" he asked.

"Yes," I replied, sitting on the edge of the bed, unsure of where to take this conversation.

He walked over and sat in my only chair, bending over, resting his elbows on his knees. It was the same chair I'd sat in not too long ago when I'd seen Huggie for the first time. "It's time to explain, Valkyrie. There must be trust between us."

I nodded once. "I know." I fiddled with the tie on my robe. "The problem is, the information I have is unsubstantiated. I'm actually not sure if it's the truth or not. I haven't had any time to figure it out for myself. Sharing it with you is difficult, both because I don't know its validity and I don't know how you're going to react. You have to promise me you won't freak out."

"You have my word. Begin." He sat back, folding his hands over his abdomen, his biceps jumping.

It would be much easier if we were in more comfortable positions, possibly dressed so I wasn't so easily distracted, but I guessed this was going to have to do.

"Okay," I said. "Here goes."

25

I took in a deep breath and blew it out. "I'm going to start at the beginning, so you have the full story." He nodded. "A few days ago, I don't remember how many, because time has blurred together, I was at work. My job in New York is to help people try on shoes at a big department store called Macy's." Fen's eyebrow quirked. "I know, don't ask. I'm sure you don't have anything so foolish in Asgard. Anyway, I went to the stock room in search of a pair of camel slingbacks, and out of nowhere I was struck by something. The force must have sent me reeling, even though I don't remember, because I woke up on top of a pile of shoe boxes." I clasped and unclasped my hands. "I never in a million years thought that what hit me had been lightning, because how could it get inside a building where there were no windows nearby?" I shrugged at my ignorance of all things Asgard. "The day went on as usual. I felt good. Then after work, on my way home, I was accosted by what I thought at the time was a homeless man. But now I'm not so sure. He grabbed me as I was coming up the subway steps

AMANDA CARLSON

and told me I was in danger. When I arrived home, I found Huggie in my kitchen, and Ingrid came in shortly after. The ettins kidnapped me in a subway tunnel and dropped me into the Norns' lair—"

Fen held out his hand to stop me. "Back up. Who was the man?"

I shook my head. "I have no idea. He was big, smelled horrible, and had a huge scar running across his face."

Fen leaped from the chair, surprising me. "What kind of a scar?"

He came forward so fast, I leaned back on the bed. "I'm…I'm not sure. But it was big. It stretched from one side of his face to the other." I mimicked the way it looked with my finger, starting from the top of one eye and tracing across to my lower jaw.

Fen began to pace my tiny room. "What were his words exactly?"

"Ah." I tried to recall what the man had said to me. I'd blocked the entire ordeal out of my mind after it happened, so I struggled to remember his exact wording. "Something along the lines of 'New York is no longer safe. You must get away. They will be coming soon.' That's about it. I was totally freaked out, so don't quote me. Why? Who do you think it was?"

"I can't be certain, but I only know one in Asgard whose face is marred by a terrible scar. Why he was trying to help you is another mystery." Fen stopped pacing and strode to me, leaning down and settling his hands on my shoulders. He smelled amazing, even though his body was completely tense.

"You're scaring me. What's wrong?"

"If it's the man I am thinking of, there might be hope for us yet."

Huge relief. "How are we going to find out if it's him?"

"We will take to the streets and search for him. If he is here, I will know it."

"Before Huggie left, the bird told me I have a powerful ally in the city. The bird referred to the ally as a he. The raven said we need to go down to the docks at midnight. He would be on a boat cloaked from human eyes. Do you think it's the same guy?"

Fen shrugged. "It may be, but we won't know for certain until we come face-to-face. What else did the raven say?" Fen sat down on the edge of the bed next to me, causing the mattress to sag. He grinned. His closeness was distracting. His body glistened from the shower. I wanted to touch him and stop having this conversation.

With effort, I focused my attention back to where it needed to be. "He said after we found this supposed ally, we needed to head to the Valkyrie stronghold in New Mexico. Do you know their exact location?" That would be helpful.

Fen shook his head. "No. It will be well hidden. But I am certain the Valkyrie Ingrid will reach out when the time is right."

I nodded. "Huggie said she's waiting for me."

"I will caution you, they will not be pleased to see me. They may even decide to engage in battle. But I will not be returned to Asgard as anyone's prisoner."

I rested my hand on his thigh, stroking it lightly. "Of course not. If they have an issue with you, we will deal with it or leave."

His expression took on a sweet seriousness. "You will need training. You are a very young Valkyrie and have no idea how to harness what's inside. Nor can you wield a weapon to any great effect."

"Hey!" I retorted. "I'm not so bad in the weapons

department. A couple of iron rods don't equal brandishing a huge broadsword, but I was impressed with my prowess, having never wielded, as you say, a weapon before I arrived in Muspelheim." He put his arm around me, and I chuckled. "But Huggie said the same thing about the training. Then he said I'd have to find my real mother, because she will be able to protect me from whatever's coming."

"Ah, so this is where the story ends. The last necessary information. Who are your parents, shieldmaiden?"

I sighed.

It was the moment of reckoning.

I pulled back out of his arms, facing him, imploring him with my eyes to be calm and listen. "Fen, you have to promise to take what I say with a grain of salt—or a grain of whatever is equivalent in Asgard. Ingrid only talked to me for a short time before I was taken, so I don't have any real facts. She told me my mother was a shieldmaiden named Leela, and Leela was her sister, which makes Ingrid my aunt." I paused.

"And your father?" Fen prodded. "He is a god, I'm assuming."

"Why would you assume that?" I was surprised he would guess such a thing.

"Because, Valkyrie, you shone clearer than any I have ever witnessed. Most shieldmaidens have a Valkyrie for a mother and a patron of Asgard as a father. Not many have gods in their parental line, but some do. By your strength and glow, it's only reasonable that you must have a god as a father."

"How many gods live in Asgard?"

"Too many to count."

"What's the difference between a god and a patron? Is a patron like a regular human?"

"That can be a good equivalent. But patrons are stronger than any human. They make up the population of Asgard."

"Oh."

"Come now, Phoebe," he coaxed. "Tell me who Ingrid cited as your father."

I gave him a weak smile. "I like it when you call me by my given name."

"I know." He smiled. "I've gotten into the habit of referring to you as Valkyrie, but I will try to change my ways. It will take time. Now tell me who he is." He'd asked the last part very softly, leaning in to kiss me.

I brought my hands up to his face. I loved touching him there.

I leaned in, savoring his fresh scent, his lips, his mouth. I broke the kiss reluctantly, glancing down at my hands, not knowing what to do with them. "Ingrid said that my father is Odin."

Fen stilled, his back perfectly straight. "That is not possible." His voice was shallow, lacking any inflection as he stood up.

"I hope you're right," I began to babble, "because I don't want it to be true. And just so you know, I have no idea if it's fact or fiction. I wasn't lying when I told you I'd never had any contact with him—"

Fen moved fast. He had one leg in his grimy shorts before I knew what was happening.

I stood, my mouth gaping. "Wait, what are you doing? Where are you going?"

"Out to find the man with the scar," he said gruffly.

"Fen, please," I implored, moving toward him. "You can't take off! We're a team, remember? I know this is not great news, but we can overcome—"

He stood stiffly as he zipped himself up. "Phoebe, if Odin

is your father, this changes everything. I must find the man, or all will be lost."

"What does the man with the scar have to do with this?" I pleaded.

"He will know the truth."

"Take me with you!" I insisted. "Huggie said I have to leave here. We are in danger. You can't go without me."

He shook his head, ignoring me, grabbing for Ingrid's ridiculous shirt that wasn't going to button.

I continued. "What if Verdandi comes while you're gone? I can't fend her off by myself. You're essentially leaving me here to die or to be kidnapped again!"

"If you possess Odin's blood, you have nothing to fear."

"How can you say that?" I argued. "I've had to fight for my life since the first moment this happened! I was kidnapped and sucked into realms I knew nothing about. And everything I encountered, with the exception of you, tried to kill me. I would be dead already if it wasn't for you." I felt like banging a fist on his forehead to knock some sense into him. He couldn't be that obtuse. I mocked looking around the room. "I don't see Odin here to shuttle me to safety in his castle in Asgard. My would-be father is nowhere to be found. Instead, he left me to die and flung my mother into a horrible world to fend for herself like she means nothing." Fen moved toward the door, and I leaped forward, grabbing on to his arm to stop him. "Odin is not my champion! You can't leave me."

Fen turned back. "It does not matter if he is here in the flesh or not. He gave you Gram and sent his loyal raven, and be well aware, it was he who struck you," he said gruffly. "It was he who sealed your fate. All this has happened because he has decreed it to be so. Odin decides whether one will receive the honor. Every daughter born to a Valkyrie does not automatically became a shieldmaiden. Your father"—Fen cleared his throat like my parentage was a hard thing to swallow—"kept you a secret, but then revealed you to our worlds in the grandest way, knowing full well he was doing so. He did not strike you without a plan. If what you say is true, there will be much standing in our way of being together." I heard anguish in his voice.

"It doesn't have to be like that!" I insisted, holding on to him, preventing him from walking out and leaving me. "We can make our own way. *Together*."

"I am a wanted man." He shook his head. "Odin will do whatever possible to capture me once again and toss me away. If you're his daughter, you will eventually come to see his way, or he will force you to bend to his will. You have no idea what kind of strength you're dealing with."

I straightened my spine, dropping my grip on his arm. "It's clear you have no idea who you're dealing with either." I placed a single finger on his chest. "I'm not going to cave just because my *possible* father tells me to. We pledged ourselves to each other last night. You're the one who saved me from death, not Odin. You're the one who's standing here with me now, willing to take on my fight, and I will do the same for you. You never deserved to be locked up in the first place. Together we can make him understand."

"He will never understand."

"If you walk out on me right now, it's over between us. But that doesn't mean I won't continue to fight for you. What Odin did to you was wrong. You said I took your heart. Why can't you have a little faith in me? Faith that I'm my own person who can choose her own path?"

Fen raised an eyebrow. "I know you're strong, Valkyrie, but that doesn't make you immune to your father."

"Huggie is proof that my father doesn't always get what he wants."

"What do you mean?"

"I mean Huggie wasn't here because my father ordered him to come." Fen looked skeptical. "He was here because he made a promise to my *mother*. The raven told me that he wouldn't tell Odin about us unless Odin asks specifically. The bird is doing his own thing. The raven could've turned us over to Odin immediately, but he didn't. He's the one who gave me information about the ally and told me where to go. I'm assuming when we get to the Valkyrie stronghold, they will offer us some protection against the Norns, and Odin as well, if needed."

Slowly, Fen nodded, his face pensive. "They may. If they decide to take up our cause, they will fight—possibly even Odin if they care about you and your mother deeply enough. The only thing that tops following Odin, for a shieldmaiden, is another Valkyrie. They are loyal to each other above all else. If there are enough of them in residence, and trouble arrives on their turf, the odds would be in the Valkyries' favor."

"Okay, then." That was a relief to say the least. "That's our plan. We find the ally and then get ourselves to the Valkyries. You're going to have to trust me on this, Fen. Just like you said before—without trust we have nothing. I didn't get a say in who my parents are." I was determined to make him understand. "In fact, I haven't had a say in any of this so far. But I do get a say in who I choose to support and where I put my loyalties. You fought for me, and I will do the same for you. My loyalty is to you first, everyone else second." I crossed my arms, daring him to say otherwise. Emotion seeped out of me, my mind not allowing me to think of moving forward without him.

Fen finally bowed his head. "Okay, Valkyrie. You win. For now." He brought his gaze up. "Although I am not happy about who your father is, I agree it was not your choice. I will ride this out to the end, wherever that will be. We will find the scarred man and move on from there."

"As a team," I concluded.

"Yes."

I glanced out the window—dawn was breaking—then back at Fen. "First, we're going to get you some real clothes and a meal. We have some time until midnight. I know a quiet diner where we can make plans."

Fen moved forward, encircling my waist, his hands moving inside my robe. "First things first, Valkyrie." He nuzzled my ear. "We will go after we pledge ourselves to each other one more time."

26

It was almost midnight. After a long day of running around New York, buying clothes, and trying to locate a fresh trail for the scarred man, I was more than anxious to have the mystery solved.

Fen had refused to elaborate on who he thought the man was, but we'd had some good, in-depth conversations about what we both wanted moving forward.

At the top of the list was freedom.

Not having anyone hunting us down was a top priority. Figuring out how to do that was the tricky part, and something we hadn't solved. It would take more than one day.

The docks were deserted and chilly, most of the boats buttoned up for the winter. The entire area had a dark, shrouded feel to it. A cold breeze shifted off the Hudson River, swirling around us, penetrating our mild protection, making my teeth chatter.

I was dressed more appropriately than before in jeans, a sweater, a new coat, new boots, and a hat and scarf. Fen looked dashing in his new jeans, big-soled boots, black T-shirt, and black leather coat.

He no longer resembled something out of a storybook running through the streets of New York and looked more like he belonged here. Even though he still came off as ethereal if you happened to stare too long. Like our waitress did. The woman almost fell over bringing him his breakfast. She had insisted he was a movie star, and we went with it. It was the easiest way to fob it off. He even signed a napkin for her.

"Aren't you cold?" I asked for the third time. "A T-shirt and leather jacket are no match for a New York winter."

Fen chuckled. "No, Valkyrie." His big arm went around me, tugging me close. "It takes more than this to cool me down. After so many years on Muspelheim, my body has become perpetually warm."

I could vouch for that. Cuddling up with him was like snuggling against a heater. Which actually wasn't all that bad, especially now.

As we neared the end of the dock, Fen stopped abruptly, dropping his hold on me.

"Do you sense something?" I asked, my voice holding some excitement. After a few false trails today, I wondered how accurate this tracking thing really was.

"Yes." He lifted his nose in the air and took in a long, decidedly animalistic breath, dragging it over his tongue, his mouth open. His face darkened. "It's just as I thought. Though, I am puzzled as to why he would be on this plane. Prepare to fight, Valkyrie."

"Fight?" I asked, alarmed. "What do you mean fight? Huggie said he was our ally, not our enemy!"

"We will see if the word *ally* truly applies. I have my doubts. As I told you many times today, the bird could seek to entrap us. We must be wary."

"I'm always wary," I grumbled. "And I shouldn't have to remind you, we don't have any weapons other than Gram." Finding a decent broadsword in New York was harder than it would've seemed.

"I will fight with my bare hands."

"Great. I'm sure my mighty fists will be a huge asset." I raised them in a mock fighting stance. "They pack quite a punch." I threw some air punches. "He'll be cowering at our feet in no time."

Fen slid his arm around my waist, chuckling. "No, Valkyrie. What you need to harness is inside here." He placed a hand on my abs. "You have incredible power inside you, enough to stun a man, or even a god, for a short time. That is a Valkyrie's greatest defense. Stun with your energy, and then go for the kill."

My stomach did a flip-flop, and not because Fen was touching me.

Other than the demons on Muspelheim, I'd never killed anything bigger than a spider in my life. "Um," I hedged. "I think it'll be a while before I can tolerate doing something like that. I'm not a very blood-thirsty gal."

Fen replied stoically, "When your life is in imminent danger, and you have no choice other than to kill or be killed, you will choose to save your own life or the lives of those you love. There is no contest."

I sighed. "Would it be too much to ask that Asgard be peaceful? Made up of big, fluffy clouds, serenity, and lots of hot yoga? Why does it have to be even harsher than Midgard? It sounds like war and fighting all the time, with more war and fighting lined up for the future." I couldn't think about what Fen had told me about Ragnarok without getting a stomachache. Too much devastation.

"We all seek power." Fen shrugged. "It is coded into our bodies from the day of our birth. It cannot be helped."

We proceeded toward the end of the dock slowly and cautiously, Fen at the ready. In front of an empty slip, second from the end, Fen stopped, tugging me behind him as he called out in a booming voice, "Come out and face me, you coward!"

Nothing happened for a full minute.

I whispered, "Maybe he's not here—"

The air around the vacant spot began to waver, like hot steam erupting out of a tea kettle. Then a small houseboat solidified into view.

It was a rickety two-story structure. The second level appeared to be an afterthought, pieced together with plywood and rusted corrugated metal. The thing looked like one strong gust of wind could topple it.

A moment later, a huge figure loomed in the doorway on the second level, which sat just below the dock line.

I cringed back, hanging on to Fen's arm.

Yep. I was a badass.

"I said, come out and face me like a god," Fen growled. "Or are you scared I will tear into your face again and leave you with a bigger scar?"

Wait, *what*?

Fen had scarred the big, terrifying man?

"I don't fear you." The low, deep voice issued from the boat as the door creaked opened. The guy was so big he had to duck to get through the opening.

I gasped as he came into view.

He was definitely the same guy who'd accosted me on the subway stairs. He even wore the same grimy hat. I couldn't smell him from here, but I was certain he would still smell like putrid old garbage, stale food, and body odor.

"What are you doing on Midgard?" Fen asked. "Seems lowly, even for you."

Did Fen just dis Earth? Sure, it was cold tonight, but other than that, it was a wonderful place to live. Much better than the realm we just came from.

"Toss your insults, wolf," the man said, a note of fatigue in his voice. "I came here for the same reason you did."

"And what reason is that? To exact revenge on those who locked you up for centuries, left to rot like a dog?" Fen snarled. "No, that can't be it. I see no bindings cuffing your wrists. I see no chains cinched tightly around your arms. I see a free man standing before me. One who has a choice whether to come or go."

The guy stepped to the very edge of the boat, a single streetlight illuminating the top of his head, casting a pool of deep shadow around him. "My freedom has been taken from me as well. And what are you talking about? You're here with the girl." He gestured to me. "You came to protect her, same as me." He seemed smug in his assessment of the situation.

But if he was here to protect me, he hadn't done his job very well. *Where were you when the ettins took me? Huh, tough guy?*

Fen seemed a little taken aback and cleared his throat before he said, "How would I know anything about this girl when I was being held prisoner in Muspelheim all these long years? It is where I've spent my days since you tricked me into taking a wager I could never win, then delivered me to the pits of despair bound by Gleipnir."

Wait, this guy was responsible for Fen's imprisonment?

Who was he again?

Fen had told me his name, but I'd been under duress at the time and couldn't remember.

"I have long regretted that," the man answered. "What

has happened between us can't be undone. The future is the only thing that matters now, and it seems our paths have collided yet again, as we both seek to keep the girl safe."

Why do you care about me? Who are you?

I had so many burning questions.

Fen snarled. He sounded like a caged animal. If I hadn't been holding on to his arm like a sissy, he would've been pacing back and forth on the dock in front of the boat like the wolf he was. "You will have nothing to do with her," he raged. "We cannot trust a word you say."

"It would be a mistake not to hear me out."

"The mistake would be not fighting me. You owe me that much."

The man took a small step closer. The next one would be from the boat to the dock, but he would have to jump to make it. "I will fight you. Then you will listen. We don't have much time."

"Remember," I urged Fen, tugging on his arm, "Huggie told us he's an ally, not an enemy. He might be able to help us." Even though he was still scary and worrisome. "We should hear him out."

"He will betray us," Fen answered firmly. "There is no trusting him. After we fight, we gather information, and then we leave."

"You would do best to listen to the girl," the man agreed. "I will tell you what I know, and then we will all leave this place together. They are coming."

Who was coming? The Norns?

The man leaped off the boat onto the dock. It was the smoothest jump I'd ever seen, almost like it had taken zero effort.

What happened next went so fast, I couldn't track it.

One moment he stood in front of us. The next, both men

were rolling around in a large mass, throwing punches. They tumbled precariously close to the edge. If they made a wrong move, they'd both topple into the frigid waters of the Hudson.

The dock vibrated angrily at the intrusion of the extreme violence on its decking. The concrete pilings groaned as the men shouted at each other, but I couldn't make out what they were saying. There was so much noise and clamor.

I glanced around, hoping no one else noticed the uproar. There were other boats docked nearby, but they were dark. I didn't think anyone lived on them.

"You will answer for your betrayal!" Fen raged as he threw punch after punch.

They rolled a few more times, the stranger gaining the advantage. "You will stop being pigheaded and listen. I am not your enemy." He lifted one of his arms, and the sleeve fell back. His hand was missing. I'd forgotten that vital piece! For a man with one hand, he was holding his own.

"You were my only friend," Fen growled, "and you became my greatest enemy. I will kill you for deceiving me!" Fen knocked him down, railing on him.

If the scarred man had been mortal, he would've been long dead by now.

"If you could end my life, which is doubtful," the man grunted while he spun Fen to the ground, "you would miss out on information that will keep the girl alive." His lone fist landed hard on Fen's chest, the sound of rock hitting stone. "And she must stay alive at all costs."

"Why do you care?" Fen huffed. "She is nothing to you!"

"You have that wrong. She is the key to both of our well-being."

Fen landed a particularly hard punch, angling his fist up under the man's chin. There was a loud crack, and the guy flew backward, sliding to a stop right in front of me.

I gaped down at him.

Fen staggered to his feet. Both men were bruised and bloody, but as I watched, their wounds began to heal. At this rate, they could keep fighting forever.

I coughed into my fist, gathering my strength, refusing to back away from this fight. "I think you guys need to calm down," I interjected. "This isn't getting us anywhere. We need information, Fen. Once we hear what he has to say, we can figure out what to do."

Fen stalked forward. "We need nothing he has to offer. I will end him, then we will leave."

I held up my hand. "No." Fen stopped, his face flashing his surprise. I'd uttered it harshly, like a command. "I know you're upset," I began, "but we are in desperate need of allies. Huggie said this guy can help us. It seems like he has vital information to share, and he's willing. We need to give him a chance to tell us what he knows, *then* you can decide what to do."

The man stood, wiping the blood dripping down his chin away with his coat sleeve.

He was taller than I remembered, and standing this close, he was terrifying. His rancid odor wafted up my nose, and I tried not to act like I noticed. His scar was dark red and ragged, just like I remembered. Fen must have been in his wolf form when he injured him.

"I will share what I know," the man agreed, the wounds Fen inflicted on him all but gone. For a moment, I wondered why the scar on his face had never healed. "But we should leave this place. Now that I have revealed myself, they will make haste."

"Who?" I asked.

"No," Fen said firmly, crossing his arms. "You will tell us here. We are not going anywhere with you."

"You are making a grave mistake, wolf. You are just as stubborn as you've always been. Your time away has not changed that."

"Before we go any further," I interjected, "I have to know why you care about any of this. About me. Who are you?"

The man turned, examining me from the top of my head down to my toes. His thorough examination made me antsy. I rubbed my arms through my coat while I waited for him to answer.

Finally, he said, "My name is Tyr. I am your brother."

27

My *brother*? Of all the things that could've come out of his mouth, that was the very last one I'd expected. My knees went weak, my arms pinwheeling to stop me from smacking on my backside. Fen rushed forward, steadying me, his strong arms rooting me in place.

I couldn't find my voice. I was too stunned. The way he'd said his name sounded like *tear*, as in the things threatening to fall from the corners of my eyes right this minute. I expected Fen to start shouting and fighting with the man again.

Instead, he responded, almost in a dead tone, "So it's true. She is the daughter of Odin."

"Aye, it is," Tyr answered, scratching the back of his neck. He seemed relieved that Fen had chosen to listen. "She is my half sister, and my duty is to protect her at all costs. The Norns have enlisted whoever they can find to do their bidding. They want her taken back to their realm, dead or alive. The price on her head is gold and riches like none has ever encountered. Things crafted by dark elves promising magic, a purse so heavy it would drag on the ground, you get the idea. Whatever their heart desires."

Fen started to say something, but I interrupted. "I don't understand any of this. I haven't done anything but live my life. I just want to be left alone." I was ready to shed some big, fat, ugly tears.

Tyr's face was downcast. It seemed like he understood my plight, which made me feel a little better. "Unfortunately, our father chose the wrong path for you. One that has the potential to endanger us all. But make no mistake, it's not your fault, sister." It was beyond weird to hear this stranger call me that. "The only thing wrong was the timing of your birth. It was foreseen that a child born at exactly the time you were would be a catalyst, one that would drastically change our worlds forever. The Norns seek to stop it from happening at all costs. It's their job, so to speak. Killing you because of this is legal in our worlds. Not even Odin himself can forbid them from coming after you. The only option for you now is to run and, when they come, to fight."

I rubbed my forehead. He sounded like Fen. Just fight when the trouble comes, no big deal. The wind was bitingly cold. I had so many questions. I didn't know where to begin. "Huggie, the raven, said that if I stay alive long enough to permanently change the timeline, the Norns will have less reason to kill me. Is that true?"

"Yes and no," Tyr answered, his voice a true baritone, deep and low. It sounded menacing, but not like before, especially with Fen standing beside me. "When your mother was pregnant with you, an old seer came to Asgard. No one knew the shieldmaiden was pregnant, as she and Odin were not supposed to be lovers." He didn't elaborate, but that was a curious thing to say. Why couldn't they be lovers? "The seer foretold of a birth that would happen in nine months. A birth that would be cataclysmic to our world. It would change things as we knew it. People took his words to heart and panicked. His predictions spread rampant among people and gods alike. All expectant mothers were sought out. The seer cleared their children based on the timing of the birth. After, we believed we'd been spared, and there was great relief. But Odin kept your mother from being interviewed. He could not bear to lose you. And being a god—and a very powerful one—he had good reason to think his child might be the one they were looking for." Tyr smiled. At least, I think it was a smile. One side of his lip turned up. "He kept you a secret, which took great skill—as much as a powerful god has to wield. But now that you've been revealed, the Norns believe you to be this child. They will seek to destroy you on those grounds alone, as will many in Asgard."

I was dumbfounded. "Why didn't he just leave me human, then? Why did he have to strike me and make me into a Valkyrie? No one would've been the wiser, and I could've lived my life in peace!"

Tyr slowly shook his head. His navy blue knit hat was pulled down, covering dark, seemingly wavy hair. I had a feeling that if he removed his hat and took a shower, he would look leagues younger. "The spell he paid the dark elves to craft twenty-five years ago to hide you was reaching its end of effectiveness. When he went back for another, they refused his bid. He had no choice but to strike you in hopes it would give you a better chance of survival."

"Okay...um," I stammered. "I'm not sure what to do with this information. But at least the reason why everything in my life has been skidding downhill like a go-kart with no brakes is becoming clearer."

Tyr seemed perplexed at my analogy. I bet they didn't have go-karts in Asgard.

Fen's arm tightened around my waist as he addressed Tyr. "So your father ordered you here to protect your sister? Is that why you came?"

"No," Tyr said. "I left Asgard many, many years ago. Soon after you were sent to Muspelheim. I have not seen my father in all that time."

"Why would you leave?" Fen asked.

"Because, my friend, what they did to you was wrong, and I let it happen. You were mine to protect, and it was a job I took seriously. I am atoning for that mistake by wandering the realms in search of answers. I've given up the life of a god in favor of finding ways to make things right."

Fen snorted. "You will have to keep searching, then, brother. Things will never be right between us."

I placed a hand on Fen's chest. His heart beat rapidly. I knew what Tyr was saying meant something to him, but it would take him time to heal from the betrayal by one he called a friend and mentor for so long. "How did you find out about me, if you haven't been back to Asgard?" I asked. "How did you know I was here and was about to be hunted by the Norns?"

"The raven," Tyr answered. "Hugin tracked me down in Jotunheim and told me of your birth and the story behind it. Then the bird came to me a few weeks ago and told me what was about to transpire. I came as soon as I could."

"You rushed to her side like a trusted brother, protecting an innocent sibling you'd never met?" Fen's voice was harsh. "I don't believe that. You have always been selfish, out for your own good and no one else's, God of War."

"Yes, that was me," Tyr agreed, nodding. "But I come here as a man trying to atone for a life of wrongdoing." He ran a hand over his neck. "The bird also imparted some very important information—facts that are just now coming to light. He told me that the seer was a fake, an impostor. What the seer said about the birth of a child was actually the opposite of what was supposed to happen. The raven fears that the impostor killed the old seer, and we will never discover the truth."

"A fake?" Fen said, his voice tight. "Only a scant few can use glamour to that effect."

Tyr nodded slowly, but said nothing.

"No," Fen replied, shaking his head. "I refuse to believe it could be him."

"Who?" I asked. I'd missed something.

"Loki." Fen's voice was as stony as I'd ever heard it. "He is blaming my father for this."

"Your father?" I exclaimed, horrified. "You mean Loki pretended to be the seer who could've caused the deaths of innocent unborn children?" I had to stop and catch my breath. "That's horrible!"

Tyr said nothing while we gathered our thoughts. Finally, he responded, "The raven believes it to be Loki. But as usual, it will be hard—if not impossible—to pin it on the trickster god who relishes in wreaking horror and havoc wherever he goes. He delights in the macabre, which you know well, friend." He directed his gaze at Fen. "During the timeframe he masked himself as the seer, he and Odin were at war over something else. If Loki had gotten wind that Leela was pregnant with Odin's child, he would've ended Odin's happiness at all costs." Tyr shook his head sadly. "It might be that we never uncover the truth."

"But if we can prove the seer was an impostor," I said, thinking quickly, "and the information was wrong, won't that prove my existence isn't a threat, once and for all?"

"That's not how Asgard works," Fen answered. "We are guilty until proven innocent. Isn't that right, *friend*?"

"Yes, you are correct." Tyr nodded. "The logic is not always sound, but that's the way it had been for us for a thousand years."

Before Fen or I could reply, there was a loud cracking noise, like a tree branch being ripped off a tree.

Tyr made a gesture to grab me, but Fen snarled, whisking me away. "Do not touch her!"

"Someone is coming, and they will be here soon," Tyr said. "We need to leave this area immediately."

"Who's coming? Are they coming through a tree? Is it Yggdrasil?" I asked as we all began to run, Fen holding my hand as we made our way back to the street. I spotted the large oak that sat twenty feet away on the main boulevard. It seemed to be glowing.

"Not Yggdrasil," Fen answered. "But it means they were granted access to Midgard by an alternate route, one that finds the beacon and takes them within closest proximity."

"Am I the beacon?" I asked, my breathing coming in puffs of air, the cold infiltrating my lungs. "It seems that with so many wormholes, Midgard should be crawling with beings from other realms." I was not happy. We'd barely had a chance to catch our breath since we landed. I'd hoped for more time.

Tyr was right behind us. "My guess is it's dark elves. They would want the bounty promised by the Norns the most and have access to other routes to Midgard, including by oak trees. Greed is their way of life."

"Can we fight them?" I asked. We'd hit a side street. It was late, but this was New York. A few blocks up, people were going to notice us running for our lives.

"Not advisable," Tyr said. "We don't know how many there are, and they will be armed with dark magic. It will be hard enough for Fenrir and me to best them on our own, but likely impossible for you. We can't take that risk."

"So what do we do?" I called over my shoulder.

"We need a place to hide," Fen replied, taking a sharp right at the corner. We booked down the next street. No one was on this street either, but our luck was going to run out soon. "You mentioned having a friend. If she lives nearby, that could work. We can duck into her building for safety. We might be able to throw them off the track since we now have a big lead."

"Yes," Tyr agreed. "I have some spells with me. If we can find a safe location quickly, I can dispatch them. It will cover our scent for a few hours. Then we can steal away."

Fen was talking about Sam.

Before I could respond, Fen added, "Your friend will remain safe. You have my word. She might have to leave her apartment for a day or two, if we are found, just to make sure. But once the elves, or whoever is after us, find we've left town, there will be no reason for them to linger. The creatures of other realms do not destroy life on Midgard. The penalty is stiff, usually death. We leave humans alone."

I glanced up at a street sign as we jogged down the next block. Sam did live pretty close, and she would likely be home. She didn't go out much, preferring to stay in and study lines or whatever it was that had caught her fancy that week.

"Okay," I agreed. "We can see if she's home. But I need to make double sure we're not putting her in any danger." What Sam would make of all this was beyond me. I smiled, imagining her stunned reaction when we tumbled through her door. "Are we allowed to tell her what we are? It's this way." I gestured toward the next block on the left before we went too far. Fen was moving fast, and I was surprised I could keep up with him. "We go down two more blocks and up one, and her building is around the corner."

As we ran, Tyr answered my question. "Yes, you can tell someone you trust about us, but whether they believe you or not is a different story. There's nothing they can do to us, so there's no harm. Even if they told a story about gods from one of the Nine Worlds visiting, no one would take them seriously. The human realm is the only one that has no clue that the others exist. The other eight worlds interact and know about each other. Because of that, we must cloak ourselves when we're here."

"Does that mean the dark elves will be cloaked?" I asked as we turned another corner.

"If they don't want to be punished, they will be," Fen answered. "If you look human, like we do, it's unnecessary."

"What do the dark elves look like?" I tossed a glance behind me. "Do they look like ettins?"

"Yes and no," Fen replied as we slowed. We had already covered three blocks and were in front of Sam's building. Hers was a regular brownstone, like mine, but her apartment was nicer. There was no doorman, but unlike mine, this building had an orderly row of buttons on the outside that corresponded to the apartment numbers. "The dark elves are a little taller and more humanlike than ettins."

"More humanlike?" I guessed that was better than more creaturelike. "Don't worry about explaining. I'm sure I'll have the unfortunate luck of running into one soon enough." I depressed the buzzer for Sam's apartment. She would likely be asleep. I kept my finger on it, tapping it on and off. It would piss her off, but she would also be more likely to get out of her warm bed and answer it that way.

Tyr's gaze was locked behind us. "Hurry, I can sense them. They are near. I tossed something behind us to mask our scent a few blocks back, but we need to be off the streets."

"I'm working on it—"

"Who's there?" Sam's voice cracked out of the intercom, sounding sleepy. "This better not be a joke. I was having the best dream *ever*."

"Sam!" I yelled excitedly into the little metal grille. "It's me, Phoebe! I need you to let me in."

"Phoebe!" There was a brief pause. "Where the hell have you been? You left town without so much as a backward glance. I spent hours—"

"Sam, I'm in trouble!" I cut her off sharply. "I'll explain when I see you."

"The door buzzer is broken. I'll be right down."

Fen watched one side of the street while Tyr monitored the other.

Tyr slid something out of his jacket pocket. It looked like one of those big chalky bath soaps you buy at a specialty store. It was swirled dark purple and white. He grinned at me. "This will make us smell like livestock."

Yummy. Tyr hardly needed to smell any worse. Add that to the list of bad smells we were bringing into Sam's apartment.

There was a noise, and I spun around.

Sam stood in the doorway dressed in flannel two-piece jammies. They were light yellow with little blue sailboats dotted all over. Her blonde curly hair was ruffled from sleep. She opened the door a crack, glancing at the guys. "Get in here," she ordered, waving her hand.

I slipped inside and just as she was about to shut the door, I said, "Wait. These two are with me. They have to come with me."

Sam arched an eyebrow at me like I'd lost my mind.

"I promise it's okay," I assured her. "I have a really good reason for being gone and for bringing two very large, strange men into your apartment at this late hour, but we have to move fast. I'll explain everything upstairs." *And I'm so sorry one smells like a sewer and now a barnyard, and by the way he's my half brother.* "Please, Sam," I begged. "Bad men are following us."

After a brief pause, she answered, "Fine. Come in." She waved her arm to usher the boys in. "But the story better be good. It'll have to top the 'pizza guy with a banana' story, or I'm going to be totally cranky."

"Oh," I told her as I walked in, "it's way better."

28

"I thought your place was bigger," I commented as Sam shut the door to her apartment. It was an asinine thing to say, but I had no idea how else to start this conversation. We were a motley crew stumbling into her home in the middle of the night.

There was no good way to begin this.

I glanced around. Her apartment was clean and sparsely decorated. New Yorkers usually had less, so the space was manageable. We all stood in the small living area, which held a couch, a table, and a few chairs. There was a tiny bedroom off to the left and a small galley kitchen to the right. Her kitchen had actual walls and a door.

"It looks small because it's now occupied by both of us and two men who are the size of at least four adults," Sam answered as she walked over to her couch and sat down, crossing her arms. "Start explaining, Phoebe, or I'm calling the cops. This is too strange, even for you." She eyed Tyr, not commenting on his stench or his scarred face.

I appreciated that.

"I know this looks...weird," I started, settling on a chair next to the couch as Fen crossed to the window to peer out, while Tyr stood by the door like a sentinel, staring straight ahead. I noted that Tyr's jacket was extra-large, and the cuff came down to cover his missing hand. Best not to let Sam see it until she'd heard the entire story. She'd already witnessed him tossing an exploding talcum bomb outside the door and had said nothing.

I didn't want to push my luck.

"This is more than *weird*, Phoebe!" she cried. "It's bat-shit crazy! First, you don't show up for work all week, and I think you left town because you were so freaked out about the stockroom incident. I actually forced your landlord to open up your apartment for me, threatening a lawsuit and pretending I was your concerned sister! When I saw your suitcase and clothes were gone, I figured you left in a hurry and were too distraught to call me. I decided to forgive you—*if* you ever came back. Now you're back, but with two guys who make the New York Giants look like kindergartners. What gives? Are they holding you hostage?" She glared in Fen's direction, and then Tyr's. "Do you need to give me some kind of sign you're in danger? Blink twice if you're their sex slave. I have Mace in my bedroom."

"No, it's nothing like that," I assured her, leaving off that Mace would hardly be an effective long-term deterrent for a god. "But the story I'm about to tell you is incredibly strange, and I don't expect you to believe it. But that's okay. I'm going to share it anyway, and then you can decide what you think. Just know that I would never leave town without telling you. You're my best friend. If I'd had more of a warning, I would've gotten a hold of you. I promise." I cleared my throat, readying myself.

This story was going to be tricky to relay in a coherent

fashion—one that didn't make me seem like I needed to be locked up in the loony bin.

Sam settled back on the couch, arms still crossed. "Well, I believe you already. I knew you would've called me. We've only been friends for a short time, but I consider you a sister."

I smiled. I felt the same way. I'd always wanted a sister, and if I'd had one, Sam would fit the bill. "Okay"—deep breath—"here goes. When I came home from work the night I was shocked by the lights, I found a raven in my kitchen." Sam's eyebrows went up, but she refrained from commenting. "Then my neighbor Ingrid showed up. You remember Ingrid, right?"

Sam nodded. "The beauty who lives next door? I've always said she should be a model. Those eyes of hers are killer, and she's got the height for it. She has to be almost six feet tall."

"Yes, she's tall, but I'm certain modeling is the last thing on her list." Was it ever. "Anyway, she came into my apartment dressed like she was ready for battle, full breastplate, toga, and spear, and told me I was in danger. Then the raven started talking to me..." I continued to unleash the rest of the sordid tale, all the way up until we'd found Tyr by the docks.

By the end, Sam was perched on the edge of the couch. "So," she asked when I was finally finished, her voice incredulous, "you mean this is your *brother*?" She scrutinized Tyr, who stood ramrod straight by the door. Sam got off the sofa and walked over to Tyr. He glanced down at her impassively. Neither of the guys had said anything during my story, but they'd both been listening to every word, especially Tyr. Fen had been watching out the window. Sam made a show of inspecting Tyr. Then she turned to me. "I guess you

AMANDA CARLSON

do look a little like him." She turned back to Tyr. "How did you lose your hand and get that awful scar?"

I'd left the scar part out. I'd wanted to hear the story from Fen first before I relayed it.

I stood and moved toward them. "How did you know he's missing a hand?" I asked her. "It's been covered the entire time."

"Just before the door closed, when he threw that stuff that blew up like a talcum bomb, his jacket came up and I saw it," she replied.

"You're not even freaked out by the fact that dark elves could be tracking us to your door right this minute?" I asked, shaking my head. "You're tough as nails, Sam. Either that, or you didn't buy my story and you're deflecting."

"Oh, I bought it, all right," she said, turning to face me. "I might be an actress-in-training, but I'm a total geek at heart. I studied mythology in college. You basically just outlined the next big-budget blockbuster movie. Odin's daughter meets up with Loki's son in one of the Nine Worlds, is hunted by the evil Norns and dark elves as she frantically tries to find her shieldmaiden mother, while escaping notice from her overbearing father, aided by a talking raven and a god with one hand, who turns out to be her long-lost brother." She shrugged. "Plus, it totally explains why you were struck by lightning at Macy's. I've been trying to figure that one out since the day it happened. It was physically *impossible* for those lights to shock you. This is the only logical explanation in my book." She crossed her arms, looking pleased with herself.

I gaped at my friend. She couldn't be serious.

If she'd come into my apartment in the middle of the night spouting the same story, I'd have made an appointment for her to see a shrink. I never would've accepted it. "You can't be for real," I said, shaking my head.

"*No* one on earth could be as calm as you are right now after hearing the story I just told."

She dropped her arms, her face falling. "Okay, fine. I'm totally freaked out." She began to pace the room, her arms tossed up. "Is that what you want to hear? I am out of my mind with fear and skepticism, and I think you might have a screw loose in a major way. But, at the same time, I'm totally intrigued." She stopped, giving me one of her intense stares. "It's hard *not* to believe someone like you, Phoebe. You've always been earnest and truthful in everything you do. I'm not exactly sure you're telling me the whole truth, but I'm going to choose to believe you for now. Is that good enough? Because it's all I can do. I mean, it's not every day your best friend turns out to be a Valkyrie. That's pretty cool to a geek like me. And if, later, I find this is an elaborate hoax to dupe me out of the fifty-seven dollars in my wallet so you can buy more Sudafed for your meth lab, so be it."

I walked over and gave her a big hug. "That's more like it. You're being totally reasonable. You're amazing, you know that? And, by the way, I'm not a meth addict. I'm not sure if that would be better or worse than my current predicament. I'm choosing to believe being a drug addict is worse, but just a smidge."

"Your brother smells like he might be one," she said, her voice muffled in my jacket as she started giggling.

Then we were both belly laughing.

Fen stepped away from the window, interrupting us. "I see nothing approaching outside. Our opportunity to escape will be soon." His fight with Tyr had left him a little rumpled, but otherwise he looked good. My heart fluttered. He was a handsome, intense man, and he was mine.

"Why not wait until morning?" Sam asked, pulling away from me. "Don't dark elves hate sunlight? I thought they turned into stone or something. At least that's what I learned in class. They forge this crazy cool stuff in their world, full of magic, but they rarely leave because sunlight cooks their brains. But maybe that's just made-up stuff? Hey, do either of you know Thor?"

Both men stared at her like she had two heads.

I was curious to hear their answers. Unlike Sam, I never took mythology classes in college. My scant knowledge came from a passing story or two in the sixth grade.

Tyr cleared his throat, his voice deep and smooth. "You are correct. They do turn to stone in sunlight." His expression appeared a little sheepish, but then he grinned. I couldn't see the family resemblance at all. He needed a shower desperately, so maybe after he was cleaned up I'd see it. "Though, on our behalf, we are not exactly sure it is dark elves who hunt us. It could be another faction. We left before we saw who was tracking us."

"It was the dark elves," Fen said definitively. "I scented them right before we entered the building. I never forget a scent."

"Well," I started, "that calls for a new plan. Can we lie low here until morning?" I turned to Sam. "Is that okay?"

"It's fine with me," she answered. "I doubt we'll sleep, so how about I make some coffee?" She headed toward her kitchen, but stopped just before the doorway. "Oh, and the bathroom is right back there. Feel free to use all the soap and shampoo you need. There are towels in the little cabinet to the left of the door." She didn't direct the missive at Tyr, but we all knew who she was talking to.

I hid my grin. Leave it to Sam to be blunt.

Tyr made a rumbling sound and reached up to scratch his neck. "I guess I could wash. It's been a long time since I've bothered with such things."

Yes, we knew.

I resisted the urge to shudder, thinking about all the buildup and the amount of scrubbing that'd have to go on to get rid of it. "Yes, that's a great idea," I agreed. "After this, we'll probably be on the road for a while. Speaking of that"—I turned to Fen—"how do we know where to go? Huggie said New Mexico. Do we just head that way and hope for the best?"

Fen followed me into the kitchen while Tyr went to use the bathroom. We both leaned against the counter as Sam made a big pot of coffee. I unbuttoned my coat, but kept it on. "Once we get in the vicinity, we should pick up on Yggdrasil, if the shieldmaiden hasn't reached out by then."

"But how are we going to travel? Plane? Bus? Car?" I asked.

"Cream or sugar?" Sam asked as she began to pour three cups.

"A little cream," I answered. I'd had breakfast with Fen this morning. The food had tasted fine, but hadn't filled me up. Sam went to the fridge and took out some half-and-half.

"Is this okay?" she asked, holding it up. "I thought you liked your coffee black."

I nodded, and she poured a shot into my cup. I lifted it and took a sip. "Ah, that's good. I usually like it black, but I'm in the mood for a little kick. This is perfect."

Once we all had our coffee, we talked about mundane things, like how the shoe department had fared in my absence. The answer was *just fine*. Then we wandered back into the living room. Tyr had been in the shower for a while, and when we heard him shut it off, we all quietly exhaled with relief.

"Not sure what to do about his clothes," Sam

commented. "But at least the first layer of grime is gone. Where was he living, anyway? The sewer?"

I shrugged. "Not sure. We found him on an old houseboat. It seems he's been roaming for quite some time." Hundreds of years.

"He never answered me about his hand or scar," Sam said. "What happened to him?"

I glanced at Fen. It was his, or Tyr's, story to tell. He shifted uncomfortably next to me on the couch. "I scarred his face and took his hand," Fen replied succinctly.

My mouth dropped open as Sam sucked in a sharp breath.

"Say what?" Sam leaned forward. "You did *both*?"

"I did, and I was justified," he answered, his face hard. "The god of war was my mentor and friend. He tricked me. Because of him I spent too long in isolation. It was small retribution."

I was a teensy bit horrified. "I...I...didn't know you took his hand, too," I stammered. It seemed excessive, but I hardly knew the background between the two of them. Who was I to judge?

Fen met my gaze, no regret in his eyes. "He tied me with rope crafted by the dark elves to ensure I could not break free." He shrugged. "His hand was near, so I took it. In my furious attempt at escape, I slashed his face with my teeth."

"Wow," Sam commented, sitting back. "That's...intense."

Fen brought a leg over one knee. "It is of no consequence. He's a god. He doesn't need to stay scarred. It's his choice."

"What do you mean?" I asked, floored by that news.

Before he could answer, Tyr came barreling into the living room. His jeans were on, and he was toweling his hair, his chest bare. He seemed much bigger with no jacket or shirt on. Huge, in fact. His muscles had muscles. I hadn't expected him to be so buff after his dirty-bum exterior. "I keep them as reminders," he answered. "Trouble's coming."

29

I stood quickly. "What kind of trouble?" I had a hard time prying my eyes off his missing hand. Why would you choose not to have a hand? Especially when you were the god of war. Hands were handy.

"I left an alarm on the door downstairs, and it just went off," Tyr answered.

"What does that mean?" Sam asked, fear seeping into her voice.

"It means the dark elves weren't so easily fooled," he said wryly. "It seems we were the fools. They have found us."

Fen was already off the couch, making his way to the door, where he laid his head against the wood and listened. "They are not here yet."

I almost let out the breath I'd been holding, but then a scratching sound came from the window.

All of our heads snapped toward it.

To my horror, there was a small man-creature with charcoal-gray skin and pointed ears perched on the sill. It looked like a garden gnome come to life—if garden gnomes were dark, scary, with thinning hair and large Gollum-y eyes. It grinned at us, its long fingernails skating over the glass.

It was toying with us.

A scream crept into my chest, but before it erupted, Fen grabbed on to my hand and tugged me to the door. "You must be quiet," he cautioned, murmuring in my ear, holding me close. "That one sees us, but we don't want it to alert its friends. We must leave now before the others arrive."

Once we were in the hallway, we heard glass shatter.

I craned my head around in time to see Tyr drop the towel he'd been holding, hoist Sam over his shoulder, and run. Sam's face was white with shock. I didn't blame her one bit for being freaked out. I was pretty sure she wasn't breathing, but I couldn't exactly stop and ask.

The dark elf cackled as it crawled through the window, kicking out the rest of the glass as it went.

Tyr slammed the door to Sam's apartment and tossed something onto it that he pulled from his pocket. It looked like another talcum bomb since there was a big puff of white smoke. "That should buy us a small amount of time," he said, moving quickly. "All the spells I have are crafted from the elves, so I guess I shouldn't be surprised they are able to break through them so easily."

We took off at a run, Fen leading us up two flights of stairs before I realized we were going up, not down. "This is not the way out!" Panic leaked around my words like a bucket with holes poked in it. I didn't want to get snatched again. The terror of landing in another place full of horror made my legs quake. Verdandi's lair and Surtr's torture were still fresh. I wouldn't be as lucky a second time.

"We must go up," Fen replied calmly. "They will be scouring the lower levels and have left guards at the exits. There is no other choice."

"But what are we going to do once we get there?" I didn't *really* want to know.

"Once we're up, we can decide. It's going to be okay, Valkyrie." He squeezed my hand. "I will let nothing happen to you."

Sam lived on the fourth floor. We made it to the eighth and final floor in a short time. I was relieved no one had come out of their apartment to investigate the racket.

"Sam," I whispered once we arrived on the top floor, "where is the door to the roof?"

Tyr slid Sam off his shoulder, steadying her with his hands. She was disoriented, clutching on to his arms. "I'm sorry, did you ask me a question?" She ran a hand up through her hair, her long blonde curls disordered from her ride upside-down. "Can you repeat it? My ears are ringing."

I grabbed her hand, squeezing tight. "It's going to be okay. I promise. I know this is overwhelming, but we need to get to the roof and find a way out of here. I'm hoping there might be access to a fire escape up there. Is the door to the roof on this floor?"

Sam grabbed on to both my forearms, her face a horrified mask. "Did you see that thing?" Her eyes were partially glazed over. "I don't…I couldn't…" She shook her head.

"*Shh,*" I soothed, stroking her arm, "you're going to be fine. This is a lot to take in at once. I promise we'll talk it out once we're safe. But, Sam, I need you to focus. Where's the door to the roof?" I coaxed. "Can you show us?"

She nodded, blinking. "Yes…it's at the end." She started moving, and we hurried after her. She reached a door at the end of the hall and turned the knob. "Oh, no." She glanced back, her face pained. "I need my key!"

Fen moved to the front, edging her carefully out of the

way. "It's no problem." He placed his hand on the knob, and a click sounded before it popped open.

"That was easy," I murmured. "I hope the rest of this turns out to be just as simple."

"Manipulating small objects is not an issue," Fen said. "Especially on Midgard. Humans could have this capacity as well. They just don't explore it."

"Good to know," I said. I was learning quickly that humans had a lot left to explore.

Fen slowly opened the door, pausing to listen. Roofs in New York City ran the gambit, but no one usually used them in the winter. Some had gardens and sitting areas, but I was pretty sure Sam's apartment building just had a plain old roof.

Fen motioned us into the stairwell. It was only one short flight up to the top. I heard a puff of something and turned back to see Tyr clapping white powder off his hand on his pants. "How many of those do you have?" I asked, my eyebrow raised.

"That was my last one," he replied solemnly. Sam was in front of him, and he helped her up the stairs, guiding her by the waist. She seemed oblivious to his help.

They looked comical together, him being large and shirtless and Sam being so petite, but somehow it worked. Never in my wildest dreams had I thought the Tyr I encountered on the subway stairs would be a nice guy. His hair was drying into long, auburn curls, and his scar even looked less scary now that he was clean. "You're going to be cold with no shirt on," I told him over my shoulder.

"I'll be fine."

Fen reached the door to outside. There was a small window, but it was dark out. "Do you see anything?" I whispered, leaning up against his shoulder.

"No, but that means nothing. They will know we must come out someplace. If they don't have elves guarding the roof, it would be surprising."

"If it's blocked, how are we going to get down?" I asked.

"They would station only one here to keep a lookout. If we can take him down without alerting the others, we have a chance to escape unnoticed."

"If we don't?"

"We fight."

That seemed like the answer to most of my questions. "How many do you think are in the building?" I asked.

"Hard to know," Fen answered. "But I would think at least ten. They believe they are tracking only us and haven't factored in Tyr. If they had, they would've sent fifty."

I arched an eyebrow. "He's that strong?"

Fen shrugged. "He's the god of war." He glanced past me to Tyr. "Are you ready?"

Tyr picked up Sam, who was still dazed. "Yes."

Fen busted through the door. I went behind him. Before I could track Fen's movements, he had a dark elf by the throat. The thing looked even worse up close. It was no taller than four feet. Its gray skin was wrinkly like a dog that had lost its fur, and its teeth were yellowed and fairly sharp—like every creature I'd seen so far outside of Midgard. It seemed the Nine Worlds were lacking in all-around good dental hygiene.

"How many are there?" Fen grated.

"You are too late," it cackled. "We have infiltrated the building, and you will not escape." Its voice was surprising, higher and more precise than I would've imagined could come out of such a creature.

Fen shook the thing disgustedly. "You will not take us today, nor tomorrow. You can tell your comrades when you see them next that the best plan is to surrender the fight."

"Oh, it is of no consequence if we win or not," the thing gloated, gulping for air, its long fingers scrabbling at Fen's hand and wrist. "We hold a much dearer prize." It gazed directly at me, its eyes widening, before it cackled again. "The ransom for your dear mother will be legendary! Much more than the paltry amount being offered for your capture. Until then," it chortled, "we will keep her well...looked after."

My hands fisted into tight balls as anger welled to the surface. The energy inside me sparked.

They had my mother. I couldn't let myself think about what they'd done to her all these years, or I would lose my mind. "There will be no ransom," I seethed. "We will rescue her from you and pay you *nothing*." It didn't matter that I had never met my real mother. Since I'd been struck, a bond had strengthened between us. I yearned to meet her, talk to her, and have a chance to love her and be loved by her.

"That would be a feat, indeed," it said, not taking me seriously for a second. "Invaldi will stop you. There is no getting into our dark realms without his permission. Trying would be futile."

"Enough!" Fen rattled it until its head seemed like it would pop off its shoulders. "How many of you are here?"

"Plenty."

"Silence him," Tyr ordered from behind me. "It matters not how many. We must leave. This human...will suffer in this cold without proper clothing."

I'd forgotten Sam wore only her pajamas. "Oh, my. Here." I hurried over, shrugging off my coat. "She can have this." When I turned back from helping Sam into my coat, the dark elf was lying on the roof in a heap. "Did you kill it?" I asked Fen.

"No, I merely stunned it. Killing an elf carries a sentence

in their world of death. It's burdensome."

"But they are the ones attacking us!" I pointed out. "It was self-defense."

"Yes, but proving that to the court is almost impossible. Come on." He gestured in front of him. "We need to find a way off this roof."

I followed. Tyr carried Sam behind us.

"Where are you taking me?" I heard Sam ask weakly.

"Have no fear, maiden. We will get you to safety unharmed," Tyr answered, his voice deep and calming.

"Did you just call me 'maiden'? Like a princess in a fairy tale?" She giggled. "I think this shitty dream might be getting better."

I chuckled. It seemed Sam would make a rebound quicker than I thought. No one could blame her for losing her sanity for a while. It wasn't easy finding out that the mythology you were taught in school *actually* existed. She was taking it better than I had.

"I see something over there." I pointed to an area on the roof that had two black rods coming up. It could be the top of a fire escape. Not every place had one that reached the roof, but some did.

Fen glanced over the side, shaking his head. "No, it's just some reinforcement. But that building over there has one." He nodded to the complex next to Sam's. It was at least a story shorter than Sam's building.

"How are we going to get there?" I asked, hoping beyond hope that Fen wouldn't say what I knew he was going to say.

"We jump, naturally."

"Um." I walked to the edge and peered down. It seemed like a mile. "I'm not sure I can make that."

"Yes, you can, Valkyrie. And even if you fell, which I won't allow, you wouldn't die."

"That's reassuring and everything," I continued, "but you seem to forget I have no training for this. As of a week ago, I was human. Humans don't leap buildings. Stuntmen with harnesses do. And won't my crashing eight stories to the ground be detrimental to the mission? The dark elves will swarm me and take me hostage instantly."

"That might be true, but you're not going to fall," he said. "All we need to do is take a running leap, and we're clear. You've got more inside you than a typical human. You must remember that."

I'm sure I would embrace my Valkyrie-ness at a later date, but right now jumping off a building sounded extreme. I tried to imagine how Ingrid would handle it. She wouldn't need Fen egging her on, that was for certain. She'd likely be across already.

I glanced back at Tyr, who still held Sam. She gazed at him with pure adoration. He inclined his head to me no more than an inch, which basically told me I was going to have to jump.

"What about Sam?" I asked. "She can't make it, and if she fell, she'd be dead."

"I will get her across safely," Tyr said, his tone confident.

Sam intertwined her arms around Tyr's neck, a bright smile on her face as she turned to me. "I trust him."

"You can't be serious." I had to keep my voice modulated so I didn't yell. "This is not a fairy tale, Sam. It's real life! What if you fall?"

She calmly stated, "I won't fall. Have you seen the size of this guy? And I understand this is real life, Phoebe. But can't a girl enjoy a surreal moment or two? Scary storybook creatures just broke into my apartment. My world has been rocked with the news that supernaturals do in fact exist. I'm happy to linger here, in fantasyland, for a while, because frankly, coming back down to earth now, in my pajamas, standing on my roof in the middle of winter, being held by a god, won't be great for my fragile psyche. I prefer to come down more slowly, on my own terms, when I'm warm and snug in my own bed wondering if this all was a dream or just my youthful imagination playing tricks on me."

I snorted. "Your fragile psyche, my—"

The door to the roof crashed open, and three dark elves ran out.

Fen grabbed my hand. "Time to go." He pulled me backward a few feet and then took off at a run.

I had no choice but to follow, gripping his hand like it was an anchor for my own fragile psyche. We hit the edge at the same time, using it to propel us forward. I closed my eyes as I cried out, "This better work!"

"Open your eyes!" Fen called back.

I pried them apart a second before we landed. We'd managed to clear the expanse with more than enough room. I let go of Fen's hand and dropped to the ground, somersaulting a few times until I skidded to a stop on the slippery rooftop. I recovered quickly, jumping up and brushing myself off. Just in time to see Tyr land effortlessly, Sam still in his arms.

The god of war made jumping between buildings look like a routine event, almost as easy as stepping over a curb after exiting a taxi.

I didn't have time to comment, because sailing over after him were three dark elves, their teeth gnashing as they flew through the night, arms spread wide, cackling like devils.

30

"Phoebe!" Fen yelled. "Take this."

I turned in time to see Gram flying through the air. I snatched it as a dark elf barreled into me. The force of the impact sent us both flying. The thing landed on top of me, skidding us both along the roof. It was surprisingly meatier than it looked.

"You're coming with us," it chirped in its high singsong voice, its breath smelling like decaying earth. "We have plans for you that involve a lot of gold and untold riches."

"I'm not going anywhere with you," I spat. "I've already been kidnapped once, and it's not happening again."

"You will come with us whether you choose to or not," it asserted. "Because I have something here that will give you little choice in the matter." It produced something out of its pocket. A black vial filled with something thick and sludgy. "You will ingest this now, and you will remember nothing."

"The hell I will!" I thrashed. But the elf on my chest had me pinned with its powerful arms. They were a lot stronger than they appeared.

"Valkyrie, don't swallow that!" Fen yelled.

"I'm trying not to," I called, averting my face while trying to rock this burr off my chest. I glanced to my left and right. Fen and Tyr were both engaged with the other elves.

Sam stood a ways away, her mouth open, her eyes wide. At least she was safe for now.

The thing continued to press the vial against my lips. "Drink, drink, *drink*!" it chirped.

I finally knocked it off of me, but it scampered right back up quicker than I could react. "Get…off…of me!" I s till had Gram in my hand, which made maneuvering difficult. I didn't want to stab the thing unless I absolutely had to.

"If you will not drink this, I will have to hurt you," it warned, clucking its tongue menacingly. "That won't harm our reward in the least. Verdandi has been very clear about that. You are to be taken dead or alive."

"I'm sure she made it clear as day," I gritted. "But that doesn't mean I plan on cooperating."

It suddenly sat up, a grin forming on its wide, uneven features. Its hand went into its shirt, and then it brandished a long, skinny dagger. The thing looked like a cross between an ice pick and a kitchen knife with a very detailed handle carved in what could possibly be bone. It gleamed in the moonlight as the elf brought it down, the tip piercing the base of my throat. It happened so fast, it took me a moment to process what was happening.

"I think I will just take you dead—" The blade went into my neck a little farther.

My hand reacted before my brain had a chance to get on board. Lightning crackled down above us. I heard Fen yell, but Gram was already in motion. The dagger hit its mark, entering the side of the elf's head with a sickening *thunk*. The thing slid off of me and toppled to the side, the ice pick falling out of its hand with a clatter to the rooftop.

I scampered up as Sam rushed over, helping me by grabbing my arm and clutching me close. "Did you...did you just kill that thing?" she stammered. "I mean, I saw it, but I'm not sure I believe it."

"I think so," I answered. "It was a gut reaction. I didn't plan on it. But it said it was going to kill me first, so I guess I...preempted it? I don't know." I bent down and picked up the ice pick, examining it. It hummed with magic. I placed my other hand on my neck where the tip had gone in, smearing the blood that still leaked from the wound onto my palm. The urge to take the weapon for myself overwhelmed me. I leaned down and pulled Gram out of the elf's head, which made a sickening slicking sound.

I wiped the elf's blood off on its own shirt as Sam's voice lowered to a whisper as I stood. "Lightning lit up the sky when you did it," she told me. "And now you're kind of glowing." There was a bit of humor in her voice. "But, honestly, it was cool to see you kick some ass, and that thing is beyond creepy. I'm not sorry you killed it, but I am sorry if you feel bad."

I glanced down at my bloodied hand. I was emitting a soft white glow, but it was fading fast. I nodded to my friend, trying to regain my thoughts. My brain felt clouded. There was a noise, followed by a cry of anguish. We both turned to look.

Tyr and Fen both had their elves by the throat, each of them stalking to the edge of the building. In unison, they tossed the dark elves over the edge, but not before I saw the reaction to my kill in both elves' eyes.

There was hatred there.

I glanced around, realizing my tussle with the elf had

taken place much quicker than I'd thought. We hadn't been on this roof very long.

Fen rushed toward me, his hands going around my shoulders. "Are you okay?"

"Yes," I answered. "I didn't mean to kill it, but it was trying to kill me." I lifted my hand to show him the blood.

He pulled me into an embrace, murmuring, "It was a just and fair kill."

"Will the drop from the building kill yours?" I asked, pulling back, glancing at Tyr, who now stood by Sam, his arms crossed.

"No," Fen said. "They will be stunned once they land, but they won't die. It takes much to kill one. Come, we must leave now." He grabbed my hand and led me toward the fire escape.

I glanced back at the dead elf's body. "We can't leave it up here for a human to find."

"Its comrades will find it and take it home," Tyr answered, ushering Sam in front of him, her slippers making no sound as she padded after us.

"Am I going to be in trouble for killing it?" I asked as Fen began to descend the ladder down the side of the building.

He glanced up. "Not if you stay out of their realm. As I said, it was a just kill. There will be no penalties in the other worlds."

"But?" I almost shouted. "My mother is being held prisoner there. You heard that thing. We have to go get her. That means I *will* be traveling to their realm."

"We can decide all that later," Fen said, his voice stoic. "Come down the ladder. The elves will be occupied with their wounded, but not indefinitely. We must move."

I followed him down the fire escape, Tyr and Sam behind me.

Once we all jumped down into the alley, Fen led us to the street, glancing both ways to make sure it was clear.

"Where are we going now?" I asked from behind his shoulder.

"We must get to the Valkyrie stronghold, as the raven told you," Fen answered.

"How are we going to get there?" I asked.

"We can use my boat," Tyr offered.

Fen's eyebrows shot up as he glanced back over his shoulder. "Why would you accompany us on such a mission?"

"Because I have pledged myself to protect her," he said. "I will see her safe. After that, I will leave if you so desire."

"Do you happen to know where the Valkyrie stronghold is?" I asked Tyr. We needed exact directions.

"No," Tyr answered. "But if we use my boat, we can take magical routes. It's not as fast as taking the tree, but it's safer and will keep us mostly off the radar."

I glanced at Fen to gauge his reaction.

He seemed torn. We needed to leave New York immediately, but taking a portal was out of the question. I wasn't going to risk getting dropped into the Norns' lair, or worse. Was there a worse? I didn't want to know. "Let's go with him," I urged. "We don't have a better solution right now, and he's proven he's on our side for now. Before I was snatched, Ingrid was taking me to Teterboro to take a private jet, but I don't think it's safe to fly, and I'd have no idea how to find out where the Valkyries keep their jet." A plane crash sounded the least desirable option out there.

Fen nodded once, making his decision. "Fine. But once we arrive at the Valkyrie stronghold, you will disappear, is that clear?"

"Whatever you want," Tyr agreed. "But the human must

come with us. It's unsafe for her to stay here. The dark elves will have her scent and will take her for questioning."

Before I could add anything, Sam piped in, "You bet I'm coming with! I wouldn't miss this for the world. Plus, you're not leaving me here with those creepy things crawling all over my building. Did you say we're going to a Valkyrie stronghold? That sounds amazing."

We took off at a fast clip down the street, Fen leading the way. Once we reached the marina, we ran toward the place where Tyr's boat had been docked.

It wasn't there.

"Your boat better be cloaked from view," Fen said as Tyr jogged up. Tyr was still shirtless, but he didn't appear to be cold in the least. Weather must be much different on Asgard. Either that, or gods could regulate their body temperature much more efficiently.

"It seems to have left," Tyr replied, glancing around.

"What do you mean it *left*?" I asked. "How can boats just pick up and leave?"

"If the boat senses a threat, it's programmed to disappear," he answered. "That's what makes it safe."

"Where did it go?" I asked. "The dark elves will be on our trail soon."

"The boat will give me a signal when it resurfaces."

"When will that be, master?" Fen asked, his voice full with sarcasm.

"My name rolls off your tongue so well, just like long ago," Tyr replied, not missing a beat.

"Don't you have some kind of key fob thingy?" Sam asked, her arms wrapped around her body, trying to keep warm. "Like cars have? We can't be more advanced here than Asgard. I mean, come on!"

Tyr looked a little disgruntled. "The boat is spelled to

protect itself and its inhabitants. That's why I live on it. It will surface soon, likely in this same place once it assesses that the trouble has left."

"But the trouble won't be gone. The dark elves are on our trail. Can't you call it back somehow?" I asked.

He rubbed the back of his neck. "If I call it back, I reveal myself."

"Reveal? To who? And how?" I paced on the dock. We didn't need any more sirens to let people know where we were.

"My father, for one," he replied. "And any others who tune in to that kind of thing." That had to include the Norns. "I have to send a ripple with my signature on it through the worlds to find it. The boat is keyed only to me, so it would get the message. But so would anyone else who's listening."

"It's too risky," Fen said.

I nodded my agreement.

"Though," Tyr pondered, "no one knows I'm with you, and I've been gone a long time. Likely no one is going to notice if I call it, as they won't know we're together."

"Can dark elves get messages easily from Midgard to their realm?" I asked. "Because they know we're together."

"Yes, in seconds," Tyr answered. "They are always linked by magic. Their leader, Invaldi, will be keeping close tabs."

"Then it's too risky, just as I said," Fen replied, crossing his arms. "The realms have to know I've escaped by now. Once the news is out that we're all together, it will be a massive hunt."

There was a quiver under our feet as the dock moved.

"What was that?" Sam asked, fear stark in her voice.

The dock vibrated again.

It had to take a huge force to make concrete sway like

that. The water in the river was agitated, lapping against the pilings violently.

My gaze landed squarely on Fen. "I think Tyr should call the boat back. This feels like something bigger than dark elves."

Fen's face hardened. "Tyr, call the boat."

"Are you sure—" Tyr started.

"I'm sure. There is only one thing that can cause a tremor like this from below the sea," Fen stated evenly.

"What?" I asked.

"Jormungand."

"No way," Sam breathed. "It really exists?"

"*Who?*" I asked as the dock tremored again, this time with more intensity. I glanced at Sam. It was strange that she knew more about my new world than I did.

"My brother," Fen stated evenly.

"The Midgard Serpent," Tyr finished. "I'm calling the boat now."

31

"Your brother is a *serpent?*" I tried to keep my voice steady. Serpent made sense, right? Like having a sibling who lived in the ocean was not totally out of the ordinary. "Why would he be after us?"

"The same reason I would hunt him." Fen began to pace. "To free myself of my bondage. My brother is a shifter, like me. He's been imprisoned by the sea longer than I've been incarcerated. He seeks freedom, and the Norns have likely offered it to him as his reward. He is here to claim it."

I swallowed. "Like, how big of a serpent are we talking about?" Behind me, Tyr stood with his head bowed and his arms high in the air. I hoped the boat appeared quickly. Though, at the moment, a boat didn't seem like *exactly* the right choice.

"Big enough to do serious damage." Fen walked to the edge of the dock and peered over the side as it shook again.

Sam came up to me, whispering in my ear, "Maybe we should leave another way? It might not be smart to get on the water with his...brother so close. How weird did that statement just sound? My life has become a figment of my imagination."

"Your life?" I chuckled. "Try mine. Do you know what the serpent looks like?" We were speaking in hushed tones.

"Think leviathan."

I made a face. "What if I don't want to?"

Fen shook his head, hearing us just fine. "We must use the boat. Once it senses danger, it will transport us to safety. That is our only option. If we go back into the city, more danger lies ahead. It seems Verdandi has left no stone unturned. Dark elves will not be all that is waiting for us."

Tyr was still chanting, arms lofted above his head. The water where the boat had been moored wavered. I hoped that was a good sign.

A splash came from our right, about fifty yards away.

"Hurry," I urged Tyr, fear clinging to the edges of my voice. "It's coming."

"Working on it," he replied. "It will be here shortly. It takes time to travel across realms."

The dock tremored roughly as shouts came from the street. I looked up to see an army of dark elves headed straight for us. There had to be more than thirty.

Sam clutched my arm tightly. "I never thought my life would end like this. Being hunted by mythological creatures in my pajamas. Honestly, it never entered my mind."

"We're not dying," I stated evenly, shoving her behind me. Fen was right—when people I loved were in danger, I wouldn't hesitate to defend them. My need to protect Sam was instinctual.

I brought my weapons out in front of me—the newly acquired ice pick and Gram. The beasties were almost to us when a terrible roar rent the air. The dark elves skidded to a stop, toppling into each other like they were exiting a clown car.

A low growl erupted behind us.

"Is that what I think it is?" Sam whispered, clutching me painfully. "Fenrir is the son of Loki, and he's a wolf. Is your boyfriend a wolf, Phoebe? Or do sea serpents growl?"

We both slowly turned.

Fen stood not three feet behind us in all his glory, dark fur billowing in the moonlight. He was several heads taller than we were, his teeth absolutely gigantic. My hand wouldn't even fully close around one. Not that I wanted to give it a try. But still.

He lifted his head and howled at the moon, which was partially occluded by clouds. I desperately hoped that any human within a ten-mile radius had not heard that.

The dark elves picked themselves up and arranged themselves in a fumbling line, seemingly unsure what to do. Then they began to chatter amongst themselves.

The pilings beneath us started to shake in earnest as something rammed itself into them. I didn't want to think about how big that something was. A leviathan could be as big as a cruise ship.

"Tyr!" I called, holding on to Sam. "You need to hurry."

"It's almost here," he answered. "Get ready to jump."

Fen paced in front of us as Sam and I made our way to the side of the dock where Tyr stood. He'd lowered his arms and muttered something under his breath, his head angled over the side of the dock.

"Who are you talking to?" I picked up on the words *brother* and *futile*.

"The Midgard Serpent," he answered, like it was normal that he hurl insults into the Hudson.

I peered over the dock. Only darkness lurked below. "I don't think it can hear you."

Tyr flashed me a grin. It was the first time he'd even attempted to crack a smile. He didn't look nearly as menacing with his happy face on. "I am cursing it. Our brother Thor has a beef with this particular serpent. If he were here, instead of grooming his two prized goats or having servants tend to his every need, he would be tearing apart the dock to get at it."

I coughed. Hard. I had to slap my chest to regain my composure. "Did...did you say 'our' and 'Thor' and 'brother' in the same sentence?"

"I did. You have much to learn, sister." He grinned again.

I was about to answer when Tyr's face suddenly changed from smiling to serious as he lunged forward. He grabbed both Sam and I under his powerful arms and, without pause, tossed us from the dock.

The open water, white-capped and rough, loomed beneath us.

I could almost imagine the jaws of the serpent coming up to greet us, gobbling us up in one massive bite. I screamed, still clutching my weapons, one in each hand, thinking this was going to be the end. I'd been such a fool to trust Tyr! All he'd really wanted to do was kill me the entire time.

The boat solidified a second before we landed.

I tumbled and rolled onto the deck, coming up quickly, my mouth poised to tell Tyr exactly what I thought of that stunt. But I was silenced as Fen leaped into the air above me, soaring fluidly, his body aimed toward the stern as the biggest sea serpent I'd ever seen—which was an oxymoron, since I'd never seen one—came roaring up out of the depths to meet him.

A scream caught in my throat.

The serpent's mouth was bigger than Fen's entire body! He was going to be eaten alive.

At the last possible moment, the powerful wolf pivoted his body, his mouth latching on to the creature's neck as they both plunged under the water in a torrent of waves.

I ran toward the back of the boat, trying to keep my footing, hoping beyond hope Fen would surface immediately.

There was nothing there, not even any bubbles.

The boat bounced as Tyr landed behind me. "Is the human okay?" he asked in a worried tone.

I'd forgotten Sam! I glanced over my shoulder. She was splayed on the deck where we'd been tossed. I rushed to her side, putting my weapons in my pockets. "Sam, Sam," I called, patting her face with my hand. "Are you okay?"

She sputtered, her eyes creasing open. "*Ow*." She rubbed her forehead as she blinked. "I think so. My brain feels like it's been cracked open. Lemme lie here for a second. I need to get my wits about me."

"Okay," I told her, glancing around until I spotted an old wool blanket. I rushed over and snatched it up and covered my friend with it. "I have to find Fen. Stay here."

"Not going anywhere," she muttered.

I rushed back to the stern and peered over the edge again. The water was dark, nothing visible. To make matters worse, the boat began to blink like it was getting ready to disappear. "We can't leave yet," I said, my voice a little frantic. "Fen is still down there!" Tyr stood to my left, glancing up at the dock where the dark elves had amassed. They peered down at us, their greedy fingers drumming, their faces smiling grotesquely. "Why aren't they attacking us?" I asked. "We're easy pickings now that Fen's gone."

"They wait to see if the Midgard Serpent will do their work for them," he told me. Then he called up to the elves, "Isn't that right? You wait to snatch the prize without doing any of the work."

"We will wait," one of them called back. "The serpent will be upon you soon enough. We are not so foolish as to get eaten."

I grabbed on to Tyr's arm. "Please tell me Fen's not gone."

"He's not gone."

"How can you be so sure?" I asked, hope resonating.

"Because he is the strongest, most capable demigod I've ever met. Plus, the serpent is his brother. Neither will kill the other."

"But what if the serpent gets the upper hand and something happens out of their control?"

"It won't."

At that moment, the boat blinked in and out of existence for a full two seconds. I yelped, grabbing on to Tyr's arm. "We can't leave without him!" I was trying to keep it together, but losing Fen now wasn't an option.

"He will be back," Tyr said in a confident tone. "If the boat leaves, we will find him another way."

"No!" I cried. "That could take too long. If he's on his own, he could get captured and sent away again. He needs our help. We can't abandon him!" He'd saved my life no less than three times. I wasn't leaving him alone.

"He is a demigod. And a powerful one at that. He will endure, as he always has."

"How can you be so calm?" This conversation was infuriating me. "You said you left Asgard to make amends. In order to do that, you have to be helpful and kind, and right now Fen needs your help. We have to wait for him!"

"The boat is spelled. It's out of my control. It will leave when it decides to leave. The spell is set up for my protection above all else."

I left his side and wrung my hands, beginning to pace. "Come on, Fen," I murmured.

A loud splash came from the bow.

I rushed along the side of the boat to the front. There was a small platform to stand on. I grabbed on to the rail and leaned over, spotting movement below, but I couldn't tell what was happening. It was too dark.

The boat blinked again. I could feel it trying to gather energy. Maybe my body was more attuned to such things now? It was fueling up for the journey, getting ready to leave, to take us somewhere safer.

"Fen!" I shouted. "You have to come up! The boat is leaving."

Something was rising to the surface quickly.

I stepped back, realizing that maybe it wasn't too smart to be dangling off the edge while a leviathan that wanted to kill me lurked below.

The serpent's head broke through the water.

It was the size of an SUV.

I gasped, tumbling backward, as it arched up in front of me. Its eyes were dark as coal, its scales jet-black and as big as manhole covers. It was focused on me. I'd never seen anything living that huge before. Water rushed off its long, sleek body in rivers, waves crashing around its body and the boat.

It lunged toward me, and I stumbled, my back hitting the wheelhouse of the houseboat.

There was another splash as Fen leaped from the water smoothly, right onto the bow in front of me. His jaws were open and snapping, his growls low and furious. His fur was drenched, but otherwise he looked no worse for wear.

"Halt." Tyr came around the corner. He held a huge harpoon gun, his muscles tense but steady. The loaded spear was bright gold and looked sharp enough to tear through a bank vault. "This arrow will fell even you," he called to the serpent. "I know you seek the freedom we all crave, but it's not going to happen this way. Go back to the deep. Your day will come soon enough."

The serpent narrowed its eyes on Tyr as it rose farther out of the water.

It wasn't interested in hearing Tyr's sound logic.

Cackling came from the dock. The dark elves had front-row seats for the show. The only thing missing was popcorn, or grubs, or whatever they ate. Once I was gone, swallowed by the leviathan, they could happily report back to Verdandi that my death had been gruesome, no doubt exaggerating their role in my demise.

I cringed back as the serpent began to sway its huge column of a body back and forth. It was readying itself to land like a wrecking ball, effectively smashing the boat to smithereens.

"You give me no choice, serpent!" Tyr yelled. "This will cause you great pain. Just be thankful Thor is not here. If he was, you'd have three of these in you by now."

As the beast came down, Tyr shot the spear.

Fen backed into me, pressing me against the wood, trying to protect my body as best he could.

The serpent let out a noise of distress that sounded like something in slow motion. It was a low eerie sound. But its body was already moving. It was coming down, no matter what. I wrapped my arms in Fen's fur, Sam the only thing on my mind. Even if the rest of us managed to survive this, she would not. I cursed myself for bringing her along and putting her in the kind of danger that would get her killed.

As the giant head of the serpent was about to crush us to pieces, the boat blinked out of existence.

When we popped back, it was dark, and we were on a small river, with high fjords running on either side.

I was screaming.

I hadn't realized I'd been screaming.

It took me a moment to get a hold of myself, my breath coming quickly, hyperventilation a real possibility. Fen, in the meantime, shifted back to his human form smoothly. He appeared normal, like nothing had changed. Except his hair was wet.

He gathered me in his arms, and I went willingly, locking my hands around his neck, choking back sniffles from the ordeal, pressing my face into his shoulder.

Tyr cleared his throat from beside us. "I'm going to go figure out where we are and see about the human."

As he turned to leave, Fen said, "We are in Jotunheim."

"How do you know that?" I said, my face muffled in his jacket, my body sagging with relief. I was tired. I could sleep for a week.

"The air here has a particular scent, as do all the realms. But we can't linger. The giants who live in these lands are dangerous."

"More dangerous than the gigantic sea serpent hell-bent on killing us with its tractor-sized head?"

"Everything is gigantic here, even the rodents."

I shivered. He rubbed my back, leaning down to kiss my neck. "We must get you to Yggdrasil soon," he whispered. "You must feed from the tree. You are depleting too quickly."

"I need to see about Sam first," I told him. "I can't believe we put her in that much danger. She could've died."

I pulled back to see Fen smiling. "What are you smiling about? This is not funny."

"Your friend is stronger than you think."

32

"Are you kidding me?" Sam's face could not have been more incredulous if we'd told her she was going to sprout wings and become a fairy. "I have Asgard blood running through my veins? How do you know for sure? That's freakin' awesome!"

"When I was in my wolf form, I scented you," Fen replied. "There's not really anything that can be kept from me when I'm in that state."

We all sat on ledges and crates on the back of the boat, discussing our next plan of attack, the moonlight bright enough to see. In fact, it was so bright it was almost like the sun. Sam sat up straighter, the bag of ice she'd been holding to her head falling to her lap. She ignored it. "I've never known my father. He skipped out before I was born. It's kind of weird that I met Phoebe pretty much on her first day in New York. What are the odds two gals with Asgard blood would meet up in the shoe department at Macy's?"

Fen shook his head. My head rested on his shoulder, his hand on my thigh. Energy leaped between us, helping me cope with everything that had happened. "There are no chances. You were sent to interact with Phoebe in some way. The reason why is just not clear to us yet. Your blood is diluted. If your father left before you were born, it is he who likely hails from Asgard, but he is no god."

"Oh well. You win some, you lose some," Sam countered, still seemingly happy with the news. "This is mind-blowing. So, I'm someone's pawn? How did they control me and make me work at Macy's? Mind games? Weird Asgardian sorcery?"

"No, nothing like that," Tyr answered, his mouth quirking slightly. The boat was in desperate need of repair, and since we had arrived in Jotunheim, he'd been back and forth trying to put things back to rights. It was a losing battle. At this point, the boat was being held together by a few nails and sheer determination. "Who got you the job?"

"Um"—Sam bit her lip—"it was my uncle Marty. He's not really my uncle by blood, he's just a good friend of my mom's. He's an ad exec who did some work for Macy's. He called me and said he heard Macy's was hiring. I didn't even have to interview. The money was better than what I was making before at a small boutique, so I took it."

"Was Phoebe already working there?" Tyr asked, picking up a hammer.

We glanced at each other. "We started the same day," I said. "But I got the job while I was still in Wisconsin. I applied over the internet a few months before I moved to New York."

"So, my pseudo-uncle Marty is from Asgard?" Sam asked. "Wow. He seems so ridiculously…normal."

"Not necessarily," Fen said. "He could've been influenced by another. Gods do their work subtly. There are enough agents of Asgard in Midgard at any given time to get most any job done. Someone could've planted information for your uncle Marty to find, then pass on to you."

"What does having Asgard blood mean, *exactly*?" Sam asked. "I'm thinking superhero with a side of badass."

Tyr paced over to a broken board, the boat rocking as he shifted his weight. "It means you're stronger than a human, more resilient, and you may possess some hidden talents depending on who your parents are." He nailed it back up.

"*Hm*," Sam said. "I'll take it. Maybe my hidden talent is dancing. I can rock out some mean moves."

"No." I chuckled. "Your talent is your huge, gigantic brain. You can remember anything. You're like a human dictionary. It's amazing."

"Ah-ah." Sam stuck her finger in the air. "You mean an Asgardian dictionary. You know, because if my brain is half Asgardian, then it's not totally human. Maybe that makes me a Humgard? Or an Asgan?"

"Stop," I laughed, "I can't take your unbridled happiness any longer."

She wasn't daunted. "I'm going to start working on my brain-to-brain communication capacity. BBCC for short. If my brain is big and magical, I should be able to figure out how to do it."

"Is that a real thing?" I asked.

"Nope, I just made it up." She giggled while pushing her fingers against her temples and closing her eyes. "But I'm planning on perfecting it nonetheless."

Tyr picked up some errant pieces of wood off the floor. "Our father was likely involved with making sure you met Phoebe. He wants to keep her safe at all costs. He will have the answers you're searching for."

Sam's eyes flew open, and her mouth fell into a perfect O.

"Odin? He knows I exist? Whoa. I don't even know how to handle that news."

"Not freakier than finding out he might be your father," I commented, yawning. I was so sleepy. Fen was right. I needed food. My energy level was sapped.

"You're right," Sam said, "you win. That's the ultimate mind-freak."

Fen shifted in his seat so I had more room, and I snuggled in. He addressed Tyr. "We need to get this boat to New Mexico as soon as possible. That's where the Valkyrie stronghold is located and where we'll find Yggdrasil."

Tyr scratched under his collar. He'd donned a blue plaid shirt, but at least this one was clean. "New Mexico is arid, if I recall correctly. There are no large bodies of water there. We might have to dock somewhere and arrive another way."

"The San Juan River runs through a big portion of the state," Sam piped in. "That's big enough for a boat this size." She looked ridiculously cute with her tousled hair and sailboat jammies, which were a little torn from all the activity, but still holding up. We were lucky to have her smarts with us. Now we possibly knew the reason why. It was a crushing relief to know she was tougher than any human and couldn't be hurt as easily.

Tyr nodded, his mouth going up in a thoughtful expression. "We can try to land there, but it will be hard to pick the right place, since, as you say, the river traverses a big expanse. Valkyries have always had a stronghold on Midgard, but they keep the location secret. We might end up too far away, and it's harder to do small jumps if we don't get the location right the first time." He glanced around him, his face pensive as he assessed the vessel that was his home. "This boat only has one or two more jumps in her before she dies completely. We'll be lucky to get back to Midgard in one piece. I called her back before she was ready." He stroked the wood frame next to him with genuine caring in his voice. "She's been my steady rock for a long time. It will be hard to let her go."

I glanced around at the rotting wood and damaged hull, the holes, and the rust. I didn't feel quite so attached, but I did feel thankful the boat had done its job delivering us from harm. "Can't you have her repaired?" I asked. "Take her someplace to have someone rebuild the entire thing?"

He shook his head. "No can do. Her magic resides in the very boards that house her. She's one of a kind, a brilliantly cobbled together piece of magic from various different elements. She's been running hard for a thousand years. Unfortunately, time takes its toll on most things, even magical ones."

"A thousand years?" I gasped, glancing around again, this time making it a point to be more appreciative of what the poor boat had gone through. No wonder it looked so dated. "Well, I hope she can get us back to Midgard. How soon can we leave?"

"We'll have to give her at least twenty-four hours to recharge," Tyr replied. "Then we'll have to decide on a rough location. The boat will materialize only on water, so that's not the issue. But we're going to have to make some kind of determination of where to go."

"I honestly have no idea," I said. "I wish I could be more help. Ingrid didn't say anything specific about the location."

Sam stood, smiling. "Do you have a map of Midgard lying around somewhere?" She directed her query at Tyr. "If I were a Valkyrie, I would pick someplace both remote and shielded at the same time. There are several places that would work in New Mexico, but outside of Mesa Verde National Park would be ideal, even though the park itself lies in Colorado, the topography leaks over into New Mexico. The canyons have skyscraper-tall walls on all sides. That's why the Pueblo Indians chose to live there. That and the cliff dwellings offered the ultimate protection from enemies. You could carve buildings into the canyon, and no one would ever know you were there." She shrugged. "It's just a thought. They could be in the mountains or shallower canyons as well. There are also some great caves."

I raised an eyebrow. "Sam," I said, "you're a godsend. Literally."

Tyr replied, "I have a map someplace. I'll go dig it up."

"I'll help you," she said, following him inside. "You guys should get some rest," she said before she shut the door. "You look like you're about to collapse, Phoebe. Sleep will do you good."

Fen made a move to stand, reaching down for my hand. "Come, Valkyrie. Your friend is right. We can sort this all out in the morning. There's a couch inside."

I went with him. I needed sleep, but I was craving energy more. I was hungry to the soul of my being, but being intimate on this boat wasn't going to happen. There was no privacy anywhere to be had, and I wasn't into exhibitionism. "Okay, but wake me up before we start moving. I want to know where we're going."

"Don't worry. You won't miss any of the action."

The boat shook so hard, I tumbled off the couch. The sofa was tiny, so it hadn't been that hard to uproot me. It was pitch black out. I'd been asleep no longer than a few hours. "What's happening?" I stood, my legs braced apart to keep me upright. "Is it an earthquake?"

Fen came bolting through the door. "The giants are here. We must leave immediately."

Sam called from above, "What's going on?" Her voice was full of sleep. She stood on the top step, wiping her eyes as she clutched the handrail to keep from falling.

"Fen says it's giants," I told her. "Did you guys figure out a location? We're going to have to leave earlier than planned."

Sam teetered down the steps. "Yes, kind of. But I don't think the boat is ready to move yet. It's only been a few hours. It's not fully recharged."

Tyr strode into the cabin from the bow side, his face set. "It doesn't matter. I'm going to have to force her to go. There's no other way. There are too many of them."

I rushed to the back to look out, but I couldn't see anything. "How many?"

"Not sure," Fen said, his voice stony. "But enough."

"My weapons are magical," Tyr added, "but I don't have nearly enough to hold them off. Plus, you two cannot withstand an attack of that magnitude. So instead, we move." He headed up the stairs, taking them two at a time. Fen and I followed, using the railings.

Tyr sat at what looked to be a control panel, pressing various levers. The boat immediately began to vibrate, but then stopped, seeming to putter out of gas before it even got started, like a car motor trying to turn over.

Tyr pounded his fist into a side panel, crushing some of it beyond repair. That wasn't going to help.

"What's wrong?" I asked. "Is it stuck?"

"If I force her to move now," he answered, "this will be the last time she ever does. The boat is too depleted. We will be lucky if she makes it to our destination in one piece."

"There is no other choice," Fen argued. "It's either take

the chance or be crushed by giants. If that happens, some of us won't regenerate." He placed an emphasis on the last bit, but he didn't have to. We all knew Sam wouldn't survive, and I might not either.

Tyr spread his arms wide across the console and bowed his head. Without looking up, he lifted a hand.

Sam placed a map in it like she'd read his thoughts. Our destination was marked with a black X. Tyr leaned up and brought it in front of him, placing it on a flat screen that sat in the middle of the panel. He had to hold it steady, because the boat was still rocking. "This is going to take some time," he said. "Go take up arms and hold them off."

Fen was already moving. I followed him back down. "Where are the arms?" I asked. When Sam started after us, I turned. "No, you stay here and help Tyr. You're not becoming giant bait."

She didn't argue, which was smart. "Okay, but if you need me, just yell."

"If I yell, that means find a place to hide quick."

She chuckled, calling after my retreating back, "I can't decide if this is the best adventure ever or the worst!"

"I'll let you know after we escape from here in one piece."

Fen had already opened a large crate that sat inside the door. He took out several spears and a harpoon gun, like the one Try had used. He handed me a spear. I took it. It felt lightweight. "This doesn't look like it would do much damage. It has to be the size of a toothpick compared to them." I'd never seen a giant, so I was imagining something as tall as a mountain.

"If a giant is pricked by that spear, they are infected with poison. It won't kill them, but it will stop them."

"What about that spear?" I pointed to one that had different markings.

He handed it to me, so now I held one in each hand. "This one will knock one out. But you must be careful, because when they fall, they fall hard."

That sounded dangerous. "Are we actually going to have to fight them?"

"That depends on Tyr and how fast his boat can get us out of here. Once the giants arrive, the boat will want to shift to a safe place on its own. That might be the catalyst it needs, and we won't have to fight. If the boat falters, we fight."

"Once they get here, why wouldn't they just step on the boat and be done?"

Fen chuckled. It was good he found humor at a time like this. He leaned over and placed a small kiss on my lips. I closed my eyes, enjoying the touch and drinking in his energy. It seemed like it had been years since we'd been intimate. "They are not that big, Valkyrie."

I was about to respond when a big, booming voice—one that sounded like it could broadcast across an entire city, no microphone needed—shouted, "Come out and fight!"

The giants had arrived.

33

Fen and I stepped out onto the back of the boat, weapons in hand. Dawn was breaking. The boat was nestled between two very tall fjord walls, which I thought would've offered us the ultimate protection. But it hadn't mattered.

The giants stood in the water, the river lapping at their thighs.

I counted twenty, all of varying heights, but all huge. Fen was right. They weren't mountains, but they were as tall as my apartment building. The only good thing was they weren't too close to us yet. The boat still had time to blink out of existence before they crushed us with their meaty fists, which certainly looked large enough to do the job.

The boat began to vibrate. "Come on, I know you can do it," I murmured, stroking the wood rail. "Get us out of here. We need to get to Ingrid."

"You do not want to engage us!" Fen shouted. "The outcome will not be to your liking. You threaten the god of war. You should know better! Go back where you came from."

"We do not seek…to fight the god of war. We want the Valkyrie…you harbor." The voice was so low and drawn-out, it sounded like thunder rumbling.

"She is under Tyr's protection," Fen called. "If you come for her, we will retaliate."

The giants lumbered forward, sending waves shooting in our direction.

I leaned over to Fen. "They don't seem daunted by your threat."

"The reward Verdandi has offered makes it too hard to resist." He shook his head. "I will relish releasing the Jondi back to their native land. Then there will be a fair fight for power here, always fluctuating. As it stands now, the giants have no natural enemies. It makes them believe they are stronger than they are."

The boat continued to rock on the waves, as well as vibrate. It was trying its best to get us out of here. "It seems to me like they're pretty darn strong. I know you said these weapons will do damage, but there are too many for me to poke at once with my spears." I shook the weapons to emphasize my point, while directing a pointed head bob to the mob that was edging ever nearer.

"Once we fell a few of them, the rest will back off. My weapon has a greater reach." He grinned as he brought the harpoon gun up and centered it on a target. "Come any closer, and I fire this! I think you recognize the gold signature on the spear."

The giants paused. "Is that…Kada you hold?"

"It is," Fen answered. "It was just used to defeat Jormungand, the Midgard Serpent."

The giants talked amongst themselves. It sounded like drums beating. The one in front, who looked fierce with a full beard and powerful arms, answered, "We will take…our

293

chances. You will only hit one…or two of us. It is worth the risk."

"Would you also risk the ire of Angrboda?"

"Who asks this?" The giant leaned down and squinted. We must have looked like ants to them.

Before the giant made his assessment, Fen answered boldly, "Fenrir the Wolf."

There was a collective intake of breath. "But you are a prisoner…of Asgard!" The statement boomed around the fjords, reverberating off the rocks. "How can it be?"

"I am a prisoner no more. I'm surprised the news hasn't reached you. I'm certain Verdandi left that out, knowing my mother, your *queen*, would not take kindly to my harassment in your lands." Fen was full of surprises. His mom was a *queen*?

"It is of no matter," the giant grumbled. "You are an escapee. Your return will triple the reward already promised to us." The mass moved forward again. "We will take you both," the giant said in confident tones.

"Come on, little boat"—I bent down and rubbed the decking like I was rubbing a puppy's belly—"get us out of here." It tremored under my hand. "That's it. You can do it."

"Get ready," Fen said, his eye against the sight, ready to fire the golden arrow.

"How's it going in there?" I called behind me. "Are we any closer to leaving yet? Because we're about to have some gigantic company!"

"Almost there!" Sam yelled back. "But don't expect us to land well, so brace yourselves."

The boat began to rev and shake like there was an airplane engine under the hull. The giants were moving faster, likely hearing the boat kick into gear.

"I will shoot if you do not stop," Fen threatened.

"Fine, do your worst—"

Fen launched the spear from the harpoon. It hit its mark, directly in the leader's chest. The giant stumbled, a look of dumb shock on his face. Why he didn't think Fen would shoot was beyond me. The guy had warning.

The giant plunged to his knees, sending huge waves crashing over the back of the boat. We were both sopping wet, and the sloshing water made it hard to keep our balance. I grabbed for the railing, almost dropping my spears.

Fen lowered his weapon and slid an arm around my waist, steadying me. "Now we see what they do."

The other giants rallied around their leader, dragging him to the side of the fjord and propping him up against some rocks.

"What did the harpoon spear do to him?" I asked as we watched the giants turn from their fallen comrade and start for us again.

Fen dropped his arm, grabbed a new golden spear, loaded it, and repositioned the gun on his shoulder. "For the moment, he is knocked out. He will come to in incredible agony, which will last about a fortnight—same as the poison in an ettin, but about a thousand times stronger."

I whistled. "I wouldn't wish that kind of torture on anyone." I thought about the pain I'd experienced from Bragnon's bite and shuddered thinking about it being even a tiny bit stronger.

As the mass of giants continued forward, Fen called, "Who's next? Who wants to—"

The boat shook us off-balance.

Fen and I both lost our footing. I went down on my backside. Fen lurched to a knee, still holding the harpoon trained expertly on his target.

The boat blinked in and out of reality.

"Come on, little boat! You can do it," I urged, trying to stand on a rocking, vibrating boat as waves from the impending giants crashed over us. Under the stress of it all, the boat began to break apart before our eyes. Boards and wood began to crack and split. "No, no, not yet!" Popping and creaking sounds surrounded us. I gave up trying to stand and began to crawl, trying to hold the boat in place with my bare hands.

"Valkyrie!" Fen shouted. "Look out!"

A giant had me in hand before I knew what had happened. It had come up from under the water. The breath was knocked out of me as I began to rise in the air. I kicked and screamed, "Let go of me!" He had my arms pinned so I couldn't move.

"Release her, or I will shoot," Fen ordered calmly from below.

The giant who held me laughed. "Someone get the wolf," he ordered. His voice sounded like a storm. "I will take this one."

"If you don't release me, you're going to be sorry," I yelled, trying to kick my legs.

Instead of acquiescing, the giant squeezed me. At this rate, I'd lose consciousness quickly, which was, I'm sure, his plan. Much easier to steal a limp, unresisting body than a steaming-mad Valkyrie.

I was angry. I couldn't let myself be the victim again. We were so close to making it out of here.

My body began to hum with energy. I had to focus on what I could use. The giant shook me for good measure.

Below us, Fen shot a spear into a giant who had brazenly tried to grab him. He loaded a new one. "Release her!" he commanded, brandishing the gun on my attacker once again.

"If I do, she falls into the current and all will be lost," the giant boomed.

I glanced down. He was right. The river ran swiftly, churning up big waves as the giants moved around. But there was no other choice. I couldn't let him take me.

The giant's fingers were wrapped around my middle tightly, and rage bubbled up inside me. "Set me down, or you will pay," I said, sparks beginning to run from head to toe.

"What is this, little Valkyrie?" the giant said, bringing me closer to his big face. "You think you can best me?"

"I know I can." I focused hard, and within a moment, lightning shot out of me. It didn't come from any one specific place. The current had wrapped around me, encompassing my entire being, and as it exited my body, it concentrated into one strike, hitting the giant smack between the eyes.

Howling in outrage, the giant loosened his grip.

Fen shot his spear.

It landed in the giant's chest, and my captor's hand opened wide, dropping me.

I flailed on the way down, knowing I was going to hit the water, searching for a way out. Once I was swept away by the current, the boat would blink out of this realm and I'd be trapped here.

I spotted Tyr, stretching off the boat, reaching his hand out to me. I nabbed it just in time, the force of changing directions that fast almost taking Tyr over the side. But he held strong and fast. I bounced off the boat, landing half in the water with Tyr's hand stretched as far as it could go.

A moment later, Tyr pulled me out.

I gasped, hacking in deep breaths as I came on board. I didn't have more than a second to cough up the water that had entered my lungs before the boat blipped out of existence.

34

The moment the boat became corporeal again, it broke apart, and we all plunged into the water, pieces flying everywhere.

Thank goodness it was daylight and we could see. We had landed on a river again, but there were no rapids, just steady movement.

"Sam!" I called. "Sam, where are you?" I wasn't worried about the gods. They would be just fine. I had to find my friend.

"Here!" she yelled. "I'm behind you."

I whipped around to see her floating about twenty yards away, clinging to a cushion from the boat. I made my way over, swimming hard. Once I reached her, we began to swim toward shore. As we arrived and pulled ourselves out, bedraggled and wet, I heard another yell.

We both looked up.

Tyr and Fen stood on the opposite bank, a ways down.

"Come on," I told Sam, grabbing her hand. "Let's walk down so we can call to them."

"Hold on, my PJ's need to finish draining another gallon of water." She sloshed forward, wringing the fabric, her jammies soaked. "This is why swimsuits are not made of flannel." She gave me a weak smile.

I grinned as I pulled her into an embrace. She'd been through a lot in a very short time. "It's going to be okay," I told her. "I'm sorry I dragged you into this, but I'm glad you're okay."

"I'm not sorry," she answered, pulling back, leaning over to squeeze more water out of her thick, curly hair. "This is the best thing that's ever happened in my mundane, white-bread life. It's even better than landing the lead on Broadway, and that's saying something. For a nerd like me, finding out that I might be from Asgard is like winning the lottery. I've always been drawn to mythology, even as a kid. Now there might be a good reason behind my obsession." She shook the bottom of her shirt out and wrung it again, water gushing out. "My quest now will be to find my dad."

"I think that's doable," I told her as we began to trek down the stream toward the guys on the other side. Tyr had begun to scale the rocks on their side, likely trying to get a better view of where we had landed.

We were halfway down when a giant squawk hit the air, followed by a telltale, *CAW-CAW. CAW-CAW.*

I looked up, shielding my eyes from the sun, to see Huggie arcing high above us. At least, I thought it was Huggie. "Does that look like a raven to you?" I asked Sam. The bird was too high up to tell for sure.

Sam glanced upward. "I don't know birds very well." She squinted. "But I think that one might have a light-colored head. Ravens don't have light heads, do they?"

I stopped walking. "No, they—"

"Valkyrie!" Fen shouted. "You must come to this side." He motioned with his hands and then cupped them around his mouth. "We are in danger!"

We jogged down to where Fen stood directly across the river, but here the water swelled, making it a bigger expanse to traverse.

"We can't cross here," I yelled back. "We need to go back the way we came and cross where it's thinner." I gestured behind me.

He shook his head. "There is no time! You can swim. It's not that far."

"What's going on?" I called, looking around, bewildered.

Sam grabbed my arm. "I think we should listen to him. Look." She gestured to where Tyr had effortlessly climbed. He was pointing to something behind him. He was too far away for us to hear anything.

"Okay," I agreed. "Do you want to cross here, or walk back to where it's skinnier?"

"Let's just go in here," she said. "I don't think we have time to spare."

Fen urged us on, pacing agitatedly on the other side, entering the water up to his knees.

I grabbed Sam's hand, and we waded in. "Don't let go," I told her. "No matter what."

She tightened her hold. "I won't."

Not even a minute after we entered the water and reached a steep drop-off, the strange bird shot down out of the sky with an outraged shriek. It definitely wasn't Huggie. Its feathers were ragged, and its head was yellow.

It was going to dive-bomb us.

"Duck!" I shouted to Sam.

We both dove under.

I lost my grip on her as we struggled to get back to the

surface, both of us needing our arms to get there. The current had picked up in this spot. Once my head emerged, I heard Fen shouting. I frantically glanced around, searching for Sam. She came up sputtering, farther downstream, moving faster than I was. "Fen!" I yelled. "Help Sam!" I pointed to my friend as I began to swim toward her.

Fen dived in after her. When he came to the surface, he shouted, "Valkyrie, you must get to safety! I will get your friend." I stopped, not knowing what to do. "Please," he urged. "I sense something is coming. Go to Tyr."

I nodded and began to swim for shore.

It didn't take me long, and luckily, the bird was no longer in sight. I climbed out of the river for the second time, feeling completely waterlogged and bone-tired. I was going to sit down and catch my breath for a second, but just before I could achieve that awesome plan, I heard a shout.

"Sister! Start climbing!" Tyr yelled from the top of the rock face. We hadn't landed in anything like a fjord this time, but tall red rocks ranged on either side of the river.

"Um, okay," I answered, turning to see that Fen already had Sam and that they were making their way toward shore. They were at least twenty yards away. I didn't want to leave them, but something in Tyr's voice spurred me on.

Things were about to go down.

I didn't know what, but I knew I wasn't going to like it.

I started to climb. Halfway up, I heard another shriek. I glanced over my shoulder and saw the strange bird circling overhead again.

Tyr stood above me, shouting encouragement. "Don't worry about it, just keep coming. You're almost here."

I began to climb again. "Whose bird is that?"

Tyr's face was grim. "Skuld's."

I froze as dread filled me. That meant the Norns were

close. They had finally tracked me down. I picked up the pace. I wasn't going to win a fight against the Norns, especially not here. We had no real protection. All the weapons had gone down with the boat.

Tyr sensed my hesitation. "Don't worry, just make it up here," he ordered. "Help is not far off."

"How do you know?" I asked, hoping against hope he was right. We would need a miracle, or Verdandi would have me filleted over the stones like an appetizer before lunchtime.

"Because I sense Yggdrasil, which means the Valkyrie stronghold can't be too far. We chose right. The shieldmaidens must live near the tree. I've also sent a message, and we should expect reinforcements. But we must hurry."

"Sent a message to whom?" I asked. I was almost to the top.

"Our father."

I froze again, almost losing my grip, rocks slipping underfoot.

"Don't worry," he reassured. "He won't come himself, but if he cares about this outcome, he will send someone."

"Huggie?"

"Possibly. But there are others he could enlist."

I reached the top, and Tyr helped me up the last few steps. From this vantage point, we could see for miles in almost any direction. Far to the right there were mesas, tall flat rock formations, to the left valleys, and mountains in the far distance.

The bird circled overhead ominously.

"If that's Skuld's bird, where are they?"

"The bird was likely sent ahead as a scout. It has no doubt announced your arrival. They will be here shortly."

"How are we going to defeat them with no weapons?" I asked. "Everything went down with the boat."

"My weapons find me when I'm in need of them," Tyr answered, like it was totally normal for inanimate objects to do such a thing. "If the Valkyries show up, it will be enough."

"Can the Valkyries defeat the Norns that easily?" That would be sweet if they could, but I had my doubts.

Tyr scratched his head. "No, but it's all about numbers. The Norns are very powerful, but they can only fight on one front. With Fen in his wolf form, me with my weapons, and the Valkyries en masse, that should be enough to deter them for the time being. The Norns will know that, because they've likely seen the outcome already, but that won't make them any more complacent. They will be rooting for you to make a mistake."

I glanced over the edge of the rocks. Fen and Sam were slowly making their way up. I was just about to call to them when Huggie appeared, blinking into existence without so much as ruffling a feather.

They come, the raven told me. *You must run, head toward the north.*

I glanced at Tyr. It was clear he'd heard the bird, too. "Let's go," he said.

"But we have to wait for Fen and Sam!" I cried. "We have to go together."

There is no time. If you do not make it to the stronghold, there is a chance the Norns will take you. They know that. They are hoping you wait.

The air around us vibrated.

It was an ominous sign of what was to come. The Norns were going to appear just like Huggie, and then all hell was going to break loose.

Fen shouted, "Go, Phoebe! We will be right behind you."

Tyr nodded his agreement, and we both took off. He muttered something under his breath, and the two spears I'd held on the boat whizzed by us, both landing in his single outstretched hand. He turned and grinned. "Not always as spectacular as Thor's hammer, but then, I have more to choose from than the god of thunder. The god of war must have many weapons. The god of thunder has only one."

He handed me one of the spears.

I took hold of it reluctantly. "I think you can wield this in your left hand a lot better than I can use it in my right. You might be better off keeping it."

He shook his head. "I will call for another if necessary. If the Norns take you, use it on them. It won't have a lasting effect, but will help until we can get to you."

"That's reassuring." As we ran, Huggie circled above us. The ground began to shake, just like the air. "I don't think we're going to make it. I don't see anything for miles and miles. What are we supposed to be running toward?"

Before Tyr could answer, there was a huge boom, a thunderclap mixed with an explosion. We skidded to a halt and turned to look.

I spotted Verdandi first.

She wasn't hard to miss. Her dress was the same putrid gray as her skin, her face enraged, as usual. Once the dust settled, her two sisters came into view. Urd still had on the ridiculous witch's hat, and Skuld looked as beautiful as ever. The strange bird circled twice before landing on her shoulder. The difference between the two of them was stark—the bird appearing half dead and losing feathers, and Skuld looking like a Disney princess.

Skuld came forward first, a bright smile on her face as she wrapped a single finger through her long, blonde hair and twirled. "You can put those things away." She pointed at the spears. "You won't be needing them."

"I will put nothing away," Tyr said, his tone absolute.

"Such a nice big brother," Skuld baited in a singsong voice. "It's very noble of you to spend your entire life searching for your pet wolf and little sister."

"Enough of this!" Verdandi stalked forward. "We take the evil spawn and leave here, as planned."

Skuld sighed, turning to her. "That *was* our plan. But I told you it wasn't going to work if we weren't on time. If we'd arrived exactly four-point-seven minutes ago, we would've had a chance. But when the wolf jumped into the water, the future was altered in favor of the girl, not us."

"You are not always correct, dear sister," Urd interjected. "The past is proof of that. I see it clearly. Things could yet change."

I watched, openmouthed, as they continued to bicker, each debating their own merits at predicting what would happen. As they conversed, Fen and Sam came over the top of the rocks. Fen held out his arm to stop Sam from nearing the fray, and I was grateful.

Without glancing behind her, Skuld purred, "It's nice to see you again, wolf. You're looking yummy as ever."

My hackles went up immediately. Her tone had been intimate.

"No need to look at me like that, child," she told me. "His heart is not for sale." Then she tipped her head back and cackled with mirth. "But I don't usually pay for anything. I'm a take-what-I-want kind of girl."

Verdandi stomped forward, obviously fed up with this conversation. "You will come with us now," she addressed me, her tone harsh. Her left arm hung a little limply at her side. I wondered if Junnal had had a hand in that.

Did she honestly expect me to say yes?

She was cocky, I'd give her that.

Before I had a chance to shoot her down properly, a strange sound hit the air, a cross between a hum and an amp buzzing too loudly. Both Tyr and I turned to see the air shake behind us. There was no other word for it.

Slowly, figures and shapes began to emerge, like mirages solidifying before our eyes.

I heard a familiar voice before I saw its owner. "She won't be coming with you now, or at any point, hag," Ingrid announced. "She's home now, and we will protect her to the death."

"Ingrid!" I shrieked as I ran toward her.

She held out her arms, grabbing me up in a big bear hug. "Phoebe, we were getting worried you wouldn't show! If it wasn't for Huggie telling us to be patient, we would've stormed the realms searching for you. You gave me a huge scare when you got carried off, but I knew you'd prevail. You've always been strong."

Huggie cawed his agreement above us.

"It feels like I've been gone for months," I said through happy tears. "I'm so happy to see…all of you." As I eased out of her arms, I appraised the women lined up in formation behind her. They were all dressed alike in white tunics and breastplates, each of them clutching an evil-looking weapon, ranging from axes to swords.

They were the fiercest group of ladies I'd ever seen.

My heart swelled with pride, and a familiar feeling rippled through me. I knew I was home. For now anyway.

"It matters not that the Valkyries have arrived," Verdandi sneered, her tone ragged and hateful. "We will take you all down."

A fierce growl erupted behind her.

Fen had changed into a wolf, and he stalked toward her menacingly, his black fur flying and brilliant in the sunshine.

Skuld began to laugh. "Now this is a party! Honestly, we should do this more often, don't you think?" She glanced between her sisters. "It's nice to get out of our cave once in a while. It's so dingy down there."

Verdandi was visibly apoplectic.

Her body shook as her fists clenched. "You will not succeed in evading us. We will not allow you to change the fabric of our world. It is unthinkable!"

I stepped forward, feeling bolstered by my backup. "That might be true, but when you come for me next time, I'll be ready."

Verdandi's mouth went up cruelly on the side. She took a step forward. Fen growled at the same time that Huggie cawed above us. "You won't win. No one escapes us. We see all."

"I've already evaded you"—I held up two fingers—"twice. The first time we met, I was green. This time, I have backup. The next time, I'll be strong and ready to fight."

Urd made a choking noise, and Skuld kicked at the ground in front of her, her bird squawking agitatedly on her shoulder. "Well," Skuld mused in a mock lighthearted tone, "it's time to go, Verdi. We will scry more. But, you're right. She will not escape us." Skuld pinned her gaze on me, and her visage shifted for a single, awful second.

I stumbled backward, my stomach heaving.

What was hidden behind her glamour shocked me. Her skin was peeling, she was missing an eye, and I was fairly certain her teeth were pointed. There were bones protruding from her cheeks, and her complexion had been blood red.

I shuddered while trying to catch my breath.

She made Verdandi look like the beauty queen.

In that instance, I knew Skuld was my real enemy. She was the one who was behind Fen being sent away. She was the one who would see my future. She was the one responsible for the horror and torture meted out by the Norns. Verdandi was evil, but Skuld was the mastermind.

She smiled, ever so sweetly, knowing I'd seen exactly what she intended. "Ta-ta!" she chirped. "It was so nice meeting you in the *flesh*. I'm sure we'll see each other again. *Very soon.*"

The ground rumbled, and in a puff of air, they were gone.

I stood there for a long moment, then turned to Ingrid, embracing her again, relief that we'd managed to evade them again seeping out of me.

"Phoebe, we're so happy to have you back. Come on, we have lots of things to catch up on, and it looks like you need to eat." She tugged me along, and I went happily.

After a moment, I realized Tyr, Fen, and Sam weren't following.

I stopped, glancing back. "Let's go," I gestured.

Tyr stared at the ground. Fen had changed back to his human form and stood stoically next to Sam, who looked unsure about what to do.

"What are you waiting for?" I asked. Nobody answered. I glanced at Ingrid. "They can come with us, right?"

She blew out a breath. "Not exactly."

"What do you mean?" I was exhausted and needed to get to Yggdrasil, which even now called to me. "They are my friends. No, actually they're more than that. They are my brother, my lover, and my best friend. Without the help of each of them, I wouldn't be standing here right now."

"I get that, Phoebe, I do," Ingrid said. "But rules are rules. We keep this place cloaked from anyone who is not a

Valkyrie." Huggie squawked overhead. "And I shouldn't have to point out to you that the son of Loki is a wanted man. We can't let them in."

I crossed my arms. "Has Huggie been inside?"

"Yes, but the bird doesn't count—"

"Of course he counts!" I sighed. "Ingrid, I'm hurt, emotionally compromised, and bone-tired. But I won't set foot inside your walls without my friends. I want to find my mom. I need to train. I know I have a ton to learn, and you have the capacity to give me those things. I'm not the same woman I was when we were in New York a short time ago. I've changed. And I'm not bending on this. If you deny us, we will go someplace else. Likely someplace less safe." I emphasized the word *safe*. "It's up to you."

"Phoebe…"

I shook my head.

Resigned, she replied, "I will have to talk to my sisters." She walked toward the group, and the shieldmaidens closed in around her.

I went to stand next to Fen, Tyr, and Sam while they discussed matters.

Fen's arm went around me, and I leaned in. "Valkyrie, you must go inside their walls," he said. "It's the only real protection you have. I can only do so much. We will escort your friend home safely."

"Don't even suggest it," I said. "We do this together or not at all." Tyr started to say something, and I cut him off. "We are not having this discussion. My mind is made up. We got this far together, and we'll figure out the next step together. Each of you has proven your loyalty and friendship. I know in my heart I need all of you here. I need to free my mother. I have so much to learn. Being here will benefit all of us."

Finally, after what seemed like an hour, Ingrid broke apart from the group and walked toward us. I stepped up to meet her. "The ladies are split down the middle," she told us.

I waited.

A grin spread across Ingrid's face. "But I cast the deciding vote." She beamed. "You're in."

"That's great—"

"But we have some conditions."

"Of course."

"The men must stay away from the main residence. They can train with you and have meals in the communal area, but they don't enter the main living space. We have some old caves a half mile down where they can stay."

I glanced back at Fen and Tyr. They both nodded.

"Your human friend can stay, but she has to agree to have a memory sweep if we deem it necessary."

I glanced at Sam and was shocked to see that she appeared elated by the news. "Anything!" she gushed. "I'm sure it won't be deemed necessary, but if agreeing gets me into that"—she gestured toward the lush valley bookended by tall mesas that had appeared like magic in front of us—"I'll do just about anything."

Ingrid walked past me, giving Fen a hard look. "Step out of line, even one time, wolf, and it will be the last breath you take. We will harbor you for now, as a favor to Phoebe. But only because you kept her alive and saw her safely back to us. That goes a long way in our world. Phoebe is special. What you've done will be honored."

Fen bent his head, acknowledging Ingrid's words, but said nothing.

Ingrid turned to Tyr. "I've heard a lot about you, God of War. You've been missing for many years. Our curiosity is piqued. If you enter our stronghold, we will wish to learn from you."

Tyr bowed his head. "I will freely share what I know."

Ingrid nodded, satisfied.

She came back to me and looped her arm around my shoulders. "We have lots to catch up on, niece! You'll have to tell us about all your travels. But first, you need to feed. You're nothing but skin and bones." She shook me good-naturedly. "Around here, we specialize in turning new Valkyries into lethal fighters. By the time we're finished with you, your muscles will have muscles. Once your weapon of choice finds you, your training will begin in earnest, and you will bloom into the great warrior you're meant to be."

"Finds me?"

"It's a process." She chuckled. "It took many tries for me to find my trusty spear. But yes, the weapon you're meant to wield will stand out starkly among all others. In essence, it chooses you. When it's finally in your possession, everything begins."

"I look forward to that," I said as we walked toward the stronghold, arm in arm.

I refused to be anyone's victim ever again.

Now for a sneak peek of

FREED

AMANDA CARLSON

– Coming Fall 2016 –

1

"Don't worry about it, Phoebe. It'll come." Ingrid's voice was confident as she handed me a new weapon. "Here, try this. It's the mighty pickax."

I took the ax begrudgingly. It felt like a child's toy after hefting a fifty pound spiked cudgel all day. The pickax was lightweight and nondescript. The blade wasn't even sharp. "There is nothing mighty about this weapon," I chuckled. "I'm pretty sure you just dug this out of storage somewhere." I didn't blame her, as we were running out of options to try. I'd been training at the Valkyrie stronghold for over a month, and the weapon that was supposed to "choose me" hadn't revealed itself yet.

I'd tried swords of every flavor and size, bows, maces, machetes, and battle axes, and that was just to name a few.

Nothing felt right.

"I'm not going to say I did or I didn't," Ingrid answered wryly. She'd been my champion since the day I'd arrived. She was up without fail every morning at dawn, tirelessly working on my skills, teaching me how to fight and defend myself, and overall being a great aunt and friend. "One never knows with these things. We have to try them all, from storage or not." She winked.

"What if my perfect weapon is not actually *in* the Valkyrie compound?" I twirled the pickax around my head, getting a feeling for the weight and size of the weapon, like I'd been taught. It was unbalanced, which made my movements clunky. I had to be careful it didn't catch on my sleeve, or worse come down on my head.

I wore the standard Valkyrie fighting regalia. The same clothes Ingrid had shown up with that fateful day in my apartment. A white overtunic, called a kyrtill, which fell to my upper thighs, soft leather pants, these were a caramel color, a sword belt called a balteus, which currently held Gram and the ice pick I'd taken off the dark elf I'd killed, and a pair of beautifully detailed arm bracers. The protective metal breast plate I wore had been formed to my exact measurements. It was held in place by thick leather straps that crisscrossed my back.

Some Valkyrie's preferred a longer kyrtill, so nothing impeded their movements. But I liked the pants. These were pretty kickass. I'd never been tempted to wear leather before, but were by far the softest pants I'd ever owned.

The only thing I'd insisted on making my own was the footwear.

Valkyries usually wore simple leather shoes, but I knew I needed more. My request had been granted, but no Valkyrie knew what a Doc Marten was, so I'd had to draw a map to the shoe department at Macy's where I worked.

The next day I'd found a beautiful pair of high lace-up boots outside my door.

Door was a loose interpretation.

The entire stronghold was literally carved out of the side

of a sandstone mesa, just like the Pueblo Indians had done with their cliff dwellings. The only thing different were the Valkyries had modern conveniences, such as beds, furniture, you name it. Things ran on energy harnessed by the sun, which is why they'd chosen New Mexico in the first place. Sunny days were the norm here. The workings were far more advanced than solar. They assured me some day humans would catch up.

Because of the arrangement we'd made to get the guys in, Fen and Tyr were not allowed in the main area. So the three of us, and Sam, had our own separate quarters a half a mile away. They were a little less high tech, but they'd worked just fine.

"Don't worry, Phoebe. You'll find yours soon enough," Ingrid said. "Our weapons have a way of knowing when we need them. My guess is you're still too green, so it's waiting to reveal itself like a present on Christmas morning."

I took a few practice swings with the pickax, air whizzing by the blade as it came down swiftly. I'd grown immeasurably stronger during my stay here. Ingrid insisted I feed from the tree every other day. I was toned and strong. My balance was much improved and I'd learned to fight with my hands.

The only thing we were waiting on was learning how to harness my inner energy.

Ingrid had insisted I wait until I was ready, as it was "a tricky thing to learn." I wasn't in a position to dictate anything, so I went along with the agenda. The only thing that occupied my mind, urging me to find my weapon and harness my energy, was finding my mother.

We had encountered a dark elf when we were fleeing New York City, and it had told us they were keeping my mother in Svartalfheim, their home realm, alluding to

316

torture among other things. I couldn't get those thoughts out of my head.

Every time I brought up the fact my mother needed rescuing, and we had to go get her, Ingrid replied, "Your mother is the strongest Valkyrie I know. She will endure. When you're ready, we go."

I swung the pickax in the air again, pinwheeling it with my arm, making my way over to a bales of hay. Each was a different shape and size. With thoughts of my mother in danger, I swung the axe down with everything I had, embedding it solidly in the middle of the red X painted roughly over the straw.

The bale exploded handily, hay flying everywhere, each side toppling to the ground, rocking like two dead weights before the lay still.

"That was great." Ingrid clapped, her voice sounding genuinely appreciative. She strode over, looking fierce as always. She wore her blonde hair in a flattop, but she was one of the most beautiful woman I'd ever seen. "That was a better than what you did with the cudgel all day. How does that weapon feel in your hands?" With the cudgel I'd only managed to spray hay everywhere, beating the bales to death like a frustrated child fisting a feather pillow.

I shrugged, bringing the ax up to inspect it, turning it over in my hand. "Honestly, it's nothing special. It doesn't hum in my hand, but I have a hard time imagining this is my weapon." Not only was the blade dull, calling it a blade at all was iffy. It was more like a tool you'd use to climb Mount Everest with. The handle was chipped and warn. It was not a weapon anyone would take seriously.

No one would run screaming if they saw me brandishing this pickax.

"No, you're likely right, this isn't it, but we gotta go with the weapons we have access to," she agreed. "Give it another try. Maybe it'll sing this time."

I eyed it. "Does this even qualify as a weapon?" I flipped it to my left hand, taking a few swings. I had mastered using both hands and pretty proud of my newfound agility. I wouldn't exactly classify me as a klutz before, but smooth wasn't in my repertoire either. I'd been a swimmer in high school, and the only thing I'd ever swung before hitting the Valkyrie stronghold was a baton in junior high and a baseball bat during our family picnics. "I think we should call it a tool from now on. If this is truly my weapon, I'm going to be the biggest pansy in Valkyrie history. It might get me voted out of the sisterhood before I even join."

Ingrid chuckled. "You haven't met Helga yet. Her weapon is a hammer. And we're not talking Thor hammer here. We're talking hardware store hammer. But," Ingrid shook her head appreciatively, "the girl can make that puppy sing. I've seen her take out more eyes than you can count. She uses that claw like it's an extension of her hand. Brutal."

NOTHING IS CREATED WITHOUT A GREAT TEAM.

My thanks to:
Awesome Cover design: Damon Za
Digital and print formatting: Author E.M.S
Copyedits/proofs: Joyce Lamb
Final proof: Marlene Engel

About the Author

Amanda Carlson is a graduate of the University of Minnesota, with a BA in both Speech and Hearing Science & Child Development. She went on to get an A.A.S in Sign Language Interpreting and worked as an interpreter until her first child was born. She's the author of the high octane Jessica McClain urban fantasy series published by Orbit, and the Sin City Collectors paranormal romance series. Look for these books in stores everywhere. She lives in Minneapolis with her husband and three kids.

FIND HER ALL OVER SOCIAL MEDIA
Website: amandacarlson.com
Facebook: facebook.com/authoramandacarlson
Twitter: @amandaccarlson

CPSIA information can be obtained
at www.ICGtesting.com
Printed in the USA
LVOW08s1040290517
536165LV00003B/656/P